Linda Svendsen

SUSSEX DRIVE

A Novel

RANDOM HOUSE CANADA

PUBLISHED BY RANDOM HOUSE CANADA

COPYRIGHT © 2012 Linda Svendsen

www.randomhouse.ca

LIBRARY AND ARCHIVES CANADA CATALOGUING IN PUBLICATION

Svendsen, Linda,
Sussex Drive : a novel / Linda Svendsen.

Issued also in electronic format.

ISBN 978-0-307-36221-6

I. Title.

PS8587.V46S87 2012   C813'.54   C2012-902058-3

Cover images: Kris Seraphin / Millennium Images, UK; © Chris Hellier/CORBIS; shutterstock.com; Grant Faint/ Getty Images

Printed and bound in the United States of America

2 4 6 8 9 7 5 3 1

For my big bro, Marc

and in honour of my grandparents

Major Louis Olaf Svendsen
9th Queen's Own Royal Lancers, South African War
CAF, 50th Battalion, Calgary, WWI
Special services, WWII

Alice Constance Moore
Suffragette and Communist

Divorced: 1914

A queen is always pregnant with her country.

SANDRA MacPHERSON

—

The most ephemeral thing at Rideau Hall
is the governor general; all the rest is history.

MME. GABRIELLE LÉGER
Viceregal consort of Canada, 1974–1979

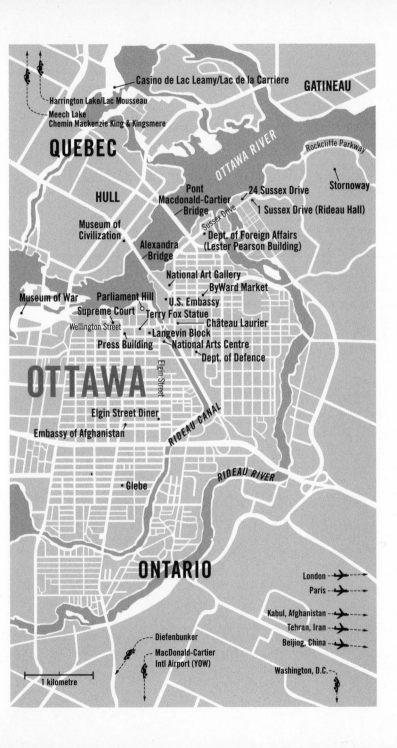

Casino de Lac Leamy/Lac de la Carriere

GATINEAU

Harrington Lake/Lac Mousseau
Meech Lake
Chemin Mackenzie King & Kingsmere

QUEBEC

Rockcliffe Parkway

OTTAWA RIVER

HULL

Pont
Macdonald-Cartier
Bridge

24 Sussex Drive

Stornoway

1 Sussex Drive (Rideau Hall)

Sussex Drive

Museum of
Civilization

Dept. of Foreign Affairs
(Lester Pearson Building)

Alexandra
Bridge

National Art Gallery

ByWard Market

Museum of War

Parliament Hill

U.S. Embassy

Supreme Court

Terry Fox Statue

Wellington Street

Château Laurier

Langevin Block

National Arts Centre

Press Building

Dept. of Defence

OTTAWA

Elgin Street

RIDEAU CANAL

Elgin Street Diner

Embassy of Afghanistan

RIDEAU RIVER

Glebe

ONTARIO

London

Paris

Kabul, Afghanistan

Tehran, Iran

Beijing, China

Diefenbunker

MacDonald-Cartier
Intl Airport (YOW)

Washington, D.C.

1 kilometre

TEHRAN ☾ STAR

INTERNATIONAL DAILY

UPDATED: 8 January 2008   16:47 GMT

MORE AFGHAN POLICEMEN KILLED

QUETTA, PAKISTAN—Two Afghan National Policemen have been killed in separate incidents in southern Afghanistan. The ANP commander in Qandahar is withholding names until the families of the victims are located.

A Taliban spokesman has issued a statement saying that the Taliban claim responsibility in these unusual taser deaths.

The Canadian Military Police could not be reached for comment.

(Courtesy NNI)

August 2008

I

—

AND TONIGHT IT WAS HER TURN. Becky couldn't sleep.
It could have been the vise of heat; it could have been the
gastrointestinal impact of the kebabs, wrapped in red leaf
"Liberal" lettuce ripped from Margaret Trudeau's vegetable
patch, served at the barbecue for Pakistan's ambassador; it
could have been Greg's freakish snore, akin to a geriatric
squirrel's with apnea. But it was, of course, her mind, live-
lier, more frenetic than Greg's BlackBerry farting beside
him on the nightstand.

Because, let's face it, the financial news was beyond grim.
The debacle of Bear Stearns in the spring. The bankruptcy
of IndyMac. Horrifying murmurs from the EU, including
whispers from the Swiss. President Bush had just signed the
Housing and Economic Recovery Act, guaranteeing billions in new thirty-year fixed-rate mortgages for sub-prime
borrowers (if lenders would only graciously write down
principal loan balances, thank you very much).

Even their Canadian banks, the busy, pursed-lip, tight-assed beavers of the global monetary team, were exposed domestically and abroad. Becky's father, Glenn, pugnacious, rattling around after his daily golf game on the tundra, texted her often to ask WTF her husband, the Prime Minister, other-wise known as Greg, was doing about this.

Her answer was: lots. They were on staycation at the summer residence pretending to boycott the Olympics in Beijing. Greg's mornings were overscheduled with confer-ence calls, financial briefings, tête-à-têtes with ministers and deputies in Finance and Foreign Affairs and International Trade, and, of course, with the Cabal of Corporate Executives, the governor of the Bank of Canada, and the IMF.

Because there was an ongoing problem with delicatessen meat, tainted and so forth, he dialogued daily with the Minister of Health, and Becky had stopped serving Black Forest ham sandwiches on family picnics for fear of listeriosis—or as Doc, Greg's Director of Communications, called it, hysteriosis.

These closest PMO cronies were bunkered nearby in rustic cottages. Since the Harrington Lake house, or la may-son de Lac Mousey, depending on your official linguistic bent, was only a fifteen-minute trip from downtown Ottawa, Greg could just as easily have been sitting in his capaciously gloomy digs at the Langevin Block chez House of Parliament. He hadn't once been swimming with the boys, or thrown a hairless leg over a mountain bike (or her, for that matter), or even cast his eyes or ears upon his gospel rock opera, a project he turned to in the sweltering summer the way other husbands liked to tear down the back porch and build a deck or thrust a fresh tree house into the parched purview of their bored kids.

And, after these meetings, Greg was icily quiet. The taciturn pattern. Becky dubbed it Brief and Brood, akin to the yin and the yang of Grip and Grin. Then he was back working the phone after supper, which was sometimes a social occasion with visiting pols or their old best buddies from Yukon ("The Northwest really wants in!"), and staying up late, stewing, or secretly gleaning details about the Democratic race down south, such as what poop of his own the priapic Big Dog had stepped into. All this while she sat unperturbed in bed updating her Day-timer—planning the children's fall schedules, which included soccer, violin and an internship for their daughter, Martha, on her eleventh-hour gap year, and Becky's own agenda involving co-chairing the ArtsCAN! (a.k.a. ArtSCAM! according to Doc) fundraiser, the Gory Horror at the GG's on Halloween and the caucus Christmas party—so that the security folks could coordinate and execute.

Sometimes Greg fell asleep as soon as his head dented the pillow. Other times he glared at the ceiling and complained about the fucking silence in fucking Quebec. One night not long ago, they had lain quietly side by side as the timber wolves howled down Meech Lake way, arousing a vociferous response from the pack skulking around Little Meech. She'd felt surrounded.

Tonight, as Greg, flat on his back, squeaked on in slumber, Becky had to get up.

The windows, all screened, were open wide. The air conditioner in their room, unfortunately, was on the fritz. She looked out on the moonlit lake, where canoes floated like comatose crocodiles, and at the well-fertilized lawn upon which various presidents and dictators had trod, holding tall glasses of iced tea or the strategically featured provincial brewsky. In the undergrowth of the sugar maples, directly to her right, Vladimir Putin had reputedly taken a *very* long leak; she hadn't been there, but security couldn't get over *it*, ever. She saw the trampoline she'd set up for their sons to play upon—surrounded by a lofty net that would catch them and fling them back before bones could be snapped or brains wing-dinged. Not far away, the inukshuk, an Inuit rock sculpture of human proportions, stood guard in its ghostly way by the ancient glacial lake.

It was then she heard the cry. Different from the melancholy messaging of *Gavia immer*, the common loon, now stirring their babies to navigate the lakeshore and avoid predators such as the black bear. No, this was definitely human. Hauntingly erotic. Indoors?

She shrugged on her Paris kimono, a gift she'd received with matching gown (and silk thong!) from President Sarkozy's velveteen-voiced Italian wife, before hurrying down the hall. Prime ministerial staff weren't allowed upstairs at the Harrington Lake house during the evening hours, but lately she never knew when she'd run into the cleaning people dashing in at the last minute to replenish stacks of plush towels or tucking sanitary napkins into a bottom drawer in the bathroom. Those for her eighteen-year-old daughter.

The boys were both sound asleep in their bunk beds: Peter on top, of course, a freckled ginger, and Pablo, so different, so dark, below. Both ten years old—one born to Becky via Caesarean in Whitehorse, the other delivered and abandoned by Conchita Maria de la Rosa, a prostitute who died in labour, God bless her soul, in Cartagena, Colombia, thousands of miles away. Becky and Greg had adopted Pablo when he was eight, a sibling *compañero* for headstrong Peter, just before Greg ran for the office of prime minister (and won a hard-earned minority for the Conservatives). Not only had the left-wing media elites treated the party as if they were the red-neck northern cousins of the American Republicans, they'd attacked Becky and Greg personally. As if any politician in his or her right mind would adopt a foreign child to influence the outcome of an election or international trade relations. *Hola.*

When she and Greg had married, after he was elected MP for Yukon (potential pipeline crossroads of the North, the territory entrusted with Alaska's back), the local press said they'd tied the knot to head off controversy from the conservative base about their common-law status. When Greg finally assumed the leadership of the Opposition in 2004 and they'd hiked to Ottawa, to Stornoway, she'd eighty-sixed her maiden surname of Holt and assumed Leggatt. That was also a tizzy-making media furor. So when Pablo, the teeter to Peter's totter, returned with them from Colombia and critics queried their parental tactics, Greg had handled the controversy in his cool, dismissive fashion. *Let me be abso-lutely frank. With all candour.* He'd even invoked the words of the deceased politician he most despised. *A certain Liberal prime minister in his dubious wisdom once said that the state has no place in the bedrooms of the nation. In this case, the nation has no place in the nursery of the PM.* It hadn't worked, although she always encouraged him to come out swinging.

It wasn't until Becky, against Greg's wishes, had invited one of the country's mid-list political journalists, a multi-platform pundit at Can Vox (appearing in print and on the small screen), along with all the grade threes at the boys' elementary school, to windswept Gorffwysfa (otherwise known as the Official Residence, 24 Sussex Drive, or in Welsh as "place of peace") for flu shot day, and Peter, her little carrot, picked his nose and ate it but nobody else saw, and Pablo rolled up his sleeve to expose his arm with the machete scar and the columnist gasped, and Pablo reacted, and Becky had crouched in her form-caressing pastel floral skirt to comfort him with such tentative, nurturing Spanish and a shy caress of his wild dark hair, that she'd punctured the blimp of public derision.

She had tried not to break down. She'd learned that from the American consultants—the agency that had been able to wangle Greg's solo stroll through Times Square at five a.m., the street cleaners just out of frame, and an interview with none other than Larry King—one of whom had studied theatre in Fresno or at the Yale School of Drama, Becky couldn't remember which. The consultant said if you feign crying in a scene, it's fake. But if you focus upon who or what elicits sorrow, and you restrain yourself, then bingo, you've hit your mark. So she'd wiped her damp eyes, thinking about one of the many cataclysmic skirmishes she'd had with her father when she was a teenager, the camera caught it, and the scribe, Lawrence Apoonatuk, set Becky up as a cross between the Virgin Mary and an Inuit sea goddess mother spirit named Sedna. The polls rose, favouring the Tories. Which worked for Greg; he studied all of them with the martyred dedication of a self-flagellating Pope. He prayed and preyed for that elusive majority.

The boys' rock-climbing helmets dangled over their headboards, ready for an epic assault the next morning on Epinephrine, Piece of Cake or Little Yellow F***er with the Governor General's son and a climbing guide. (Becky had talked to Greg about changing the vulgar names of the sites, and he'd agreed that it was an embarrassment to the region but said it wasn't serious enough to play to the base nationally.)

Their room was cool, the air conditioning blasting. She stepped over the circus of Bionicles to switch it off, opened the windows and listened.

The boys breathed quietly. In the corner, the gerbils, Mr. Fuzzy and Señor Wuzzy, seemed to be up to no good, rearranging the aspen shavings and corncobs in a cage that, in daylight, resembled the colour-coded interior of a model of mammalian intestines.

Becky decided that she'd heard an animal in heat or had imagined an animal in heat, both of which were equally probable.

She closed the door to the boys' room and treaded toward Martha's chamber at the end of the hall, passing her few chosen William Kurelek "Ukrainian Pioneer" paintings, which she loved for their obese blue skies, their flat open promise, and the teensy-mini-weensy atomic blast hiding in plain sight on the horizon. She always had to hunt for it.

The door was ajar. Her daughter wasn't there. The scent of Hannah Montana cologne hung in the air. The iPod was parked in its dock. Oh, Martha.

The Prime Minister's Security Service (PMSS) presence at the Prime Minister's country residence was casually formidable. Security manned in-your-face formal posts at the main entrances to the National Capital Commission's holdings in Gatineau Park, off Chemin du lac Meech, and a lake lockdown (maintained in ways she didn't know—frogmen?). Four RCMP lived on site in a guardhouse within hailing distance of the mansion, and there were plainclothesmen dotted around Gatineau Park in the guise of fishermen, mostly. The property itself was rigged with a variety of motion detectors, high-tech alarms, heat sensors and surveillance cameras that usually revealed white-tailed deer, lost mountain bikers and the occasional hippie wanderer in sweat-wicking underwear sucking on a joint.

After a quick check through the rest of the house, Becky slipped on her Smurf blue Crocs (Mother's Day present— from Greg), unlocked the front door and headed out, down the porch steps to the cool, wet lawn. There were lights on in both PMO cabins. Probably Doc, the hirsute British Columbia wunderkind with a beard as mangy as a pygmy goat's, who wasn't her favourite, and who never slept, was spurring his own aides to keep busy online adjusting the national political conversation on partisan blogs. Either that or he was engaging in Skype sex with his gal pal on the left coast. His arrogance accrued daily.

As she turned to the cabin of the Chief of Staff ("Call me Chief, rhymes with Dief"), the light was immediately extinguished. This senior appointee was clean-cut, scentless, with beautiful marble fingernails. Very aware that he was probably watching her—as Chief saw everything, knew everything, and if he could sleep beside Greg, as well as occupy just about every conscious second of Greg's life, he would—she moved on. He derived from a murky military background, his CV sprayed with unreadable Middle Eastern names.

Televisions flickered in the RCMP guardhouse. The country had gone Olympics nutty—watching Michael Phelps and his washboard abdomen and the epic sorcery of the opening ceremony, with the little lip-synching singer, and the Beijing Weather Modification Office, in the thick of the monsoon season, shooting rockets armed with silver oxide to seed the clouds and dispense with any rogue raindrop before the global gathering at the Bird's Nest stadium could be leaked upon.

From where she stood, she could see in the window. Corporal Robard, alone, dug into a plate of nachos while the security camera images of the mansion's front door, dock, roof, driveway and more were displayed on the screen he wasn't watching. Robard's partner, the popular Shymanski, must have been on patrol and the other two off-duty and in bed. Becky decided not to bother them—yet. Something didn't connect for her: the animal sensuality of the sound she'd heard and her quiet, well-behaved daughter last seen after the ritual brushing, flossing, etc.

"Mom?"

Becky whirled. "Honeybee."

And Martha was there, in front of her, wearing her Vimy Ridge T-shirt and Bermuda shorts. Not far from the house, by the trampoline. Had Becky walked right by her when she'd come outside? Had Martha been in the woods? Her tall, dark-haired, serene teen, who'd witnessed her dad castrating the Opposition in the House of Commons at "Take Your Child to Work Day" in grade twelve, who stood solemn-eyed for long hours in the rain on Remembrance Day, whose favourite escape was an episode of Sunday night's tame *Heartland* on the taxpayer-funded national broadcaster (which Doc called the *Communist* Broadcasting *Corpse*), and who displayed gratitude, if not delight, for an above-the-knee and practical navy blue skort. Innocent, humourless, deferential to every-day citizens, Martha had been conscripted by Greg to his cause more than ever this summer.

"What are you doing?" Becky asked. "It's the middle of—"

"I forgot my iPod, Mom," she said quickly. "That's all." Her usual ponytail was loosened, the elastic tight around her wrist. "But no worries. I found it. Over by the inukshuk." She gave a pat to her pocket.

Her daughter wasn't given to lying, never having had cause or opportunity. Becky wondered what would have suddenly created the need. "Let's go back in," Becky said, touching her girl's elbow. "Before we set off the alarms."

Becky took a few Croc steps in the direction of the front porch, but Martha looked back toward the forest.

He emerged from the entrance to the trail farthest from the single sodium arc lamp blazing over the parking lot. RCMP corporal Taylor Shymanski slowly, *hop-bump*, concluded his perimeter patrol and raised his hand in a wave. *"Salut, madame."*

"Salut."

Shymanski was the latest addition to PMO home security; he was also the youngest. A well-known and respected face. Eastern Townships–raised, a Ukrainian sausage-and-poutine guy in his mid-twenties. He'd worked with the Afghan National Police, training recruits, and had also toured central Canada with his Afghan counterpart, Lieutenant-Colonel Aisha K. They'd spoken with opinionmakers and participated in think-tank panels about what was and wasn't happening on the ground in Kandahar. She was a widowed thirty-something police detective whose true surname couldn't be revealed in order to protect her family. Last February, Shymanski's Toyota SUV had been destroyed in an explosion outside the governor's palace. He'd lost his right leg in the blast, and Aisha K., in the same incident, had been abducted and was eventually presumed murdered. It had taken months to reassemble him with the prosthetic limb and a minute for the GG to pin on the medal. All of this had been a huge trauma, and Greg had taken the kid under his wing. This summer he'd kept the young man—wiry, affable, with furry seventies sideburns and a prematurely wise face—close. Becky privately suspected this particular Afghan file was still on simmer.

He took a while to approach and came up beside Martha.

"Salut, madame," he repeated. *"Mademoiselle,"* to Martha. "Is everything all right?"

"To be honest, I came out because I thought I heard something." Becky was aware of Martha's breathing. "An animal."

"Probably me, madame," Shymanski said. "Crashing through the bush."

"What did it sound like, Mom?" Martha asked.

"High-pitched," Becky said.

"Flying squirrel," Shymanski offered without hesitation.

"You think?" Becky noticed that Martha was taller than him, possibly because of his slight stoop.

"Sure. They're bouncing off the sugar maples tonight."

"Get out!" Becky said, ever so awkwardly.

Martha looked down.

"They dodge around trees like Sidney Crosby on the rink." He waved his crutch in the moonlight. "They have these long flaps of skin that stretch from their wrists to their ankles."

"It's true, Mom," Martha said. "Corporal Shymanski showed us—"

"On the night vision."

"Right," Becky said. "Peter and Pablo told me about that.

I bet that's what I heard, then." But she suddenly had the sensation of being locked into a soundproof booth, like the ones on TV game shows, and while the show went on and on, she was stranded with her thoughts. Becky found Shymanski pleasant and sympathetic; he could shoot the breeze and, obviously, a weapon or two. But how did a man his age rebound from loss and horror to live and buckle up his plastic limb next to his very real balls every day? He was trying not to look at her daughter's long legs, so skinny, in the moonlight. Her 110-pound baby with flushed cheeks and erect nipples. The quiet and sisterly presence that had provided the background hum to the PMO the last few months as Becky played camp counsellor to Peter and Pablo.

Becky wound it up quickly and all said their *bonsoirs*.

Back in the vestibule, Becky gave Martha a piercing glance. "Your iPod's by your bed, honey. It wasn't outside."

Martha missed a beat. She was such a sheltered eighteen— it would have been endearing if Becky hadn't been so distressed. "Did I say iPod, Mom?" She dug her phone from her shorts pocket. "I meant—" she said, her palm glowing.

Side by side, they walked up the staircase enveloped in what Becky discerned was the dying aroma of the Disney-trademarked cologne and the drying vestiges of Corporal Shymanski's most intimate essences. Becky felt seriously ill. How had she and Greg missed this? She'd talk to him first thing in the morning.

2

—

BUT THAT WAS NOT TO BE. At 6:30 a.m., Becky sprang from the shower to wrath from the sky, to a battle of helicopter blades chopping into her consciousness. She wrestled open the steaming bathroom window, damning the National Capital Commission, their stingy landlord, and saw Greg down on the lawn frozen in a Camp David tableau. He sported his best Levi's jeans, which her tailor had lassoed in at the waist, and an untucked maroon polo shirt that camouflaged her considerable achievements (and influence on the official residence's chef) in caloric reductions. On his head, covering the bald spot overemphasized by his black fringe: a vintage Tilley Endurable.

A man she'd never before seen jumped down from the helicopter onto the specially hydrated emerald lawn. With his understated Kennebunkport vibe and the squint of a seasoned weekend sailor, he towered over Greg as the PM shouted a boisterous welcome, then patted him on the back, a consoling gesture partnered with a brisk finger pointing at the whirlybird then his ears. Greg laughed; he got it. They ambled up to the sun porch while aides bounded over, reaching for the man's briefcase. They were waved off. Hurrying in from Lawn Right, Chief, with damp hair and exquisite chinos and cuffs, looked sharp in a self-obsessed way. He had Doc in tow, in Ray-Bans, with his polo shirt sprouting fur at the collar. Here was their date at the OK Corral, and that was A-okay with them. They dashed in the back door.

None of this was on the schedule.

Becky dressed quickly in a Lida Baday sleeveless pantsuit, coriander cotton twill, a higher-end outfit she kept handy for emergencies and summits, and went downstairs, to where the staff was scrambling, with CNN on low in the kitchen, to lay out a quick breakfast buffet in the sunroom. Peter and Pablo torpedoed each other's cereal bowl with sliced banana and blueberry bombs; the scent of sunscreen and insecticide wafted from their pitching arms. She cornered one of the aides who'd tried to confiscate the helicopter man's briefcase. "Who is he?" she asked.

"Don't know," the aide said. "Only the PMO has the intel."

"Well, you're in the PMO."

"My level's not that high."

"It's not Nintendo," Becky said.

Just then she felt the breath of Doc on her shoulders. "Greg has requested your presence."

"I'll let the boys know," Becky said. "They're supposed to go rock climbing."

"You're wanted. Now."

"Who's in there?"

Doc just gave her his bespectacled look.

Becky waited in the doorway while Greg set himself up in the white wicker loveseat, his legs crossed hombre-style, with the American directly across from him in a matching armchair (mental note: dye these hickory maple, ASAP). The American removed the lavender-stuffed Daughters of God throw pillow (hand-stitched by two sister-wives), which colourfully illustrated artisan cheese production on Noah's Ark. Doc and Chief immediately stepped into the three and nine o'clock vantage points, placing their tiny notepads on the side tables in synch, with matching gel pens, BlackBerrys and tall glasses of water. Both men were hyper-alert.

Becky then made her entrance, aware of her buff and freckled arms, her cloud of honeysuckle spritzer and a hint of breast for good measure.

"I'd like you to meet Rebecca Leggatt. My wife."

Becky was always secretly pleased at the response; she savoured the immediate and visceral disconnect. The leading edge of a question seemed to quiver, then linger: How had *he* gotten *her*? Why had *she* settled for Greg's lumpen sourness? It was a mystery to plebeians and patricians alike, and wormed its way into the flow, and the pauses, of conversation.

Becky shot out her hand, which was enclosed by both of helicopter man's smooth clams. The American was memorizing her sweet hide, she hoped, and imagined it goose-pimpled in the salt breeze on his catamaran, yacht or similar aquatic transport. At forty-six, she could pass for ten years younger if the lighting was favourable.

"Rebecca, this is Alexander Manson. He's recently taken on the advising role in DC."

"Pleased to meet you," Becky said. "Welcome to Harrington Lake." She'd heard about the speedy dismissal of Fuchs, the ex-adviser, whom she'd quite liked because Greg appeared solid as a brick and semi-brilliant next to him.

"The pleasure is definitely all mine. Your husband thought it would be valuable for us if you sat in."

Becky fake demurred.

"Given that you've busted in on a family holiday," Greg prodded.

"Right," said Manson. "And I'm here on my own. As you know, our Canadian ambassador's taken some time off this summer."

"He's disappeared," Greg said.

"Gone back to the Okefenokee," Manson said. "And conch soup."

"He's just counting the days until he's a civilian." Chief had to add this.

Pastor Grant, Greg's campaign and spiritual adviser, respirated heavily from the Okanagan on a speakerphone set on the glass coffee table. Becky engaged in eye semaphore to remind Greg that Pastor Grant's ears and big mouth were there, but Greg wouldn't look her way.

"The gist is," Manson began, "the future. It's become very clear that we're in the middle of a financial *Titanic*. Our Federal Reserve guy, Big Ben, he's looking at a nightmare. Paulson. All of them. And we're looking at it spreading to Europe. And beyond. Iceland—it's cracking. So this is the abyss. We're here.

"As you all know, John's putting up a helluva fight. McCain's can-do. For the right. A helluva thing. But it's too close to call. Right now. Might be different tomorrow, but today we've got Chocolate Jesus. We've got his iPod apostles. We've got his posse running amok.

"Here's the lay of the land, globally. Mexico, Calderón. Right wing—it was hard to do, but we got him there. Cost us. U.K.—Brown's Labour is as good as right, and we've got the Conservatives ready to carve his carcass any second. Sarkozy in France, check. Merkel, check. Dutchies, going righter by the minute. And then there's you guys. Our invisible paperweight. Our secret weapon. Here in the free north strong and true."

After a pause, Greg said, "We lost our man in Canberra." Greg still hadn't got over Labour's defeat of the right coalition down under. The former PM had been a mentor.

"Temporary. A glitch." Manson stared at Greg. "We're on it."

Greg shrugged. "I have a stepbrother there."

"We need Canada to stay with us," Manson barrelled on. "No matter what happens. A few years south of the 49th— it's a hiccup. There's a lot at stake.

"With your minority government here. Risks. It's been analyzed. A couple of our tanks checked this out. Especially with this economic backdraft about to burn the markets. And the feel-good 'Yes, Whatever' goddamn Dem ticket. Even though you run this country like you're already president, a lot can happen. You with?"

Becky looked at Greg. He seemed smothered in thought or else the man had had him at *president,* which they sometimes joked about, particularly during frisky pillow talk.

"So you see an opportunity," Greg finally said.

"Check."

"You recall we passed a four-year election law based on a campaign promise and we're not due for another election until 2010?"

"Yes."

"At your suggestion."

"Of course."

The brain trust sucked this up.

"You know that our editorial-savvy citizens may not be as prone to media amnesia as folks in the rest of the world."

"I'm sure they're just as dumbed down as most. Mired in debt, hockey tickets. Costco, child care. And here's the but," Manson said. "Wait for it. We'd prefer to lock you guys in now. For real. For as long as possible. Because we don't know the bottom. We need you to do some heavy lifting if the U.S. of A. sidelines for a spell."

Doc took a sip of his water and spilled on his pet beard.

Manson spoke. "Of course, we'll lend you a hand."

Chief made eye contact with Greg.

"Any obs?"

"No," Greg said, looking at Manson. "No obs. It's a go. It's a green light."

It was exactly then that Becky understood that any discussion of contraception for Martha or a transfer to Nunavut, or even Haiti, for poor peg-legged Corporal Shymanski was going to be delayed or even forgone. Because this had to do with the majority, Greg's majority, and that always came before family. Life would only be better for the family, in the long term, if Greg's policies, which happened to be hers, came to fruition. If she was honest, she also felt a steady thrill at the prospect of nasty partisan combat once again.

"What about the Privy Council types?"

Greg flicked his finger in a missile-like *meh*.

"What about the King? God Bless Him. Don't you have to get Charlie's permission?"

Queen Elizabeth's early abdication in favour of her senior citizen son and longish farewell tour in 2007 had rocked the world—especially Greg's, who despised the *environmentality* of the freshly dubbed Green King. Hankies had been wrung. However, royal PR wizards had polled globally in the U.S. and it had been determined that the Charlie brand, with solid William as chaser, would provide the sentimental narrative and economic bump for Britain, particularly if Elizabeth II role-modelled retirement to the millions of greedy boomers refusing to exit the job market.

"Our Governor General represents the Crown in Canada and it's purely ceremonial," Greg said.

This would have been the time to mention King Charles's

flirtatious comments to the Canadian GG on royal occasions. Greg didn't.

"We've cut the apron strings." Chief seemed pleased to hear his own voice again.

"And so has the King," Manson said. Group chuckle.

"The GG is Commander-in-Chief," Greg elaborated, and then, at Manson's evident alarm, "In title only."

"We'll have to change that."

"In good time. Bottom of the list."

"So a date-stamper then?"

"A speech reader." Doc.

"A cheerleader." Chief.

Greg summed it up. "A few Royal Ass-ents."

"Royal what?"

"You heard me."

Becky led the laugh.

Doc stepped in on it. "She hands out medals."

"Like the Medal of Honor?"

"More like wineries. Wellness. Even books." From Doc again.

"Cups, mostly," Greg cut in. "You know the Stanley Cup?"

"Hey, I played D at Harvard with a crazy Canuck."

"Well, Lord Stanley was Governor General, although we've scrapped any Brits serving in this role."

"Yes, we seem to have moved from Brits to economic migrants," Chief said.

Greg pressed on. "This one will probably come up with her own cup too."

"Pilates," Becky enunciated, turning the exercise regime into a specialty coffee.

Manson laughed with lazy luxury, and peeked at Greg again with the Becky question in his eyes.

Greg stood, indicating the conclusion of playtime. "The role is to consult, encourage and warn. End of story."

"Heard this gal's a maverick."

"That's John McCain," Greg said, and again Becky laughed and leaned low to pick up an orange juice from the coffee table.

But Manson couldn't quite let this subject rest. "A real wild card."

"Only in that she was installed by the previous government for reasons I won't get into."

"Wasn't she wearing fur coats to promote the Eskimos and so forth?"

"Fashion. Take it from me, she's not wild anymore," Greg said, nodding toward Becky. "My own secret weapon's neutralized her."

Manson happily turned to Becky. "Even though she's black."

She nodded. "The new white."

"So Amen!" shrieked Pastor Grant via speakerphone. "Let's drop the goddamn writ."

Manson exploded out of his chair. "Amen!" he shouted. "I hear you, brother. Amen! Hallelujah!"

"Amen! Amen!" Chief and Doc stood and gathered around Manson as Greg folded over and finally severed the connection on the speakerphone.

On cue, Becky extended her hand like a semi-precious gift. "When you next see her"—Becky looked into Manson's sea-damaged squint—"give my love to Laura."

He took her hand and squeezed it firmly against his damp heart. She didn't let go.

3

"LISE, TU LES AS TROUVÉES?"

Lise dug through the storage bin on the deck. *"Un instant."* She was still pre-caffeine and hunting for her hiking boots. They'd been muddy and she'd left them outside, but the help had moved them when restocking the rustic Seven Dwarves–sized cottage.

René, her husband, tousled and purposely unshaven, waved acknowledgement from the patio flanking their cottage. He was languid in the hot summer morning air, enjoying his own post-coital perspiration. Niko fidgeted beside him, swatting at a frenzy of bugs with his red hippie bandana.

"Maman, maintenant." Niko's voice was as low as an elephant seal's.

Her son, her sixteen-year-old only baby, now seemed to be growing by centimetres hourly, akin to a cinematic alien infant time-lapsed into a six-foot filial aberration, with hairy dirt on his upper lip and a bouquet of taut whiteheads on his chin that pierced any person's train of thought with their eminent squeezability.

"Race you," René said, and they took off out to the road, where Becky and her boys, and other rock-climbing types, were to meet them at eight sharp. It was 8:05.

Lise wandered back inside and found her boots under the kitchen table. She sat to lace up. Slumming it in this cottage, with its kitschy mix of Moroccan carpet and Kirkland kitchen mats, and now gulping that first bullet of bitter espresso Lise was relieved to be away from 1 Sussex Drive, the Governor General's official residence—hers—in Ottawa. Not because she found the thirty or so hectares of Rideau Hall—a Victorian villa with ice rink, tennis court, toboggan slide, rock and other gardens, art collection, and what René called a wet dream of a wine cellar, with vintages as tenderly aged as him—onerous or tiring, what with the constant glad-handing, flag-waving, flower-sniffing and air-kissing, and the pressure of back-door intelligence-gathering and deal-making, but because it was a boon to be utterly free of a certain newly installed staff member. Miss Margaret Lee Yeung.

And to be able to walk around naked, if so inclined, and think a wholly banal thought.

"Maman!"

Lise grabbed the insecticide and headed back out the door. Niko was impatient, and it was unlike Becky to be late, she who didn't even seem to make a pee stop that was unscheduled or non-tactical. But they'd all been stirred by a helicopter or two, earlier, and Lise surmised that something had come up for the Prime Minister. Trade glitch? Border skirmish? Bee sting and anaphylactic shock?

"Je m'en viens," Lise said.

Before Niko could bellow again, René started chasing him around an archaic maple. *"Je vais t'attraper, Niko man."* He grabbed at his shirt, ripping it, and wrestled him to the ground.

"René!" Lise called. *"Sa chemise!"* But she wasn't mad at all.

Niko turned onto his back, regained his own two feet and returned the favour; René was pinned under his stepson. *"Y'm faut un stunt double! Un stunt double!"*

Niko exploded with happy guttural honks and this brought such pleasure to Lise.

For the camaraderie was new, born from Niko slowly accepting the loss of his own father, Brett Neeposh, the Cree academic and environmental activist who'd mysteriously drowned seven years ago. They'd been inseparable. Brett had been raised near Lake Mistassini, on the land, but had also snagged a degree in environmental law along the way and a gig at McGill. On Niko's sixth birthday, Brett had paddled with his son, leading a convoy of canoes, down the Ottawa River to Parliament to protest a uranium find on their trapping grounds.

Lise had been moved by Niko's ever so gradual gravitation toward René, her second husband and a Québécois movie star (who'd scored as an undercover drug and arms dealer in a César-, Silver Bear– and BAFTA-winning foreign film, among others), as his stepfather. The relationship had fostered the best in each of them. Which made it all the more damaging that René was hoping to pack his bags in a few weeks and disappear to Europe. She'd been aghast when he dropped the news on her last night.

Lise stepped further into the clearing and doused herself with Deet, showering her strong legs and ankles, her tank top and arms, and rubbing the poison around her delicate stalk of neck, down her back.

They'd only been married five years. She'd been a high-ranking children's charity fundraiser, the star of *oui*Care, and with her inheritance could afford the job. She also produced *oui*Care's "program" on the NGO Channel, with healthy ad buys from cash-fat corporations looking to bolster their philanthropic profile. She met René, the middle child and sole son of a Liberal MP and former minister, on location in Freetown, Sierra Leone—and he'd told her about exchanging his Grit *rouge* heritage for the peripatetic career of a rogue thespian. When Lise had hired him as celebrity guest empathizer for her infomercial about child soldier reconciliations, she witnessed his gently sure touch with traumatized kids. She fell hard. She wanted that in the life of her own fatherless AfriCree boy. *Et pour elle aussi.*

They'd been shocked by the offer of this Excellencies post, although she'd had hints (from corporate sponsors) that the RCMP had been digging for detritus about her parents and her past. The Mounties had even flown to tiny St. Bertrand, the African nation her now-deceased parents had fled for flusher Canadian pastures (and tax credits for textile factory owners), to interrogate the former head nun at her private school. Despite her many trips to that continent, Lise had successfully avoided dropping in on *le vieux pays*, even though her older sister, Solange, had repatriated, marrying a doctor and settling in the capital, Jolie Ville. Lise supposed she considered herself estranged from her past, even as her public and now political profile had been built upon it. Her viceregal coat of arms prominently featured St. Bertrand's smoking volcano; twin egrets flew away with broken slave chains falling from their wings. Canada, or Quebec, was represented by a fleur-de-lis pennant stuffed in the beak of a Canada goose.

The invitation to Lise had been extended by the pre-Greg prime minister, a Liberal, for complicated reasons that included Quebec. She and René both knew that Canada had been complicit in the removal of the first democratically elected president of St. Bertrand, Jean-Louis Raymond, a regime change brought to the country by Bush. French-speaking military from Bushy-tailed allies including Canada had been helpful in this covert operation, although the Canadian media hadn't covered it. It was clear that the then PM could kill two birds with one stone by appointing a St. Bertrand expat and Québécois African to the highest title in the country. The First Nations blood connection was a bonus.

René had argued vociferously, almost recycling his performance as Louis Riel, that they had to be *inside* the system, ultimately, to change things. "If you don't have a seat *à la table, alors, tu es au menu.*" He'd gone on to vent about the example of his father. "'We must be the change you want to see,' was what he always said."

"Gandhi was the one who said that."

"So they were both right," René said, undeterred. "For you to have any power—and prestige is power—to implement change, say, for Africa, *et moi pour le Québec,* this position is what we need."

But she'd not really wanted to become the Governor General and Commander-in-Chief.

When the last woman to hold the office had taken a circumpolar tour (because the site beneath the melting Arctic Ocean, claimed by *tout le monde,* potentially housed the biggest oil reserve on Earth) at the request of Foreign Affairs and International Trade, bringing along an entourage of ballerinas and buskers and cartographers, she'd been blasted by the Opposition (Greg) and the media. The then PM *avait fait le poireau et s'était tourné les pouces,* allowing the Auditor General to add up the cost of caribou, caviar and dry cleaning, which really aired the GG laundry.

But René had been insistent.

Now the viceregal consort had this incredible opportunity. He'd gotten off the phone with his agent and almost collapsed with the momentousness of the offer. Not so much financial as creative prestige.

"It's the writer-director of *In Bruges,*" he'd said to Lise the night before.

Niko had left for a hootenanny with Becky's kids; Lise could speak freely.

"René," she said, her mind clipping at a breakneck pace, *"c'est vraiment formidable* and won't it interfere—"

"It's Benicio del Toro."

"Yes! Yes." She paused. "But won't it take you away for the fall? The Official Schedule—"

"There will be a hiatus," he shrugged. "In the shoot. It's not like there's going to be an election."

"But Greg and the Privy Council have set this up—the African mission, St. Bertrand."

"I'd have to miss it."

"I don't want you to."

"Your sister's there."

"It's not about Solange. It's about I don't want to be there without you."

"But you haven't been back in decades."

"Well, it's always on the brink of civil war or elections or natural disaster—"

"Lise," he said, "I can't express to you how important this opportunity is." He was wearing a white silk shirt, unbuttoned, and was tanned and compactly strong. He casually stretched out on the couch.

"And Niko," she went on. "If you're away, and I'm doing the Official Schedule on my own, he may as well be an orphan. This is not good. Not what I intended. Why I didn't want to be the head of state in the first place."

"Perhaps he can stay with Maxim and his parents—"

"Maxim's mother deals."

"Or another friend—"

"He doesn't have any."

He paused. "I see."

"St. Bertrand is sketchy," she said, easing down beside him. "So is Foreign Affairs and International Trade—like dealing with the CIA."

They had made up before midnight, *bien entendu*. He played the trooper and murmured about plums—there would be other plum roles, plenty of plums, a plethora, in his personal fantasy orchard. He'd taken a shower to cool off and collapsed beside her, naked, on his side, facing head to her big toe, on the sheets. He'd bent his knee and placed the firm rough ball of his foot, just so, and explored her area with a consistent mellow pressure until it grew so sweetly intense that she slid all the way down to his end, where his legs scissored her and secured her sex to his willing mouth.

When she was thus engaged, doing her duty for Canada and by her spouse didn't seem so contradictory. "Take the role," she'd advised.

Becky and her boys roared up the road in her practical Jeep, stored at Lac Mousseau, with Peter's hand pressed to the horn. They were closely tailed in a four-wheel drive by the rock-climbing guru and the personable RCMP corporal. Becky pulled over, climbed out of the driver's seat, and handed her keys to Corporal Shymanski.

"Lise!" Becky said. "Chick hike."

"But—" said Lise.

"Give the boys a break," she said, winking at René.

It occurred to Lise that an hour of alone time with Becky might not be a bad thing. *"D'accord,"* she said.

Corporal Shymanski awkwardly fitted himself behind the wheel of Becky's Jeep. Niko joined him, riding shotgun, and Lise saw Niko looking down at his own hairy legs next to the prosthetic of the Mountie. René swung in with the guru in the four-wheel drive and Peter and Pablo threw themselves in behind. Pablo wasn't as garrulous as Peter, who took after his chatty mother. Both of Becky's boys were athletic, which was to be expected with Becky practically throwing Peter onto an ice rink in his cruising diapers and hiring a fitness coach for Pablo before he could pronounce Greg's surname. The Leggatt boys had been livid at not being allowed to attend the Beijing Olympics, and when Becky had explained to them that they were trying to help the poor Dalai Lama and nice Tibet, Peter had apparently put up a photo of Monsieur Lama and hurled darts at it. In his temper, Peter took after Greg.

And now René and the monkeys were gone.

Becky set off up the trail at a blazing pace, the same way she'd charged into Rideau Hall with a French vintage the day after Greg's minority victory. "Howdy, *voisine*," she'd said, as if in a cameo on *Desperate Housewives*. "Pinot!" She was always chairing 10Ks for charity—fundraising for a potpourri of cancers, parrot literacy. Her gams and glutes had been whittled to seduction.

"Did you hear, Lise?" She talked over her shoulder—she always had to be in front.

Lise struggled to keep up. "The helicopter?"

"No, no, that was just a forest fire drill. No, about John McCain."

"*Pardon?*" Lise said, trying not to audibly pant at the grade. "What about him?"

"He's choosing a woman!"

"What?"

"As running mate—can you believe? And not just any woman. Our next-door neighbour and best friend, Sarah Palin, governor of Alaska."

"How do you know?"

"Greg and I put her forward! I met her at a Midnight Sun golf tournament last year, and she's just the ticket for the ticket—if I do say so myself! Her husband drives an Eskimo sled-dog taxi. She's a volunteer firewoman. She delivered her own baby in a kayak."

"Ms. Can-Do!"

"Hell, make that Mrs., yeah. Makes Joe Biden look like Captain Kangaroo."

Lise dropped to one knee to retie her laces and change the course of the conversation. Easier said than done.

"It will be interesting to see what happens to Obama's poll numbers now." Becky jogged on the spot. "Especially since he's got all those spurned Hillary supporters breathing down his neck."

"And Hillary." Lise was back on her feet and charging.

"Yes, and her. Divisive for the Democrats and the country." Becky smiled at that misfortune and pulled ever so slightly ahead of Lise again. "Besides, I wouldn't want that woman mad at me."

"Have you ever met her?"

"Yes. OMG."

They hiked silently for a few minutes, the tramp of their footsteps sounding vaguely military in intent, or so Lise thought. Their heels kicked up smoky dust.

Becky glanced over at her with a good hostess grin. "How's roughing it in the bush?"

"*Formidable!* It's so kind of you and Greg to ask us."

"The taxpayers' pleasure. And you're not missing Margaret Lee too much?"

"Oh, God," said Lise.

Margaret Lee, Lise's newly appointed adviser, stuck to her like cerebral Velcro. Although she'd been a long-time civil servant and supposedly non-partisan, in reality she was at the epicentre of the right wing. Greg Leggatt, in his infinite tactical wisdom, had seconded her to Lise as soon as he could—posting her predecessor to China, a country his government opted to overlook, treating it like the Asian version of Monaco or an overpriced teacup dog breed—cute but *qu'est-ce qui se passe?* Greg had been adamant about the miniature regime change. *Lise, I want you to have all the support you need. Peggy's served at the top-drawer embassies.*

René performed a decently mean Greg Leggatt, sticking out his stomach and speaking in human dial tone. *Lise, I want you under surveillance and surrounded. Peggy's led our evil witch hunts . . .* It had been funny until.

"You have no idea who Greg had in mind for your secretary. Do you remember Scott Serf from the Mulroney administration?"

"No."

"Trust me, you wouldn't want Scotty running your office. He'd be telling you which bra to wear."

"I don't think so."

"And snapping it."

Lise laughed sharply. *"Non, non, non."*

But Becky seemed quite carried away with this image, and her mirth spilled out on the trail, bouncing back off the foliage.

Lise sighed; she occasionally deployed this on Margaret Lee.

"What?" Becky quickly read it.

And then it tumbled out of her mouth, right out of the blue. "René has a problem."

Lise saw Becky hesitate, the hitch in her stride. But she kept going. She didn't look at Lise. "What's up?"

Lise plunged ahead. "He's been offered a part. *C'est incroyable!* The role of a lifetime. With the director of *In Bruges.*" When Becky didn't say anything, Lise knew she'd never heard of it, let alone seen it. "He's already won an Oscar for Live Action Short."

"When?"

"A couple of years ago."

"No, when is it happening?"

"This fall."

"Piss on his bliss," Becky said. "He can't do it." She was speed-walking up the path, and Lise hoofed it to catch up.

"He must."

"The state visit to Africa," said Becky.

"Yes, but he wants to reschedule. In the spring."

"Your entire mission? To the fucking continent?"

"No, just his component."

Becky pulled her non-carcinogenic water bottle out of its charity-logo harness and popped the lid. "He doesn't have a component. You're the dynamic duo. And it's Africa. You can't turn those boyos on a dime. It takes them a month to respond to an e-mail, they have to plug in their laptop and there's no electricity." She gulped the water.

"Becky," Lise said. "That's insulting."

"You've said worse about St. Bertrand, Lise. You know you have."

Lise took a deep breath, then smiled. "True, but I'm from there. I'm allowed to say it. Nobody else can." And she meant it.

Becky indulged in a very long swig, which gave Lise time to reevaluate.

She elbow-checked Becky's arm. "*La merde*—it happens, eh?" she said teasingly.

Becky almost choked.

"You okay?"

"Yes," Becky said, then, "No, I'm still recovering. 'Shit happens.' René wants to make a movie." She was laughing.

Lise moved into what appeared to be a warming portal.

"It is a huge opportunity for him, *c'est magnifique*, and consort or not, he has to be able to pursue this."

Becky considered. "It *is* all about the optics, of course. And René will shine a positive light on Canadian culture—"

"He plays a priest."

"I like *that*."

"Yes." Lise didn't mention that this was a gay priest, positive only in that he had AIDS, and other issues, including the ethical question and quagmire of euthanasia.

"Good. Greg can push the Privy Council around. And I'll have my work cut out with Greg."

"I see what you're saying," Lise said.

"Well, I'm always after Greg to promote culture, particularly in Quebec. That's no secret. And it's definitely beneficial to see Canadian actors on the *world* stage."

Lise understood this to mean that she was happy to see Canadian actors stray away from the indigenous and subsidized Canadian trough. Mooch Lake. Any actor with a credit in a non-Canadian work meant that the citizens hadn't had to pay for it.

"Look at that Sandra Oh," Becky went on.

"*Sideways*," Lise said.

"*Grey's Anatomy!*" Then Becky chuckled. "A priest! René's not exactly typecast, is he?"

"*Non. Non.* He's not."

"What does Niko think about all this?"

"*C'est le plus difficile,*" Lise said. "We haven't told him. He'll miss René. And when I'm away too, in Africa, he'll be lonely."

"Nonsense," Becky said. "He'll stay with us. At 24 Sussex. He gets on so well with Martha and the boys."

"We couldn't ask that."

"You didn't."

"Oh, Becky, no."

Becky was on a roll. "And here's an idea. Does he like Corporal Shymanski?" Becky hopped on one hiking-booted foot.

Lise laughed, as she got it. "Yes. Yes, he does."

"Well, let's get Shymanski transferred to Rideau Hall. He'll be a big brother for Niko. A mentor." She hauled out her cell and tapped a memo to herself. "By the time Shymanski travels on with you to Africa, Niko can come to us."

This didn't entirely make sense to Lise, but she sensed an enormous favour being dangled. "Becky."

"I'll keep a close eye on him. Security will be tops—nobody taking off to play hockey. I'll treat him like my own."

This sounded too good to be true. And it was, because she didn't want her son inhaling the same air as Greg Leggatt. Becky, sure. Greg, no.

"And don't worry about bothering Greg," Becky said. "We barely see him."

"Becky, I—"

Becky, misreading, stopped on the trail and turned to face Lise. "It takes a village."

Lise was pulled into Becky's arms and pincered in a titanic hug, misted with Becky's athletically feminine perspiration. She also inhaled Becky's hair volumizer—definitely a white-girl product. She didn't think it was a good time to remind her that *It Takes a Village* was the title of the Antichrist Hillary Clinton's children's book, the conceit of which was cherry-picked from a clothesline of African proverbs, translated from Swahili, or lifted from the Kihaya culture, or even Yoruba. Lise had picked up this information on her *oui*Care travels.

When Becky let go, Lise found herself stupidly upset.

Becky patted her shoulder awkwardly. "Lise, it's okay. It's no biggie. We're the moms of non-Caucasian boys."

She was always going on about this. That women were bound by their children, and their children were friends, swimming tethered in the fishbowl of sharky Ottawa with its lobbyists, ambassadors, politicians, pundits, math teachers, choirmasters, coaches, counsellors, pediatricians, dental hygienists, tutors, hairdressers, barbers, hangers-on, and the *de rigueur* atheists and racists. It was a place where a misfired confidence could result in the fall of the nation, or an intelligence leak could sink a trade deal that would sustain a whole region or, worse, kick the flying buttress out from under the carefully constructed and robustly bolstered self-esteem of a beloved child. A tough and treacherous place, and as mothers, they had to stick together.

Becky produced a piece of pristine folded Kleenex from one of her multitude of mini-pockets.

Lise blew her nose passionately then stabbed the tissue in her back pocket. *"Merci,"* she said.

"Sa na fey rien. Moving on." Becky led again, a certain spring in her step. "Let's leave it that I'll ask Greg about

René when I spot an opening. He's been preoccupied with the Hill."

"With everyone on holiday?"

"Everyone but him."

"But Greg must be so pleased," Lise said. *"Pauvre Monsieur Triste.* The Leader of the Opposition—his polls are abysmal."

"True, but all our bills are blocked in committees."

"The Senate, *oui.*"

Becky went on. "Greg is very frustrated. He's thinking hard about proroguing this session and calling a fall election."

"Quoi?" Lise hadn't known she could screech like that, but the man had just amended the law thirteen months ago and created a four-year fixed election-date cycle. He'd made a big deal about this. He'd overhauled Parliament. *"Pourquoi?"*

"Greg's always the first to call a spade a spade."

"He'll be called a flip-flop." In her distress, she said *fleep-flope.*

"Maybe. For two days, until a volcano somewhere, or the inevitable change in the media cycle."

Becky was right. The media definitely knew which side their *pain* was buttered on.

Lise summoned her own considerable personal majesty to deliver her ultimatum. "He would have to have my permission. *Bien sûr.*"

Becky became quiet, but Lise was exhausted. In ominous silence, they passed a meadow being plundered by pairs of ravens, foraging for those relentless young beaks back at the ranch. Becky's posture became *plus dur,* her spine a ridge of steel. She dropped back.

That made Lise even more uncomfortable.

"Becky," she said, coming to a halt. "Look."

Becky approached and stopped. Hands on her hips, a leg jutting out, and Lise knew exactly what she'd looked like on the first day of her sophomore year.

"Growing wild," said Lise. She pointed at the edge of the trail. "A garlic *bébé.*"

"So it is," said Becky.

"I'm going to pick it. For René's salad."

"Don't."

"Pourquoi pas?"

"It's Crown land, Lise."

"Il y en a beaucoup!"

"You can't pick anything on Crown land."

"Ah, but I am *la grosse légume, n'est-ce pas?"* Lise crowed. "I am the Big Cheese! I am the Crown, *n'est-ce pas?"*

Becky cast such a chilly look upon her that Lise froze and took immediate stock of her own weight, muscle and fortitude. It wasn't conscious; she just did it. In that humid forest in the subdued light of morning, she realized that there wasn't anybody else around. Lise would even go so far as to tell René later that there was a homicidal glint in Becky's eyes.

"I wouldn't touch it if I were you," Becky said.

"Becky! Are you serious?"

"Yes, Lise. I. Am. You are only the *representative* cheese."

The women stood staring at each other in the woods.

LINDA SVENDSEN

Then Lise shrugged. "Hey, *c'est la vie*." She looked up at the sky, the colour of laundry rinse water just above, darker beyond. *"Regarde ces nuages*. I'm going back."

"See you," said Becky, not budging.

Lise headed down the trail, but she turned around and took another look.

Becky bent.

Then swooped.

Then swallowed.

[46]

4

—

AT THE GATINEAU HOSPITAL EMERGENCY, Becky kept her
head down as she trailed Greg through the waiting room—
stacked with children of August and their broken bones, the
elderly succumbing to heat prostration and poor nutrition,
and a young addict, stretched thin as a rubber, dangling
between this realm and the next, muttering in what might
have been Cree. She crossed her fingers that there were no
listeriosis casualties on site. The four security stayed so close,
Becky didn't dare speak to Greg for fear of how he might react.
It occurred to her that the only reason a few people noticed
Greg, the Prime Minister, was that their security detail was so
actively casing out the ill and their companions. Otherwise,
he was any other slightly sunburned bloke—some dude with
a blistering rash climbing up his neck—who had the bad luck
to end up here on a ravishing summer evening.

Becky had waited to brief Greg about her conversation
with the GG. She'd stewed while Martha had prepped and

departed for a friend's pool party back at Manotick, while overseeing Peter and Pablo's tent set-up on the lawn (for their sleepover, with soon-to-be-gone Corporal Shymanski in attendance to chase the bears), while watching Greg shoo away Doc and Chief, who had jumped on their blowers to the election machinery, summoning them from family reunions and RV excursions and ATV treks and Bible camps all over the rural free world. She'd restrained herself until she and Greg had settled into the extraordinarily uncomfortable matching wicker chairs on the porch. In her straw bag, she'd placed a copy of the late Eugene Forsey's book parsing Parliament in case she needed to refer to it.

She knew Greg would be incensed at what Lise had so softly threatened. So she approached it carefully. She offered her personal assessment and deeply held beliefs about Lise's psyche. African female: economic migrant heiress in a racist province. Married down: Cree terrorist. Then widow: grief, guilt, single mother of a biracial boy. Married up: Québécois Caucasian Liberal blood. And simultaneously down: lapsed Catholic, aging thespian, black sheep. Overcompensatory grandiosity. Mercurial decision making.

"Cut to the chase," Greg said. "Will she or won't she?"

"She's surrounded with the best advisers."

"I know, I put them there. Will she or won't she?"

"She will. Eventually."

"What did she say, exactly?"

"She said you would have to have her permission."

Greg rose up. She rose as well. He paced back and forth, breathing heavily, on the porch.

"Greg?" she ventured.

He whirled in the dark, picked up the fig-scented candle in the glass vase from Indigo and threw it off the porch. Then he raised his chair and booted it, and kept after it, down the stairs and out across the grass. She saw the boys, in the midst of shining flashlights in each other's mouths, cease and desist and scramble after their extremely upset father to illuminate him sending the battered wicker into the lake with an anticlimactic splash.

"Dad?" Peter asked. "Dad? What happened?"

Shymanski, crossing the grass on his one bare foot, a bag of marshmallows and graham wafers in hand, paused.

"What are you all looking at?" Greg said.

Shymanski was stunned. The boys too.

She removed herself immediately. Let him deflect. She fled, praying that none of Greg's display was on the security cameras, and that nobody else had seen, not even some rogue Soviet satellite in space. While she brushed her teeth, her cellphone pinged. A text message from her dad. Up late again. Or up early for golf. He sometimes teed off at midnight in the summer. She couldn't read it right now. Couldn't deal with him too.

About two in the morning, Greg woke her. An excruciating band of pain stretched down his left side and a cluster of pus-filled blisters was hiking up toward his face.

"Shingles," she said.

This had happened before, on his first day of service as Leader of the Official Opposition, another time of unanticipated and gargantuan stress in his life, mostly caused by the grassroots and Tory diehards. She had prevailed in keeping the media away from him, although they soon learned that no media was very interested in what the Leader of the Official Opposition did anyway. They had to hustle for coverage.

"We have to go to the ER," she said.

"Oh, fuck that," he said.

After she'd alerted Corporal Robard, they had sped through the winding and cruelly dark roads of the National Commission Park, past a quartet of raccoon eyes, blazing like those of combative Tamil illegals stashed in the wilderness. Greg was now at this older Quebec hospital, in the hands of the young Pakistani emergency doctor along with an exhausted fourth-year female resident whom Greg refused to look at or answer. It was herpes zoster; they might have to boost the acyclovir because of the attack on Greg's face, which in a worst-case scenario could affect his eyesight, leaving him blind as Tiresias or Andrea Bocelli. The resident referenced both.

While Becky stayed away, full fathom five, soothing herself with a bottle of water, hugging the hall of the Emergency exit, she couldn't help remembering what Greg had said as he kicked the chair into Harrington Lake.

"That woman's going to learn her place," he said.

HEY EVE
(with thanks to Lennon/McCartney)
From *Temptations: The Rock Opera*

Hey Eve
Don't be afraid
Take a big bite
And you'll feel better
Remember to chew and swallow it down
Then your eyes will open so wi-ide

Hey Snake
Don't tempt me now
I was told to
Ignore the fruit on the tree
And hang with Adam here on the ground
Our Father is watching over us now-ow

Hey Eve
I'm covering my ears
Take a big bite
Go 'way and leave us alone
Remember an apple a day-ay-ay
Our Father will whack you with a stick-ick-ick-ick

Hey Adam
Let's have some fun
Eat this apple
And let's go wi-i-i-ild
The second you join me in this sin
La La La La La La La La La La La

Fa La Fa La Fa La Faaaaa
La Fa La Faaaa
Hey Eve
Fa La Fa La Fa La Faaaa
La Fa La Faaaa
Hey Snake

WORDS AND MUSIC BY GREGORY LEGGATT

septembre 2008

5

———

"ARE YOU GRANTING THE DISSOLUTION?"

"I haven't been asked yet."

"*Mais*—when you are?"

"I can't discuss it," she said.

René was hunting and gathering—toothbrush, razor, dental tape, and pomegranate moisturizer for alpha males—in their master bathroom. His leather toiletries kit was swollen. "The Toronto *Blob* says you will."

Lise perched on the edge of the tub. "Good for them."

"But are you going to say yes?"

"Tune in tomorrow." Lise pinched his closest buttock. He'd gained weight for the role of Father Benedict and his jeans were no longer lifting and separating.

"I am disgusting," he said.

"Nobody will see when you're lost in your cassock."

"Ah, but when it's off—" He zipped his kit and flew from there to the master closet.

She followed and watched as he flipped through a stack of soft Easter-pastel cardigans.

"On Can Vox breakfast radio—"

"*Oui.*"

"—the Chief of Staff said it was a done deal."

"Amen."

"The Director of Communications also said your approval is a formality—"

"*Fini.*"

"—like the Throne Speech. The PM puts the words in your mouth—"

"*C'est tout.*"

René lifted the entire stack of sweaters and placed them beside a mound of professionally rolled yoga pants and trousers in the suitcase resting open on the Duxiana bed.

"René," she said patiently, "the GG usually *does* act upon the advice of the Prime Minister and Privy Council. It's in the Letters Patent."

He looked her in the eyes. "She is also called upon to consult, encourage and warn."

She stared right back. *"Bien entendu."*

"So are you going to grant his request? To dissolve this Parliament?"

"That is my executive privilege, René." She'd had it. "You're being a big fat viceregal bore." She knew he'd be upset at *fat*.

"Okay," he said. "Okay, Lise. My hope, *mon vrai espoir*, is that permission for an unnecessary election wasn't bought."

"What are you talking about? How *bought*?"

"By making them grant me a leave. For my film."

Lise walked out of the bedroom and slammed the door. *Vice-reine*-style.

Ten minutes later, they bade their farewells in the Rideau Hall foyer.

Niko was with them. Becky had expedited the Shymanski transfer, true to her word, and he already seemed to be fitting in. Niko had screened *In Bruges* with him the night before and they were quoting lines. Niko didn't seem affected by René's impending absence at all.

Lise and René embraced in front of the portrait of Her Excellency Adrienne Clarkson. He held on to Lise tightly even though she was still pissed at him. *Complètement.*

"*Va t'en,*" she whispered.

He nudged his hip bone against her in a way that made her want to press hard back. Then he hummed a few bars of "La Vie en Rose."

She melted. "Phone me," Lise coaxed.

"*Tous les jours, ma chère.*"

"Every day."

"No missions to Kandahar."

"*Non.*"

"Promise?"

"*Oui.*"

"I'll be back in November. For the hiatus."

"*Oui.*"

"I'll mail you my absentee ballot."

She shot him a look.

René had the habit of kissing her as if they were completely alone even when they were in a crowded formal reception or a Loblaws. Particularly in a Loblaws. He could make their contact singularly urgent. He did so then. Niko broke in between them, with his body odour and acne and endearing adolescent bravado, and Lise thought, *Toute ma vie est là*.

She caught a glimpse of Shymanski watching them, resting his back against a wall. She had the feeling he would have happily embraced them all too. He looked like a man who unfailingly called his mother; this perhaps explained his connection with Lieutenant-Colonel Aisha K., his older Afghan police partner, who had disappeared. Or died.

Margaret Lee appeared and shook René's hand. "Goodbye, Your Excellency," she said. "Do break a leg."

"Ah, Margaret Lee," René said, "I will miss you most of all."

He disappeared, pretending to flee his aides-de-camp, out the door. Lise put her arm around Niko.

"You'll be okay, *Maman*," he said, then turned to Shymanski and shadow-boxed him to the Long Gallery. She suddenly heard Niko hammering "Chopsticks" on Glenn Gould's practice Steinway, accompanied by Shymanski's steady chords.

In the afternoon, Lise accompanied Niko to his therapist. Dr. Pelletier's modern home office, in the Glebe, faced out on the Rideau Canal. The interior light was beautiful, calming, even on dark days, and when Lise joined Niko in his sessions, it felt as if her son could fully accept losing *son cher papa*, handle being a half–First Nations boy with his famous African mother representing Charles, the King of England, and deal with a hip French-Canadian-Caucasian stepfather who sometimes sucked the aforementioned mother's complete attention. In the winter, while Dr. Pelletier calmly reframed their thinking errors, she heard the ice-skate blades whisking by on the Canal and, outside, walking back to the car, she inhaled the scent of roasting chestnuts in the cold air. Small things that gave order and clarity and major hope. She kept her faith: he was a lonely teenager in a tough hierarchical milieu. She understood why Niko was drawn to the slightly older Martha, who was unspoiled, grounded, and didn't play social games. Lise thought she would have been a wonderful friend for Niko if she hadn't been so Christian.

Today, though, Dr. Pelletier had run interference at his door and asked if she minded if he and Niko met alone to set goals for the school year. Lise did not.

"*À plus,*" she said, and eased back to the car. Corporal Shymanski waited behind the wheel; he was an excellent defensive driver. "I've been kicked out," she said.

"Do you want to return to Rideau Hall?"

"We'll just have to turn around and come back."

In the end, she decided she wanted to sit on a bench in the shade by the Canal; it was so hot, and too humid for joggers, and they were basically on their own. Lise asked him about his prosthesis, if he was happy with his lighter carbon-fibre composite leg, was the suction suspension comfortable? She'd had experience talking to other transfemoral amputees, who were also veterans, and was able to engage in the details without exhibiting either horror or pity.

Shymanski provided a few updates about muscle atrophy and the physio he was undertaking.

"It was a tough thing that happened," she said. "For sure."

"It was," he agreed.

She noticed steps to the water near the boat tie-up, not too far from them. "Why don't we go over there?" she suggested. "We can put our feet in the water and cool off."

Shymanski smiled. "Foot."

"*Oh, mon Dieu,*" she said. "How stupid of me."

"No worries. Let's do it."

They headed over; she had to, at that point, having been completely insensitive after referencing his prosthetic leg. She slipped out of her sandals and sat down at the edge, lowering her feet. It was lovely and cool. She didn't want to check and see what Shymanski was doing— it was taking him a while to remove his New Balance sneaker. She played with her feet, skimming the surface, rotating her ankles, and suddenly his big white foot loomed beside hers. He stood and kept the prosthetic with the other New Balance shoe dry on shore. She had to give it to him—he was game.

"Do you ever hear anything about Lieutenant-Colonel Aisha K.?" she asked. "Or is the case closed?"

"They don't talk about her," Shymanski said. "Not to me."

"She was an extraordinary person. Look at the response to her here in Canada."

"Yes, Your Excellency." Shymanski nodded.

She sensed a well of deeper feeling—loss, bitterness—but he wasn't going to spill. She also had a bad habit of projection; after all, it was *her* husband who'd left that day.

"She was like a rock star, wasn't she?" he said.

"*Oui,*" Lise said. "You knew her the best of all of us."

"That's true," he said, then laughed. "Even though she could be hard to know. With the burka, you know."

"For sure."

"Your Excellency," he said, "I know I probably shouldn't ask."

"It's okay," she said. "Go ahead."

"Do you know why I was transferred from the PMO detail? Was there a reason?"

"Yes, there was a reason. Rideau Hall needed you. You and your skill set."

"*Merci,*" he said. "*Merci beaucoup.*"

"*Il n'ya pas de quoi.* Should we head back?" Lise said. Niko became impatient whenever she was late.

That night Lise retired early, emotionally exhausted from the day and the prospect of meeting with the Prime Minister in the morning.

Lise couldn't get Shymanski and Lieutenant-Colonel Aisha K. out of her head. The Corporal had seemed haunted.

The whole Lieutenant-Colonel Aisha (Arabic, meaning "alive") K. phenomenon had begun with an enigmatic photo of her on the front page of the furthest left right-wing national newspaper, there being no left-wing national newspaper. It had been back in 2006, before Greg became Prime Minister. An above-the-fold, full-colour, full-length profile of Lieutenant-Colonel Aisha K., covered crown to toe in her blue burka, arm extended, and an elegantly manicured grip on Bulgaria's very own Arcus 98 DA (Double Action) military pistol, pointed convincingly at the left margin.

Trop fou, Lise had thought: you expected to see a camouflaged Afghan woman offering a platter of battered figs, or tossing a couple of underweight goats around her neck— anything but this *tableau noir*. The country learned how single mother Lieutenant-Colonel Aisha K. home-schooled her children and then was chauffeured to work at the ANP by RCMP counterparts (Shymanski) because Afghan women weren't allowed by law to drive. And because of Taliban death threats.

It was catnip propaganda.

Nobody knew what she looked like. Nobody had seen her face; nobody in Canada or Afghanistan, not even border control, could talk about the insolent jut of a hip, a set jaw, a cast-downward glance, the rogue mole in an unforgettably delectable place.

Mansbridge fawned, Radio-Canada *s'est fendu en quatre aussi*, and Strombo cracked the audience up when he leaned over and said, "Seriously. Undercover?" and she threw her long limber fingers, a festival of ornate rings, toward the boom mic and laughed rather mannishly. Then she was filmed at target practice competing against the hunkish rookie Shymanski, two-legged at the time. The Liberal PM commanded Lise to throw, ASAP, a reception.

Lise, the neophyte, complied, *tout de suite.* In a flash of populist genius, she wore her official military uniform to further the cause. Becky, then wife of the Leader of the Opposition, arrived in a lower-cut frock, white Colombian lace. Nobody cared about the redhead with the Conservative cleavage.

Lieutenant-Colonel Aisha K. was mobbed. Of course, there were finger foods, halal; Lise's people had spoken with the guest of honour and she'd agreed to take sustenance before the function and nixed any liquor. All doable, and Lise was sailing along with full-hostess prowess until the non-Greg Prime Minister, juggling seven midget halalburgers in one giant fist, spilled his cranberry juice down Aisha's baby blue linen breast.

"Suivez moi," Lise signalled, and led Lieutenant-Colonel K. through the imposing double doors and upstairs to her serene private quarters.

Lise took Aisha right into her walk-in closet and unzipped a garment bag. *"Voici, madame,"* said Lise. She handed over her Afghan burka, a claret brocade, a *bonne chance* hand-me-down from the most recent ex–Governor General.

"Shukran," Lieutenant-Colonel K. said. She instantly cast her damp garment up into the air. In a rustling shimmer of fabric, she ducked out from under.

In those three, *peut-être quatre, peut-être six secondes*, Lise had glimpsed the burka-liberated back of her head, an *au courant* shoulder-length pageboy crushed from crowd-pressing heat, slimmer shoulders than any Afghan sack suggested, and when she pirouetted with a smile, Lise saw Aisha full-on, all-face, with her intelligence, humility and luminous clarity, which made her, *magiquement*, extraordinarily beautiful. She also sensed a frighteningly hard edge. The closet exploded with the scent, the olfactory circus, of Aisha's perfume—Hawaiian plumeria? Lise had wordlessly draped her in her own heavier duds.

Becky had met them at the bottom of the stairs. "I heard about a wardrobe malfunction," she said, laughing.

The next day her quote had become a Life section headline across the country, with a photo of the new gal pals posing under a portrait of the Earl of Minto.

But the press hadn't caught Becky's pointed aside in Lise's ear. "Did you see her face?" And Lise's affirmative nod.

Lise's private phone rang around midnight. She'd fallen asleep in a puddle of letters and papers, and it took her a minute to figure out where she was before she could search for the phone. She picked it up.

"Turn on Can Vox," Becky said, and hung up.

Lise flicked the remote.

And there was René, much younger, giving a speech to a gathering of long-haired, bespectacled, semi-Orwellian ragamuffins about the sovereign nation of Quebec, and how he would die fighting for its freedom from the English "master-bators." Lise recognized this immediately. It was a clip from *Jeune Lévesque,* for which he'd been nominated for a Jutra, and which could sometimes be caught late at night on the cable dumping ground for young Canadian *auteurs.* Lise watched, entranced with his youth and verve, but she also found herself thinking about what had been happening in her life at the time this film was made. Niko had just been born, colicky, and she and Brett would have been taking turns walking him around the flat and singing with Youssou N'Dour CDs.

Journalist Lawrence Apoonatuk appeared following the clip and began his interrogation of a person Lise could only characterize as a Smirk.

"Can you identify the person in the clip?"

"René Claude, consort to the Governor General of Canada."

"Where did this event take place?"

"In Quebec City. We found the tape in an apartment that was about to be demolished."

Lise screamed.

"And do you think, potentially, that this is a grave embarrassment · to the Office of the Governor General, Commander-in-Chief, and to Canada in general?"

"It would suggest that Madame Lavoie and Monsieur Claude were not sufficiently vetted by the former minority Liberal government who initiated the appointment."

"But Monsieur Claude is the son of a former Member of Parliament."

"In this case," Smirk said, "all I can say is that this nut fell far from the tree."

"My God," Lise said. *"C'est un extrait!* A cleep! *C'est* Jeune Lévesque!"*

She phoned Becky back. She didn't care if she woke Greg up, or whomever. This sort of slander was poisonous, malicious, and she would need the Prime Minister to denounce this immediately, publicly, now.

Becky's cell rang and rang.

Talk about *une nuit blanche.* It took Lise the rest of the night to appreciate the tactical beauty of Greg's move, for she assumed she saw his hand in it. A kerfuffle in the Governor General's office, a radical separatist consort, and the citizen public would be attacking her and René, writing incendiary letters to the blogosphere, and the cartoonists would caricaturize her with a ring in her nose, while Greg quietly got his way about dissolving Parliament. Breaking the very law he had initiated.

In the shimmering morning, Lise looked out the windows of the viceregal bedroom toward *la Colline du Parlement.* She could see the Peace Tower and families at its foot in the early morning queue for the crooked little elevator to the top, seizing the last seconds of the Labour Day holiday. Education *and* fun. When she angled herself the other way, she could see the six limousines in the Prime Minister's convoy, approaching Rideau Hall on the Prime Minister's personal promenade, to park at the Prime Minister's personal entrance, which was logically positioned next to the Governor General's study with its Napoleonic desk. Lise marvelled. Six cars. *Quelle production! Grosse Corvette, p'tite quéquette.*

She paced into and out of her closet. She was ready: in her Teenflo turmeric pantsuit with Hermès scarf and Comme-ci Comme-ça heels. Her hair was coiffed without a smidge of lacquer; anger locked every curl in place.

Let him cool his heels. *Attendez-moi, monsieur.*

She knew that Margaret Lee, Henchwoman and Crony, would be extending her chilled hand in greeting, slightly dismissive of valiant old Clark the Privy Clerk (arriving in the last car, complaining of construction near the Langevin Block and some fuss at the U.S. embassy), and ushering King Greg into the Governor General's study as if she herself were the GG. And who knew? She might very well be on the short list of future Excellencies.

Let King F—ing Tut rest his royal butt.

Her reverie was broken by her personal phone emitting urgent heart monitor soundings. She knew who it was. *"Bonjour."*

"Excellency, the Prime Minister is here with the Privy Clerk." So smug, so full of her Margaret Lee-ness and sanctity.

"I'm unavoidably delayed, Margaret Lee."

"I believe the honourable gentlemen have busy schedules today."

"I repeat: unavoidably delayed."

"Very well." Perfunctory.

Lise had time to check her laptop for the weather in Bucharest.

They half rose, the two of them, when she entered her study. Even that irritated her. Margaret Lee had ushered the Prime Minister and Clark into the study before she'd authorized it. The protocol was such that even if the Prime Minister utilized his private entrance, he should collect his blazing thoughts in the Victorian waiting room until she was ready for him.

"Excellency," said Greg. She honed in for the double cheek-peck. Today's aftershave was reminiscent of a homeopathic remedy and Niko's Axe.

She smiled professionally. *Sans la cordialité.*

She moved to Clark and did the same again. As the highest-ranking non-political official, his main chore was to ensure continuity of government.

"It's lovely to see you both," she said. "I understand there's a request."

Clark bowed his head.

"Please." She indicated the seating opportunities.

"Before we get into the specifics, Lise, I wanted to brief you on the very recent business with René," Greg said.

"Yes. I was going to mention that."

"Please don't worry about it. Doc's going to address the problem at a press conference today. As a tag. He'll confirm that it was an audition tape for a Quebec movie of the week—"

"A feature," said Lise.

"Okay, a feature movie."

"It was not an audition tape. René was actually cast as René. It was a *cleep*."

"Too many Renés," said Greg. "It doesn't matter if he was in it or not, actually. It becomes too confusing for the public if we give them details."

"He was nominated for a Jutra."

"We don't want to go there, Lise. Let's focus on it being an audition tape, because if we get into the casting and the award, then the press will think he was sympathetic to Lévesque. So, René auditioned, blah-blah, and His Selfness is out of the country, unavailable for comment. Should blow over in a week—tops. The country's getting back to school and has other fish to fry. Half the journos are cruising the Mediterranean anyway. The Toronto *Blob* types."

"Not Lawrence Apoonatuk."

"Maybe not him. But everybody else. We're trying to figure out who sent this to Larry. Does René have any ideas?"

"I haven't told him."

"Oh," said Greg. "I see."

A silence in the room.

Clark, privately designated Corporate Puppet by René, simply stared at her, his briefcase hidden behind his calves.

Lise couldn't breathe. Out in the corridor, Corporal Shymanski answered questions from the PM's security team in a low tone. Then a knock at the door. "Ah," said Lise, as coffee and tea were delivered with rosemary-scented cookies from a biscuit boutique in the ByWard Market. Clark was all over those.

Greg cleared his throat. "Now, Lise, as you know, I'm steering a minority government in the House of Commons with an Opposition majority in the Senate. I have laws pending that I can't get passed in committee."

"Primarily Senate."

Margaret Lee tapped into her netbook, propped on her lap, with her tiny fingers bulleting.

"Yes, but I'm sensing that everyday Canadians are growing restless. They've elected us to see some action and I suspect we'll only be able to effect change if we go back to the citizens and ask for more support for our progressive agenda. Further, the Opposition has finally laid out an environmental plan, which doesn't make any sense, and the shit is hitting the fan."

"Their kind of wind power," Margaret Lee said.

Greg chuckled.

Lise said, "I have a concern and would like to discuss this with my constitutional adviser."

"Oh, but she's away until next week," Margaret Lee piped up again.

"Why wasn't I informed?"

"You were."

"Then I would like to consult with the alternate."

"Unfortunately, he's not available either. It's that time of year."

"Constitutional scholars—they all flee civilization as they define it," Greg said.

"They're in Muskoka," Margaret Lee said.

"Or maybe they're all on a cruise too," said Clark.

"The fixed election is a new law."

"It's not a law, Lise. It's not binding. Language, language, language." Greg added gently, "It's not in your prerogative to deny me."

Clark nodded, which she took as a threat.

Margaret Lee stared at her.

"I'm not comfortable," Lise said.

"What would make you so?" This from Greg.

"A conversation with the constitutional adviser."

Greg turned to Margaret Lee. "Peggy, who can you reach?"

Margaret Lee scurried from the study.

"*My* concern," said Greg, "is that we're into a delay of hours or days. I'd like to dissolve the House of Commons before the MPs file back for the fall sitting and give everyone the time to prepare. If the writ drops right after Labour Day, the election can happen quickly, following Thanksgiving."

"Before the U.S. election," Lise said.

"Well, it's not timed to that," Clark sputtered.

She had a quick thought for the Leader of the Opposition, Monsieur Triste, whom she sometimes saw jogging with his dog, a brown Labrador, past the Princess Anne Gate. He was a decent chap, despised by the corporatariat in his own Liberal Party. He'd been handed the reins to the losing team after the last election (when the RCMP announced a criminal investigation of an ex–Cabinet member, revealed to voters at the dawn of the campaign). Monsieur Triste was also from Quebec. *Une sorte de frère.* Maybe he could pull this off, win a snap election?

"All right," Lise said.

"You're sure you don't want the adviser?"

"No," Lise said. "Do it."

"Oh, thank you," said Clark.

Greg leaned over and performed a somewhat clumsy high-five with the Clerk.

Margaret Lee could be seen through the door to her office, back turned, on the phone. But with her sixth sense, she adjusted, read their body language and shot her fist up high as she hung up.

Greg took Lise's hand. "Becky wants me to tell you that you should come over while René's away. I'll take Niko and the boys to a Sens game."

Lise managed to smile. "Oh, yes. That will be nice." She retrieved her hand from his slightly sweaty grip. *Va te faire foutre.*

October 2008

6

—

MA-JOR-ITY.

Ma emerged from her pressed lips like mother, *maman, ma belle,* while *jor* sat, take-no-prisoners, final as *force majeure,* followed by the double-beat, put-a-skip-in-her-step rhyming cousin of *I Am Pretty,* the closer: *ity.*

Majority took her whole mouth to say. It was so worth it.

In the four weeks since the writ dropped, Greg had lost thirteen pounds and gained ten and twelve points, respectively, on the Tory-friendly Rippo and Karp-Deem polls. He was almost as Bic-skinny as the whiny Grit leader and surging ahead in all the prime-ministerial-attributes categories, while a Green Party candidate had been discovered on YouTube caressing the banjo in what looked like a marijuana forest, inspiring the appropriate ripostes. The country hadn't even blinked when Lise predictably crumbled and dissolved Parliament; after all, the NHL teams were back in training.

Greg was at the airport in Charlottetown, P.E.I., this morning, an hour ahead of Ottawa time, and he was being fully covered by the campaign media, which was how Becky could keep tabs on her front-runner as she climbed a mountain in the home gym at Sussex. She flipped between the news channels and watched "Follow Our Leader," as Greg cajoled the country not to worry about the financial cratering occurring everywhere in the world.

She could taste it: *majority.* The word she dared not wish for aloud in non-Con company. She wanted to celebrate.

She would, in fact, be celebrating that night. With Greg on the road, and Ottawa's civil service sitting stunned in pubs, 100%-cotton knickers in a twist over the election call, she'd invited a couple of the corporate wives—Sonja, Maya and Sasha—along with some lively hockey-forward live-ins and spouses—Avalon, Atlantys and Tamberlyn—and the Cohen twins and, of course, Lise, and Apoonatuk, all of them Sussexing it over to 24 for appies, highballs, flirtations with the secret service, and a suitable chick flick to give them ninety-three minutes to sober up and walk a straight-*ish* line to any Lexus. The goal, beyond neighbourliness, was to thank the chequebooks for their largesse and the ongoing show of Tory support. She saw such nights as her country's equivalent of a one-night-only bonk in the Lincoln Bedroom at the White House. She and Lise also wanted to ask the gals to pony up for ArtsCAN!, which now loomed large on their calendar—right after the election. The gals seemed pathetically star-struck about the GG.

Of course, Becky knew the media would go gaga over her, Becky, if Greg would only allow it. The country would fall in love with her infectious snicker, quasi-Olympian health, sunny self-deprecation and stilettos. His fear, and it was one she shared, was that she might be too candid in her remarks and send them back to the drawing board. They only allowed Becky to play to the extremely loyal base, where she could extol motherhood, gerbils, crampons and croutons.

Becky was also secretly pleased that the unleashing of Lise's consort for his Euro vanity project had clinched Becky's dispatch of Corporal Shymanski to Rideau Hall. Greg had asked questions, but then consented; Shymanski wouldn't be too far away. As for Martha, Becky had kept her busy. Her daughter was quieter than usual, if that were possible, and going to bed very early, but Becky thought this was a plus. She always knew where she was.

Lise had cooled to her since René's *Lévesque* movie clip had conspicuously surfaced. They had seen each other at a few official occasions and been dutifully friendly, as one would expect, and Niko had chilled with Becky's boys. But Lise had cancelled their statutory yoga date. Also, perhaps more tellingly, they were both at Hair on George and Lise had pretended not to see her, even though they were kitty-corner to each other and visible through the checkerboard glory of the dazzling mirrors. The GG had left first, darting into the dodgy elevator. Becky would make it blow over.

Becky had also invited some of the female Cabinet members, who had Greg's back on the Hill. They were the ones with glossy, nipple-grazing hair, uniformly haughty demeanours, suits with satin blouses and an uncanny ability to *mea culpa* at a crispy finger-snap from Chief. (It had been her idea to "photo prop" the young women and stash the plump crusaders in the Antarctica of the backbench.) None of them could attend, though, because they were stuck in their ridings fighting for their seats. Pity.

Becky stepped off the Stairmaster and downed a glass of water. Through the window she could see the Gatineau hills, trees screaming with their customary autumnal fire, and the first tremble of morning traffic on the Alexandra Bridge and buses bearing workers to the Hill. And vice versa: drones from the Glebe on the schlep to Gatineau.

Sarah Palin was on the TV. There was ye olde clip of her at the Republican convention. "Lipstick on a pig." Great line. Viral. Too bad she had to wear glasses. Although maybe it made men pause to mentally remove them, and a pause was as good as a vote.

It was almost time to wake the kids. No practices that morning, no Pro-D, no anything extracurricular. She had time for crunches, a pelvic series, maybe a plank. She slid onto her yoga mat and positioned herself facing the TV screen hung from the ceiling, and started her count.

The coverage was back on Greg and a mystery voter, on the other side of the country, who had some pressing questions for him. Suddenly her father appeared live from Whitehorse, and was he in those horrible golf pyjamas? Were they shooting in her parents' Yukon living room?

Wasn't that her blown-up high school grad photo with her hair in a zombie perm? And then Greg, whose big head filled the other side of the split screen, waited while Apoonatuk breezed through the coy and obligatory intro; Greg didn't know he would be dialoguing with his father-in-law until Glenn spoke.

"What in hell are you doing about this economic melt-down, Prime Minister?"

Becky saw Greg blink in recognition of the voice. She heard Doc curse in the background.

"Not to worry, Glenn, uh, Dad. Frankly, with stock prices dropping, it's a good time to buy."

Greg raised his lip in Smile 101 and Glenn glared directly into the camera.

Becky's heart hammered. WTF and who the fuck. How had this breach happened? She was off the mat, reaching for her phone. But then she hit her brakes: in a campaign, this was essential to the tool kit. Greg couldn't control every byte and bump, and neither could she. It was a sneak attack by the usually obsequious Apoonatuk, who worked for a broadcasting corporation asking for the moon from the CRTC, but it was not her job to control Can Vox, and God knew nobody could muzzle her father. Was Greg handling it? Yes. Grimly.

"Oh, they're saying it's time to board the plane," Greg said. "Save a place for me, Becky and the kids for Thanksgiving dinner, Dad."

Was it likely to impact the final outcome? No. She wanted to text Apoonatuk and cut his Sussex family access, but held off. The PMO was actually very resourceful in these instances. They spanked bad.

The interview ended without Glenn resorting to any further inappropriate word usage. Greg gave his stock wave and climbed aboard his Airbus. Doc ran up the stairs behind him. They were taking off for Montreal. Apoonatuk waxed on, in his studio, reminding the audience that Becky's dad was a successful entrepreneur, as was Becky herself, with her former Party Time business, which catered birthday bashes for underprivileged kids and theme parties for, quoting Becky herself, "those special children known as adults."

Where did Apoonatuk get off? Breathe.

Then the breaking news. Headlines about the plunge of the stock market in Asia. The Hang Seng. The Nikkei. The DAX. Wall Street was diving into the raptures of the deep. The TSX tagged along for the dip.

Becky swallowed hard. *Mamma Mia!* would be the best flick for her party. Meryl Streep, who really should have gotten a handle on her menopausal weight, nonetheless was pursued by three handsome middle-aged men, mouths wide open, packages apparent.

She hit speed-dial to her dad and got his voice mail.

After breakfast with Peter and Pablo, with contraband cantaloupe snuck to Mister Fuzzy and Señor Wuzzy, their gerbil castle-condo placed carefully on the buffet in the dining room, and after signing Pablo's ESL test, which he'd been invited to redo, and ensuring that clean gym uniforms were squished into backpacks that couldn't be over so many crippling kilograms, Becky walked her sons to Rideau River Elementary. Martha had already been chauffeured to the National Gallery of Art, where Greg had "volun-told" her to do an internship during the gap year. Actually, Becky and the boys were driven as far as Acacia Avenue and then followed by security as Becky led them—the boys arguing loudly about which book was more evil, *Warlock* or *The Giver*, both of which Becky had domestically banned for pagan content. For the ten minutes it took to travel the route, she inspected the front doors of the various ambassadors' residences—the nation who needed to launder (and hem!) their flag, another country whose mansion could use Debbie Travis for a colour makeover—and Stornoway, where the Leader of the Opposition could be seen swaying in his tai chi poses on the raked lawn, intimidating the Iranians across the street.

The public school, predictably, was composed of older buildings, portable classrooms and an afterthought sort of playground. At the entrance, Becky made nice with the other moms, none of whom ever mentioned the election. Everyone also pointedly avoided talking about the markets and their instantly eroded net worth and dramatically scaled-down foreseeable futures. She lent her purple Sharpie, fished out of a foxhole in her Coach hobo bag, and highly recommended her own Ottawa U. orthodontist to a newcomer from the Netherlands. She always looked out for the NATO allies. A text dinged in her pocket. Her dad, getting back? But no, it was the National Gallery curator's senior administrative assistant, who had just sent Martha home with flu symptoms. Becky didn't linger. Some of the women were avoiding eye contact with her. . . . Whatever.

Martha rested her forehead on the toilet seat in her personal bathroom, which Peter had taken to calling the Ben. "Martha's in the Ben again," he'd say when they were summoned to supper or for a prayer circle. Martha's bedroom had been Ben Mulroney's room, Peter informed her. Becky thought that the former prime minister's son had done well by the Mulroney name, unlike his own father. Greg couldn't bear to hear the surname in any variant and even flinched at *macaroni*.

"How you feeling, honeybee?"

"I don't feel well, Mom. Thank you for checking on me." Martha was subdued.

"Of course, sweetie." Becky crouched beside her and stroked her hair. "What are your symptoms?"

"I threw up at the gallery. On my blazer. I feel as if I might faint. I'm tired."

Becky felt her daughter's forehead, which was slightly pimply on the hairline, oily and coolish, clammy.

"Do you think you might vomit again?"

"I don't know, Mom. I wish I could tell you." She dropped her chin and retched.

As Becky pulled Martha's hair back, the hair band slipped into the bowl and Martha gripped the edges of the toilet.

Becky didn't think twice. She plucked the hair band out of the puke, a mash-up of Martha's tiny breakfast, and tossed it in the sink. Then she washed her hands, dried them and squatted back beside her daughter, rubbing circles of mother comfort onto her back.

That was the downside to galleries. Tourists were attracted from godforsaken parts of the world, embarking and debarking through a diabolical maze of germ hubs—airports. Or groups of schoolchildren, with their sneezes and snot, contaminated door handles, benches, water fountains and toilet seats. Martha had probably picked up a virus, which would be contagious, but more importantly, time-consuming for the prime caregiver.

She stayed low beside her daughter, aware of the beeping vehicles outside. Vans delivered booze and bouquets.

Martha flushed the toilet, pushed down the lid and rested her head upon it.

"I'm calling the doctor," Becky said.

"No, Mom. Please."

"Yes, Martha. I don't want everybody to get this."

"They won't. I promise I'll stay in my room. I don't want to see anyone anyway."

Martha looked up at her for the first time. Her daughter's face was pasty, puffy and pale green. Becky took her hands in her own and almost got brain freeze from the chill.

And so it happened, in the middle of the day, when Becky had umpteen demands upon her, especially in the fervour of a campaign and in the waning hours before a gathering, that she hauled up a tray of hot tea and digestives, crawled onto the bed of her daughter, snuggled an arm around her vomit-scented girl and hung out. The doctor was on her way.

Martha's room was comforting in its Martha-like ways, with the unicorn poster, collector spoons from her father's relatively recent international treks and the ubiquitous stuffies. Her laptop, with CSIS-installed controls, sat cold on her desk under a Jesus wearing jeans and hanging from a mother-of-pearl cross—Martha's hip memento from Bible boot camp. Like a princess behind her moat, Martha had a view of the Ottawa River, the steep drop and the secret service decoy boats.

"So how did you fall in love with Dad?" Martha asked.

"Boring," Becky sang.

"It's not boring, Mom. It's as good as Genesis."

"Well," Becky said, "we'd only been dating for a little while."

"How dating?"

"Oh, going to a movie, Sunday brunching—that sort of thing."

"He never goes to movies."

"He did then. And then our dating took off and became more regular because we both belonged to the Federal Agenda party. It was brand new and he was magnificent."

"How regular?"

"Well, we'd see each other every weekend and talk during the week."

"Did you fool around?"

Becky went on super-high alert. "No."

"Never?"

"No."

"Never?"

"No. What do you mean by 'fool around'?"

"Kiss."

"And?"

"Hold hands."

"And?"

"That's all."

"Okay," Becky said.

"So, how did you know it was love?"

"It just gradually occurred to me. To us."

Becky wasn't about to reveal that moment, even though she remembered. It was Greg's oldest stepbrother, Paul, the verbal one, who'd introduced them. She'd always thought Paul was sort of sweet on her. She'd met him a few times at political fundraisers and he'd caught her eye. Paul, however, was engaged and on his way to clerk in the Attorney-General's office in Australia, and she suspected he'd asked if she wanted to meet his brother to somehow corral her, to keep her in the circulatory system of the Federal Agenda.

The son of Becky's parents' friends was tying the knot and Becky roped Greg in as her date. Her dad had started reminiscing at a spontaneous champagne breakfast. He remembered when Lance, the bridegroom, had brushed a pony's teeth with his toothbrush, he remembered when

Lance had stolen a penguin; there was an animal piece to Lance. By the time Greg arrived, in a suit jacket that was scrunched and too short in the sleeves and had a distinct Zellers air to it, and Glenn drove them all to the church in his buff waxed Cadillac, it was clear that Glenn would not be driving the Cadillac to the reception. Becky had thought it would be her. If her mother, Nancy, had intervened with Glenn, he'd have had a fit, which would have been tricky.

But Greg approached her father in the parking lot. "Glenn," he said, "I've always wondered how this model handles . . ." And, so easily, Glenn slid into the back seat, gloating; Nancy scooted in beside Greg and patted his shoulder appreciatively; and a few minutes later Greg had looked at Becky in the rear-view mirror, her father oblivious beside her, and Becky had felt a stirring heat between her legs.

Later that week, coming home from a Federal Agenda meeting, she asked him to pull off the road. He did, and she climbed onto his lap and kissed him into the shock of her lust and, it had to be said, wantonness. He'd started to cry. Becky wasn't a virgin, so there was God's overview to factor in; she was fallen, a divorcee. He told her he also didn't know if he could love again. He wasn't over his former girlfriend. They'd had a long-term relationship, but Nina's illness (she'd been diagnosed with depression) had sapped his political purpose. When he abruptly terminated their engagement, she'd been institutionalized. He didn't want to talk about it. Becky observed he was typically male in that he couldn't stop talking about it. *There, there. That's in the past,* Becky had said. And then he'd surrendered to her. "Miss Riding Secretary," he called her in the heat of it. In the morning, he proposed by fax.

Martha said, "So the first time you consummated your love was on your wedding night?" She dipped her cookie into the tea and it softened and melted away.

"Actually, the day after. After the wedding party, we fell asleep." And she'd been woken up in the night—that unforgettable snore. "This is intimate stuff, Martha. Between a mom and daughter."

"I understand, Mom. So who was your first husband?"

"His name was Aidan van der Merwe."

"From South Africa."

"You've been googling."

Martha nodded. "Sorry, Mom."

"That's okay," Becky said. "It's best just to ask directly, though."

"So why did you divorce?"

Becky took a breath. "I am so glad you asked that. Thank you for inquiring. That's a really good question, honeybee." She paused. "I married way too young, sweetie." She sighed, dropped her chin. "He was older. He was experienced. He'd travelled. And I made a premature and purely emotional choice."

She didn't mention he was fun, that she'd never laughed so much.

Martha was quiet. Reflective. Becky prayed really hard for a bullseye.

Security phoned and announced that the doctor had been cleared. Becky started decluttering Martha's bed. "He was a dreamer," she said, still feeling Martha watching her. And then came the knock at the door.

During a stolen lunch in her own study, Becky phoned Apoonatuk and disinvited him as token male at the all-gal gathering that night. He'd only been asked to cover Part One—drinks—as he was on his way to a charity event at the Westin, but she wanted to let him know there would be fallout for inviting her father on the show to ambush Greg and quiz him about the supernatural stock market crash. Apoonatuk protested—playing up the humanizing optics of the segment. Becky didn't touch that one.

Then she tried phoning her father again. She left a message this time. "Hi Dad, Becky here, you were in fine form this morning, love to talk to you." She ate some celery, picked at the Gouda, and peeled the skin off her gala apple and devoured it.

Her cell rang, she saw it was Glenn and she answered. "Hi Dad, it's about—"

"Are you calling to give me shit too?" he started. "Your goddamn mother, the goddamn assholes at your goddamn husband's PMO, they're PO'd, and since when do I have to kiss everybody's holy asses to get permission to speak in this country? Last time I voted, this was a free country with free freedom of speech."

"Dad, calm down."

"The hell! Here I was trying to do your goddamn husband a favour, maybe insert some family into his campaign, why in hell he doesn't get you out there with your legs and your looks is beyond me, and those cute kids, and the little South American one too, and the whole global financial system is on life support, and your husband's lackeys are phoning me and fucking lecturing me right and left and—I'm not donating one fucking cent to this illegitimate turkey called the Conservative Party of Canada. And I'm not shutting up. You've never picked the right man, Becky. Your heart's in your—"

Becky heard her mother in the background, yelling at him to stop, just stop.

The line went dead.

At the party that evening, Becky noticed there was a moment when both sides of the room were engaged in discussing the American election. The corporate wives were exchanging tidbits about Cindy McCain and rumours of a lover and also about Sarah Palin and the nasty interviewing techniques of a certain female anchor.

"Why didn't she just interrogate Sarah about Dostoyevsky?" demanded a thrice-married high-tech mogul's wife.

"One of the oligarchs," deciphered a Cegep-graduated figure skater.

Meanwhile, the hockey wives were full of admiration for Michelle Obama and her Target and Toledo wardrobe mash-up, intermingled with knowing comments about

Barack Obama's tight butt and cerebral sexiness. "His brain goes right to my clit," said one, setting them all howling.

They seemed to have completely forgotten that their hostess's husband was battling for his own return to office. But that didn't bother Becky. It was something she'd laugh about with Greg on the phone before turning in. *That's Cana-dumb for you*, she'd say. *So busy gawking on the front porch, anyone could come in the back and rob the place blind.*

The women spilled through the main floor, waltzing between the dining and living rooms, and pieces of epic Canadian art and outdated floral drapes resembling castoffs from Buckingham Palace. For Becky, it was a bit like home, before Ottawa, when a house party meant a keg in the back of the truck and a group howl at the moon. *Mi casa es su casa*. Yes. And the pitchers of *mom-jitos*, the recipe her mixologist had concocted, were going down swimmingly.

All Becky had to do was relax and mingle and foster goodwill among the insipid women. The boys had worked with the tutor and were now off at violin with an aide-de-camp. Martha was resting. Dr. Cambridge had spent considerable time with her, even asking Becky to leave the room for a few minutes, and she'd advised Becky to let Martha stay in bed and skip her internship the next day. If it was Norwalk, it was mild. When Becky had pressed and asked for a firm diagnosis, the doctor said she'd know better tomorrow. She spoke of a swab. "All will declare itself," she'd said with a shake of her stethoscope.

Lise, as she always did, worked the rooms, the main hall

and the corridors. Outfitted in a sizzling golden shalwar kameez, vintage, a gift from the current president of PEN International and one of Mahatma Gandhi's descendants, she went on a spree of hugs and flesh kisses, posing under Pachter's iconic flag portrait on the entry stairway, complimenting highlights and new geometric cuts, laughing too forcefully at their jokes, tearing up at a confidence, dragging the Indonesian transgendered chef in to praise the mango-cilantro prawns. She cradled the sweet six-week-old infant, Tiramisu, conceived out of wedlock in a Tuscan villa; nobody knew if it was a boy or a girl. She remembered everything the women had ever implied and shared raunchy confessions about René's adventures in the acting trade and his day of shooting with, yes, Penélope Cruz! No, they didn't embrace, *merci, mon Dieu.* Corporal Shymanski, with his limp, shadowed the GG and Becky noticed that he needed to shave. She was relieved that Martha was in quarantine.

Lise kept avoiding Becky, or so it seemed to her, bare shoulder inclined a little the other way, gaze aimed at Becky's forehead rather than her eyes. Out of nowhere, though, while Becky was in the midst of inviting the first line forward's main squeeze to a prayer brunch, Lise pried her aside, steering her into the stainless steel kitchen.

"Lise"—Becky sing-songed her name so she wouldn't sound snarky—"I'm just about to start the movie."

"It has to wait," Lise said.

"I've wangled a screener, and it's the singalong version." This was courtesy of Tory allies at the New York PR firm, the ones who'd coached her in how not to cry and who'd put Greg so uniquely on Broadway.

"*Un moment,*" Lise insisted.

Becky tried to keep cool. Everybody knew that guests hated it when their hostess abandoned them—the backlash could play out passive-aggressively in the deposit column.

Lise planted herself against the huge Fisher & Paykel refrigerator morgue in the industrial kitchen, swishing the staff out into the pantry. In the glittering Indian garb, offset by her gorgeous caffe latte skin, against the steel backdrop, she resembled a glorious animation dropped into a techno-logical wasteland.

"We need damage control, *tout de suite,*" Lise said sharply. "Do you know what he's just done?"

"Who?" asked Becky, though she knew instantly exactly whom Lise was talking about.

"The PM. Quebec."

"What?" said Becky. She'd spoken to Greg just before the arrival of the first guests and updated him about Martha's flu, and how Martha would have to cancel a few campaign stops with him.

"He's denigrated the arts. He's said the *majority*—"

Becky tingled.

"—the *majority* of Canadians don't give two cents about ballet and opera and esoteric literature and don't want to subsidize it for the pleasure of the elites."

Becky's first thought was, *He's right.* Her second thought was, *Minority, minority, minority, minority, minority.*

"You can imagine what's happening. The artists in Quebec are very upset, the First Nations are upset—it's all about culture, identity. A few of the anglo artists—the Ghost of Peter Gzowski cult, the Ghomeshi gang and a couple others, also on the blogs—all furious. Culture is subsidized, identity is subsidized—why has he done this?"

"I had nothing to do with it," Becky said.

"And the ArtsCAN! Our gala! How can I work with you as co-chair? Where is my credibility as Governor General working with you on this?" Lise's eyes were wide. "What are you going to do?"

Becky thought about it—the carefully cultivated list of corporate sponsors and spouses, all delighted to be rubbing anything with Greg, with her, and the Canadian luminaries who had fled the shallow Canadian turtle dish and become fast-swimming, sleepless celebrity sharks in the translucent global ocean. The waste of money, relationships and months of strategy.

Becky spoke carefully. *"Mamma Mia!* I'm starting the movie. Then I'm going to call my husband. Can you stay with the gals?"

Lise nodded. "Make him feex eet."

Becky punched in the lock code for the swimming pool. It had been the same for years: 1217, December 17, Mackenzie King's birthday. She pulled out her BlackBerry and plunked down on the end of a chaise longue. Steam rose from Mila's Jacuzzi and she knew she was barely visible to security. So be it. She needed to be somewhere she wouldn't be disturbed.

She punched Greg's direct number and received his voice mail. "It's Becky," she said. "The kids are fine. Call me ASAP."

She stared out the window into the dusk. The garden was just about under cover of darkness now, with the last stalks starting to rot from the root.

She called Doc.

"Becky." Clipped, Mr. Importante.

"Give me the leader."

"He's with Chief."

"Interrupt."

"No can do."

"Not good enough."

Pause.

"All I can do is give him the message—"

"*Get him!*"

Pause.

"We're coming in for a landing here in Winnipeg. Have to end. The pilot's waving at me—"

Becky knew that pilot, the congenial Trenton commander. "Doc."

The phone went dead.

She was about to call Greg back and leave a caustic version of her original message when somebody appeared at the pool entrance. Silhouetted and in uniform, he wasn't anyone she recognized from the 24 Sussex staff. She had the insane feeling that she was in danger. She eyed a kayak paddle glistening on the deck six feet away. The boys hadn't put it away again. Here was the sting: an official residence full of inebriated guests singing an ABBA hit with the Governor General and here she was, far from the literally madding crowd, by a roiling hot tub haunted by the ghosts of prime ministers' families past, with unnurtured children, and the lonely, loyal, preoccupied wives. Security was anywhere but upon her. Oh, for the *cojones* of Madame Chrétien.

Then she realized from the man's gait, as he walked toward her, that it was Corporal Shymanski.

"Madame Leggatt."

"Corporal Shymanski. What are you doing here? How did you get in?"

"The door—it was unlocked."

Becky stared at him, supremely ill at ease. "It locks automatically."

"Martha gave me the code."

She was supposed to have the indelible upper hand, the authority of her husband's office as chief executive of the dominion, but she didn't. She felt violated, even threatened. "I need to get back," she said. "My guests."

"I am wondering how Martha is."

"She's sick."

"I'm sorry to hear that."

"She's probably got a virus. We all have to keep washing our hands. Take one of my party favours when you leave." Becky got to her feet then, and moved past the paddleboards and mini-kayak. "I've packed little pocket-size dispensers. Rosemary and lavender. So soothing."

Corporal Shymanski stepped in front of her.

Becky made herself taller, using some of the Mountain pose techniques—pushing the balls of her feet, in her high heels, against the tiles, pressing on the inside of her thighs, pretending there was a string, make that steel wire, lifting the crown of her head to the low ceiling.

"It was you who transferred me to Her Excellency."

Becky's voice was measured, calm. "You should not be addressing me. This is inappropriate."

"It's important."

"You're out of line, sir."

"We both care about her."

"Her Excellency?"

"Martha."

"Corporal, the conversation is over and you're out of here."

"Elle est enceinte."

Becky heard, *Elle est* a saint.

"She's pregnant."

Becky couldn't breathe. This couldn't possibly be happening. Yet, like the illustrations in the Christian pop-up books she still read to Pablo, events of the past weeks sprang from the page like a giant Noah's Ark, or Burning Bush, so to speak: her knowledge of their relationship, Martha throwing up, the secrecy, her questions about Becky's love life—all loomed, leered, waggled their collective misery at her, sticking out of the flat, uniform, linear, orderly and distinguished progress of her constructed life.

"That's a lie," Becky said.

It was hard not to recollect Corporal Shymanski's record

in Kandahar at the Provincial Reconstruction Team and his heroic work with Lieutenant-Colonel Aisha K. She didn't know much about him, but in a way she didn't have to: they kept him close in Ottawa and that told her just about everything she needed to know. He was a boyish young man, desperate to reconnect with normalcy, and he had targeted her very young, serious, just-about-married-to-Jesus daughter. They'd been together or in close proximity all the hot summer. She had to tell Greg what had gone down; she could not possibly tell Greg.

"That is why the doctor is coming back tomorrow," Shymanski said. "Tonight, Martha's thinking about what to do. She needs your support. We need it."

"You were supposed to take care of her, not pass on Stockholm Syndrome."

"She is eighteen, Madame Leggatt."

"Don't tell me my own daughter's age." Becky pushed him. "You don't know what you're talking about, sir. We have never had this conversation."

After the guests had ebbed away, singing "Money, Money, Money," and Corporal Shymanski had escorted Lise back across the street to 1 Sussex Drive, and Pablo had woken from a nightmare about that book he hadn't read, *The Giver*, Becky checked in on Martha.

She was sitting up in her bed with her sketchbook across her knees. She'd drawn a unicorn and was adding shadings to its very pointy horn.

"I spoke to Corporal Shymanski," Becky said.

"I know," Martha said.

"Why didn't you tell me about him?"

"I didn't want him discharged."

"You kept on seeing each other after the transfer?"

"Yes. He was on afternoon shift at Rideau Hall, so we'd meet on my lunch hours."

"To do—?"

"Just walking. On the Hill or down by the locks."

Becky sat down on the edge of the bed. "It's not the flu, is it?"

Martha fixed her steady gaze on Becky's face. Then she opened her bedside drawer and passed Becky the pregnancy test wand, two blue lines, the aroma of pale urine steeped in Jamieson multivitamin, the assurance of health.

Becky couldn't help herself. "This is very serious. This is a crossroad." She wrapped her daughter in her arms and didn't think she could ever let go. This was one fucking epic maternal fail.

"I love him, Mom," Martha said over Becky's shoulder. "He's a good person. He's been through so much."

"He should have worn a condom."

"I wouldn't let him."

"Oh my God, Martha," Becky said.

"I wanted to give him pure love. Who else is going to love him with one leg?"

"Terry Fox had one leg!" Becky let go of her. "Everyone adored him! He could have had any girl in the country! And their mothers too."

"This is different. And Taylor may have PTSD."

"It doesn't mean you're under any obligation to love him, honeybee. You're just eighteen. This is your first— relationship. Your first obligation is to love yourself. To figure out what love even is, for God's sake!"

"That's not Christian, Mom."

"Oh, yes it is. Jesus had terrific boundaries."

"Christianity is about sacrifice. That's what Dad says."

Martha was tucked into her pink pyjamas with her hair tied up in a tight topknot. It didn't seem possible that she could have had intercourse in the underbrush with a one-legged military Mountie. It would have been beyond Becky's capability or empathy, at age eighteen, to make love with a physically challenged man.

"I do love him, Mom. But I don't want to have a baby."

Becky took her daughter's hand.

"Not right now. Not yet. He's not ready."

Becky was ashamed at the relief flooding through her total Beckyhood. She wanted to walk her fingers up Martha's back and croon "Itsy Bitsy Spider." Becky wasn't hearing *marriage*, nor vaunted *motherhood*, and so she had finally found her window to fix this problem. "It's about you, honeybee," she said. "You first." But she also knew it had a lot to do with Greg.

It was midnight when Becky threw on jeans, poncho, Roots cap, boots, boy glasses, all to hide her ginger-ness, and told security, "Car."

Greg had not returned her call. She couldn't stay in the house another second. When she was younger, just after she got her driver's licence, she'd borrow her mother's Honda Civic and head out on the country roads, the radio loud, Top 40, button-drunk, always pushing toward the next hit, any way she could get her autocratic father out of her head.

In Ottawa she was imprisoned, tethered like a Clydesdale.

It took only a few minutes to drive past seemingly quiet embassies—the U.K., France, Saudi Arabia. She turned the corner by *Maman*, the huge and ghastly metal spider outside Martha's National Gallery of Art, past the newer U.S. embassy, which insisted itself upon the city like an armed fortress. Past Revenue Canada. Past the Governor General's private entrance at the Château Laurier, with its ominous fading grandeur. She steered through the heart of the National Capital Region, the War Memorial, the Peace Tower, and she caught sight of the very human-sized sculpture of Terry Fox, with his own prosthetic toothpick. She cursed.

All the way down stately Elgin until the city became a neighbourhood, with laundromats, nail salons, barber shops and shawarma parlours. She parked the car by a fire hydrant and tucked into the diner, which was busy with a few post-clubbers and locals. She took a booth at the back and hid behind the brontosaurus-sized vinyl menu. She ordered the mac and cheese, and pulled out her BlackBerry. If she could have, she would have driven to Toronto and then carried on to Niagara Falls, over the border, and disappeared.

On the smartphone she drafted her resignation to the

ArtsCAN! (ArtsCAN'T!) board, cc'ing Lise and bcc'ing her husband. Sent it.

She pondered the Sarah Palin option, wherein she'd believed that the little Down's syndrome baby had been the daughter's, because the daughter had dropped out of school, and Sarah had hid her own pregnancy, and the age discrepancy was so slight as to easily throw her daughter's baby into Sarah's very own flock. Of course, Sarah hadn't lied; she was just that kind of go-fer-it gal, you have your Down's syndrome baby and run the state too.

She briefly mourned being a grandmother.

She devoured the mac and cheese. Didn't even taste it.

On the way home, Becky turned on the radio in the car for the news. It had proven to be an effective way to keep track of her husband, and sure enough, she heard Greg right at the top of the segment. He was in Edmonton, where a female reporter with a sexy voice asked him if he thought he would be punished for his inflammatory comments.

"About the stock market?" Greg asked.

"About the arts," the reporter said.

Greg replied, "Do you like punishment?"

In other news . . .

Mid-October 2008

7
———

WHITEHORSE, THANKSGIVING MONDAY. In the dining room, from behind her mother's room-shading California shutters, Becky spied on the campaign media shivering outside. They'd already sussed the backyard of her childhood, a lost bend in the Yukon River, one of them repeatedly kicking the old Canol pipeline marker left by the U.S. Army builders in the 1940s and salvaged by her father.

Upon the appearance of Greg, her mother, Nancy, and the kids, the coven of photographers, cloaked in Gore-Tex and toques, sank into a group squat to snap pictures. The reporters loitered by the chartered campaign bus parked like a circus caravan in the middle of the crescent. There was a huge close-up photo of Greg on the side, and the reporters, who looked as if they'd been cast into the territory from the dark caves of his nostrils, were now leaning on his colour-enhanced salmon lips. Doc lurked, mouth-reading.

From the kitchen, the aroma of roasting bird combined with butter-larded pie crust made her gag. She would have opened the window but didn't want to draw a lens.

It was time to talk turkey. Gobble-gobble. The cue to spin the Tory tax cuts—underwritten by the surplus built up by the Liberals but disguised as Conservative largesse. But Greg was in free fall, politically and, well, privately. She could see he was pretending to listen to the kids, raking a few fake leaves hauled in from the riding treasurer's trailer pad, but he kept turning his back on them and checking his CrackBerry for the latest from a key internal poll.

Tomorrow: the election. Showtime. Leftovers and giblets, oh my.

Becky and Greg were back in their home riding to celebrate the holiday with her parents and to produce a photo op—no Q & A—with the whole family, including the gerbils, who flew coach on the campaign plane. Becky, in full apron, camped in the kitchen, baking pumpkin pies—with real pumpkin! Her father had been kidnapped and taken to Mountain View golf club to be awarded the Pierre Berton Fellowship trophy. There he would be feted with an open bar and serial toasts to keep him far from the home fires. Glenn and Greg were not talking—not since the financial world tilted and Glenn had shed a host of vital retirement shekels.

The next morning, Becky and Greg were to cast their votes together at Audrey McLaughlin Elementary; how Greg wished Elections Canada could find a church basement in their riding, rather than a school named after the former NDP doyenne.

Becky, too, wasn't talking to Greg, and hadn't done so since Doomsday the previous week. The day after the trifecta of gaffes, he took a personal nosedive in the Karp-Deem, which then extended to a party slide on the Rippo, on top of which he didn't return her call about ArtsCAN! and the kaput co-chairmanship. As Lise had predicted, Greg's comment about the arts had alienated Quebec and urban voters, all of whom seemed to pursue an artistic sideline, working as extras in American movies with mammoth Canadian tax credits, or crocheting dog vests, *click-snick*, for boutique consignments. It was suddenly a nation brimming with citizen artists or those who knew, had begat or maintained one. Anne Murray and Denys Arcand were insulted and organizing. Even if the PMO itself was able to bury the "punishment" line, Becky remembered it. She heard it in her head.

Greg had criss-crossed his country, bent over backwards, done his utmost, bolstered a nervous Tory newbie, hugged a Sikh there, shalomed a Jew here, and pitched in and pot-latched. He'd relied on blanket apologies for epic errors in governmental history, a smattering of dollars for curling sheets and warming huts, and a stance on crime that buggered everybody's minds given that excellent statistics shouted that crime had fallen. His stylist was on task keeping him looking consistently Trudeau-esque. Very PET, with the dark fringe highlighting his shiny domed bowl.

The handlers, domestic and international, were simultaneously in premature bereavement and crisis mode. They'd
counselled Greg in the debates to drink tepid tap water, stay
calm while the opposition chorus Chicken Littled itself, and
to sound-byte in the sock-footed singsong of kindergarten
English—which had backfired, as the citizens phoned the
Communist Broadcasting Corpse to complain either that he
was on Ativan or else unbelievably condescending.

The Opposition, whom Becky could not bear to look at,
were rising in the polls. These were the ones who'd give out
Pampers to every infant born on the gibbous moon or
donate their Air Miles to al Qaeda. The female demo-
graphic, as ever, eluded her husband. They didn't want him
at their book club or bake sale, buying into the summer
timeshare at the lake, at Snowshoeing for Tibet, or Scouts.
Even inviting Martha to co-write his gospel rock opera
wasn't switching on the father-daughter wow factor.

The situation almost made Becky wish she were in
Victoria with Lise, sponsoring a soporific girls' conference,
with rich radio bytes and pro-feminist op-eds. And the Tory
brain trust would not release Becky and let her win the
bitches back. She had to perspire in the pantry to appease
and please the base.

She hadn't told him about Martha's delicate condition. Like
her, he was against abortion. They'd had long and frequent
discussions about this over the years. She knew that if he
learned about Martha, he would send her away to Switzerland
to carry the little Shymanski to term, and then give it, their

grandchild, up for adoption to some decent Heidi in Lucerne and forever be done with it. God's will, wipe one's hands. A version of breed, flee, love. He wouldn't have permitted Martha to marry Corporal Shymanski, even if she'd wanted to, because their followers frowned on teen marriage.

Outside, Martha piggybacked Pablo and Peter tried to pick up his grandmother. Greg loomed like a hundred-foot Macy's balloon float, bobbing and ineffectual.

"Put Gramma down," Martha said to Peter.

After Becky had assured, reassured and promised her daughter that she wouldn't burn in hell, Martha had made plans for a medical abortion. Dr. Cambridge's prescription medications were now contained in Becky's newest Fossil purse flopped on her mother's microwave trolley. Becky's legs shook.

Becky's cellphone rang. "Hello."

It was Lawrence Apoonatuk, high on her shit list, and she killed his call.

Then her parents' phone trilled its ring tone, "I Say A Little Prayer for You." Becky picked up. "It's Thanksgiving, Larry."

"I can't reach anyone at the PMO."

"Everyone's with their families."

"Let me play you something."

"Larry, I don't have time—"

"You will for this."

She caught the insistent voice of the tai chi master, the Leader of the Official Opposition, so beloved by women in the country, who probably felt sorry for him and wanted to wipe his brow. She quickly realized that this was the friendly election-eve fireside chat that would start to go national in the east, Newfoundland and Labrador, very shortly.

"Give me a minute, Larry."

Becky headed out of the dining room and up the stairs, past photos of her mom and dad's various anniversaries, photos of Becky and her parents in Hawaii, to her girlhood bedroom, preserved in peak high-school Mausoleum. She sat on the edge of her three-quarter bed with the vintage Eaton's catalogue bedspread and Cabbage Patch doll.

"Play the clip," Becky said.

She heard Apoonatuk, the interviewer, lead the Leader of the Official Opposition down the garden path of finances, pensions, medical care and the environment, and the answers, in simple English and complex French, were as she would expect. By the book. Stump. And then Apoonatuk asked a simple atomic question. "If you'd been Pierre Elliott Trudeau, would you have invoked the War Measures Act?"

The tai chi master was floored. Becky heard the fatigue in his voice, his awareness of the political tripwire, and she couldn't tell if he'd drawn a blank on the definition of "invoked." At first. But then he said that he never would have been Trudeau, and he couldn't comment on a different time and place, and in trying not to be drawn into a divide between English Canada and French Canada, he ended up sounding moronic. But this was a *taped* interview for television broadcast. He had gone into it at 95% strength and 95% preparation because he knew the unspoken rule book allowed him to *correct* any mistakes. She heard him ask for a do-over in a most plaintive and unwinning way. "I *dewn't* understand."

Apoonatuk punctuated the scene. "Picture this. He's waving at his handler now. She's panicking. Drowning man."

Becky heard the handler patiently disentangle the question, a sapper defusing a bomb.

"I request a do-over," repeated Tai Chi.

And then, silence. Becky replayed this in her mind. It was delicious.

"Becky, I want to be best friends with you again," Apoonatuk said. "This will go to air in the next thirty minutes. Up to you—do-over or original?"

Becky considered her options. Greg stood behind Peter and Pablo, awkward, always awkward, looking less like the boys' suburban buddy dad than a neighbourhood eccentric. She saw the photographers exchanging looks and Doc started to herd them. "We're done here, we're done." And then they all heard a loud car, make that a Hummer, travelling down the crescent toward them. It was Becky's dad driving, moving in a straight enough line, slowing for the turn into the driveway until he suddenly gunned it and crashed directly into Greg's bus photo, caving in one of the chins, actually rendering Greg's face leaner, craggier and more appealing. Cheekbone!

"Call you back," Becky said.

She hung up and raced downstairs and out into the yard. Glenn, quite stunned, was still behind the wheel, and her mother was shooing the reporters and photographers away. "The boys are upset," she said. "Please. Give us some space."

And indeed the boys, upon hearing that they were upset, commenced crying, Peter the loudest and most distraught. "Grandfather," he wailed.

Becky took him in her arms, aware that Doc and an aide were confiscating the cameras of the media while flushing them out of the area. Another aide called 911. A reporter blurted out, "Hammered in the Hummer," but they knew that if they regurgitated the incident they were virtually cutting off their genitals in Ottawa.

Becky saw that Greg had the driver's door open and was reaching out to Glenn—"I don't think we need an ambulance, Rebecca"—and then his BlackBerry buzzed. Becky couldn't believe it, but he turned away from her dazed father to check the message. She released Peter and moved toward Glenn, whom she was quite ready to maim, when she heard it. "Fuck," Greg said.

She'd heard *fuck* before. That was nothing new, and no biggie to the PMO staff who routinely sought SSRI medications to deal with the stress of quotidian access. She knew he'd just seen the results of the internal poll and that the number wasn't peachy. She'd got that. But despite her knowledge of his temper, and her prescience about his moods, and her perfect attunement to the pitch of his intonation, she was not prepared for what he did next. He kicked the door of her father's Hummer, which prompted her dad to get out of the vehicle, very quickly for him, brandishing fists.

Since even Greg mind-blindingly realized he couldn't deck or be decked by his father-in-law, his foot found something else demolition-ready at knee level. He pulled his leg back and his leather loafer exploded, knocking the gerbil spa out of the lawn chair, where it spun in the cool tundra air, scored with piercing squeaks, and tumbled across the brown lawn. Security couldn't have been more surprised if he'd pulled one of their weapons and shot at them.

Becky was on the move, but her dad got to Greg first and threw a punch. Missed.

Martha screamed.

Peter started to cry again and Pablo joined him.

Security snapped into position. Glenn, who was none too steady on his feet, finally remembered that the jerk on his property also happened to be the Prime Minister. The RCMP detail pulled Glenn away from the PM with what sounded to Becky like endearments.

The boys were on top of the gerbil palace, Pablo prying open the door. He got Mister Fuzzy out and handed him to Peter, who ran, yelling "Triage," into the house with his grandmother by his side. Pablo had to dig for Señor Wuzzy, who seemed to be pinned under the wheel. He held out the gerbil to Becky. It wasn't moving, seemed dead, and Becky didn't hesitate.

"Give me," she said to Pablo, his big brown eyes full of too much for one his size. She fell to her knees and thumb-covered the tiny nostrils, pursing her lips to fit around the little stitching of its mouth, and breathed. The taste wasn't very nice, a combination of pellets, a vague rotting veggie flavour and the tang of rodent gut, but she was determined. Martha crouched beside her and Becky concluded that her life was beyond bizarre when she was giving mouth-to-mouth resuscitation to a pet gerbil while the pills that would abort and kill her grandchild, cells splitting and complicating right beside her, sat in two clear safety-proof bottles in the makeup pouch in her purse on the microwave trolley next to the turkey platter.

Inhale, exhale. Inhale, exhale. Inhale, exhale, inhale, exhale. Pablo hiccupped loudly in her ear. *Inhale, exhale.* Señor Wuzzy's precious perfect gerbil whiskers, stiff as a stunted whisk broom, tickled her lips.

She wouldn't look at her husband or her father. "You're out of here," she finally said to them both, heading into the house with the dead pet cupped in her palm and her other arm over the shoulder of her slumped adopted son.

She left damage control to Doc and his team and then she mothered. She spoke to Margaret Lee Yeung, the GG secretary, her old connection. *Have you left Victoria yet?* Lise would have wrapped up her capstone at the young women's conference. *Can you make a stop in Whitehorse?* What was a lift on a Challenger among friends? Then she folded Pablo into her arms and asked him where he wanted Señor Wuzzy to be buried. This turned out to be 24 Sussex, near the other non-living prime ministerial pets. Becky found an old mini-cooler in the garage and a pink face cloth from the guest bathroom and a frozen gel ice pack . She lovingly wrapped the gerbil in the face cloth then tucked the bundle into a sandwich bag. Pablo stuck with her; her mother kept Peter and his annoyingly frisky survivor away from them. "We'll bury him tomorrow," she said to Pablo as she closed the cooler.

"Will there be music?"

"Yes," Becky said. "Holy hymns."

"I'll sing."

"Yes."

"I sang when my mama left."

Becky knew this wasn't the case, but now wasn't the time to rewrite the family mythology he was fabricating. It was his Colombian piece.

Pablo pressed against her.

Greg came in the back door and saw them. "Pablo—" he started.

Becky turned herself and Pablo so that their backs faced him. She didn't care who saw—Doc, security, the Toronto *Blob*.

She heard the despair in his footsteps as he walked back outside. Everything was a disaster. Her mother's dinner. The family. The election. The smell of the cooking bird permeating her brain. The death of her child's pet and her husband's unconscionable behaviour and the imminent abortion.

She stepped into the bathroom with her cellphone. Apoonatuk immediately picked up her call. "Original," she said.

Martha took the dose of mifepristone at the airport, with a few sips of Dasani. On the flight, she held the cooler containing the dead gerbil in her lap. Becky sat beside her in the rear of the jet, far away from Lise, Niko and her staff at the front. Lise was wearing her reading glasses and pretending to pore over a huge black binder. Margaret Lee had run her solicitous interference. Becky told her to thank Lise for the lift, and Margaret reported that Lise had said, *"De rien."* The GG was obviously still overly miffed about ArtsCAN!

Peter had opted to stay in Whitehorse in order to accompany his dad to the poll the next morning and miss school, and, Becky suspected, to skip the melodrama of the gerbil funeral. The PMO was in rewrite to explain the absences of Becky, Martha and Pablo at the historic event tomorrow— and were flying in Greg's parents from Thunder Bay. Becky couldn't stand Greg's stepmother, Rose the martyr, who was sliding into early Alzheimer's and continually misidentified Becky as Greg's first fiancée, the compulsively glum Nina. "I'm so happy to see you," Rose would say. "You don't seem down." Becky had given up on setting her straight, and besides, from what she'd heard from Greg, Nina had been Becky's exotic opposite with her butt-length black tresses and Salvadoran heritage—sharing only a penchant for dresses, preferably white and sleeveless, for God's sake.

Grief-stricken Pablo was asleep on Becky's other side, knocked out by a slyly potent melatonin she carried for jet lag.

Corporal Shymanski, whom Becky had hoped would be dispatched elsewhere, sat beside Niko, playing Nintendo DS. Taylor kept staring at Martha, and Martha stared back, until finally Becky had to insist that she wear a sleep mask. Then she slid one on too, and promptly dozed.

When she woke up, Martha wasn't beside her. Becky looked around wildly.

Martha balanced herself in the rear of the Challenger. Corporal Shymanski was with her, his head close, a hand pressed against the magazine rack.

Becky couldn't help herself. She unbuckled her seat belt and took three steps. "Excuse me," she said.

Martha and Shymanski turned toward her. Both had tears in their eyes.

"Excuse me," she said. "There's going to be turbulence and Martha needs to sit down right now."

"Madame Leggatt," Shymanski said.

"Mom, please give us a minute."

"Sit down," Becky said, "now."

Martha obeyed immediately, seating herself back by the window, and promptly covered her damp eyes with the sleep mask. Her shoulders shook.

"This is not human," Corporal Shymanski said to her. He was smouldering, as if she'd displayed effrontery beyond measure.

"Take accountability," Becky said. "You're the man. She's a girl."

"I'm not talking about Martha," he said. "It is about the government. Your government." He made his unique way to the front of the cabin to join the rest of the GG's dozing security team.

—

The drive to 24 Sussex was rote, silent and slow, with the Ottawa darkness everywhere. By the time Martha was asleep, and Pablo nested in, snug in his hot-air balloon pyjamas, beside Becky in the master bedroom, and the staff had stored Señor Wuzzy in the empty fridge, Becky had brushed, flossed and surfed all the RSS feeds and news channels. The coverage of the Official Opposition leader's massacre of basic Canadian English on this particular occasion was phenomenal; the seed had been planted. What if he couldn't understand a question at the Security Council? What if it was World War III? Would you want him representing us on the world stage? Could he connect with intergalactic aliens? They had been fed the doubt with double helpings of turkey, dressing, cranberry, mashed potatoes and pie à la mode. God bless Can Vox.

It was freezing the next morning: election day. After the short private funeral, Becky ordered the car, packed their bags, and she, Martha and Pablo headed up to the Harrington Lake house. They stopped at Pharmasave while Becky ran in and bought extra overnight pads; she already had the painkillers with codeine. The hills were frigid with frost. Ski hills talcumed. She convinced herself that she was voting—for her family.

The house was freshly dusted, with a full larder. She settled Pablo into a marathon *Land Before Time* rotation and shook out the misoprostol for Martha. The cramps started immediately and the bleeding was heavy. Martha squeezed in beside her brother and Becky covered them both with a Hudson's Bay blanket. Outside, the inukshuk stood with its stunted stone arms.

That night, Becky watched Greg, accompanied by Peter and Greg's father, as he made a few unmemorable remarks about the overwhelming endorsement of the Conservatives. Blue streamers fell, and Peter managed to look delighted and surprised—and even slightly ADHD? Greg's dad was predictably humble; how had he produced this magnificent and puffy dump of DNA? Indeed.

Minority. Minority. Minority.

Late October 2008

CANADA
Special Committee on the Canadian Mission in Afghanistan
Comité spécial sur la mission canadienne en Afghanistan

EVIDENCE number 1,
Témoignages du comité numéro 1

REDACTED COPY – COPIE RÉDACTÉ OCTOBER 23, 2008

From: MP13, KANDAHAR (ex officio)
Sent: October 21, 2008
To: ███████ ; DEF C4; DFAIT C4
Cc: ████████████████████████████████████
████████████████████████████

Subject: FOLLOW-UP TO MY MEMO DATED January 28, 2008, ████ –
Kandahar-████████ **in Training Unit**

SECRET

1. To date, there has not been any response to the memo dated January 28, 2008, subject line Kandahar – ████████

2. The earlier memo is hereby embedded:

To: ████████
Sent: ████████
Cc: ████████████████████████████████████
████████████████████████████████

Subject: ████████ – ████████ – ████████████████████████

Reference: ████████

1. On ████████████████████████████████
████████████████████████████████
████████████████████████████████
████████████████████████████████
████████████████████████████████
████████

2. As requested by ████████████████████████
████████████████████████████████
████████████████████████████████
████████████████████████████████
████████████████

3. An interview was granted with ████████████████
████████████████████████████████

███████ ██████ which pointed to ████████████ .

4. ██
██
██
████████

5. ██
████████████████████████████████████ the deceased's
mother.

6. ██
██
██
██
██
██
██
██
██████████████████████

7. The tally of missing █████████████████████████
████████████████████████████████

8. ██
██
██████████████████

9. ██
████████████████████████ request ██████ interview
██████████ .

10. All further ███████████████████████████████
██████████████████████████████████ the mission.

11. Robust ███████████████████████████████████
██
██
██████████████████ hearts and minds ████████████
██
██████████████████████████

12. ███
██
██
████████████████

13. ███████████████████████████████████
███████████████████████████████████

Canada's image.

25. ███████████████████████████████████
███████████████████████████████████
███████████████████████████████████
███████████████████████████████████
███████████████████████████████████
███████████████

Document Number/Numéro du document: D - 711 - 358
Receipt Date/Date:

Redacted by: AG

8

—

A WEEK AFTER GREG'S Minority Resurrection, Becky ventured to the National Arts Centre for the ArtsCAN! gala. Incognito. She didn't tell Greg; she wore a Sudbury nickel ball gown and a long dark witch's cloak, and entered through a side door after the gin- and bling-saturated reception and speeches, which avoided directly addressing the arts and culture cuts inflicted by Greg. She hunched in the lighting booth far above the sold-out house. She was there when Gordon Lightfoot performed "The Canadian Railroad Trilogy," and the crowd sang the words by heart, and she cracked up with everyone when Itzhak Perlman introduced Cohen as "that old Jew," and Leonard then sang "The Future" and received a standing ovation. She did the disappearing act when Lise, in an indigenous Bjork-like gown glued together from goose feathers and cedar bark, delivered her closing remarks about the integrity and longevity of Canadian culture.

In less than two minutes she was home, and Greg, in his Research in Motion hoodie, halted her right at the door. His fingers were dusty with Doritos and he was livid. "Let's talk in my study."

She was ready. "About?"

"You know what *about*."

He turned and walked ahead of her up the grand staircase, past *The Painted Flag*. Becky took her time, lifting the thin, flirty hem of her dress. His tread was heavy. It was his executioner's gait, and so she didn't wait for him to launch when they walked into his dimly lit lair.

"I don't care about your"—finger quotes—"feelings re the gala. You embarrassed me in front of folks I cultivated assiduously, and you threw away years of our work, particularly in Quebec, indulging in petty comments and cuts. So don't bludgeon me now."

Greg installed himself behind his desk, which was clear enough to reflect the portrait of Prime Minister Diefenbaker at his back. The boss. "Wedge issues win."

Becky remained standing.

"This isn't about any finger-quote feelings." Middle finger. "Or your finger-quote gala."

Becky took a breath. Okay, then no need to confess she'd sequestered herself in the lighting booth, engaging in entertainment espionage on the national and corporate elites. "Then what?"

He stared at her as if he might actually take action. Her tissues, her muscles, seemed to recollect the kicking-the-gerbil-cage moment and her heartbeat sped up. In the same way she knew where every washroom in Ottawa and Gatineau was located, so did she know the site of every panic button at 24 Sussex, the Langevin Block and Greg's Centre Block office. She'd never considered, though, that she might push it because of her trepidation re him.

"Martha," Greg said.

He leaned back and folded his hands in his lap. He kept interlacing his fingers different ways, the way he did when he was awkwardly posed in an Asian preschool or gurdwara kindergarten. He looked uncomfortable, as if he were talking to the TV news anchor he most despised. Then he was faux friendly to her, a warning. "I sat down with our oldest child tonight. Asked if she'd like to perform in *Temptations* at the 2010 Olympics."

Adrenalin shot up Becky's stem and her arms were flooded. "And?"

"She fricking lost it."

"How so?"

"Said she didn't deserve to participate in a gospel rock opera." Greg stopped there.

Becky stayed still.

"So I asked why. Why would a beautiful, innocent girl like herself not deserve this?"

"Right," Becky said. She noticed that the ridiculous floral curtains were drawn, which was unusual. She had to stand and be able to move quickly, manoeuvre.

"Do you know what she said, Rebecca?"

Becky shook her head.

"She told me she was a murderer." Becky watched Greg finger the family portrait, the one with the very heavy pewter frame, a gift from Chancellor Angela Merkel on the occasion of the G8 summit in Hokkaido, Japan. "She said, 'Dad, Dad, I don't know how to tell you this. I killed my child.'" He paused. "'Your grandchild.'" Greg's eyes were fierce and reddened. "Is that true, Rebecca?"

"Greg," she said. Then she just nodded.

He hurled the frame directly at her, and she was only five feet away. Becky ducked, which probably helped her miss Greg's second throw of a dancing soapstone polar bear, personally carved by the oldest Canadian shaman, because she instinctively stayed low and zigzagged while bolting for the hall. She slammed the study door behind her. "I'm pressing the button," she said, her voice ragged and bass. "If you come near me, I don't care what happens."

His phone rang then. Through the door, she heard him pick up.

"Hey, Bob, yeah." A pause. "Yes, we're throwing the furniture around tonight." Pause. "Right, yes, better than an ulcer." Nasal snicker. "Well, you know what the little women are like with the crockery. It gets busted. You take care now. Good night, Bob."

Becky didn't wait. She slipped off her heels and flew downstairs. In a few minutes she had barricaded the living room and set herself up on the couch. She didn't care if she slept in her ball gown, covered with her witch's cloak, holding the metronome from the grand piano with the panic button electronically stitched to the bottom.

If only the Corpse's top comedian could see her now. He'd held a fake sleepover with Greg and Peter a few years back, all running amok at the Diefenbunker, and he'd yelled to Greg, "I'm the king of the castle and you're the dirty rascal, husha, husha, we all fall down." Then Greg had locked them in. Peter had panicked. The comedian had become very irate and ratings for the show went through the roof. Maybe you had to be there.

She woke up at three in the morning. She smelled something burning, and was disoriented, not knowing where she was, or even who she might be. For a minute she thought she was back in her parents' home, lying very low in her old room after a parental debacle.

She looked up to see Greg standing over her in his ridiculous pyjamas. She didn't know why he couldn't wear bottoms and a T-shirt the way her first husband had. He wore Joe Fresh checkered flannels, and it was a distinctly unattractive look, unless she actually wanted to jump the bones of Beaver Cleaver's dad, and he was also holding a plate of scorched toast. Anger. Hunger. The lethal combo pack. She had mentioned this to him in the past, pre-campaigns.

He spat at her. "Who was the father?"

She said, very evenly, "I am holding the alarm. If you trust your thugs to keep this out of the *National Pest*, so be it."

He was silent, just breathing over her.

"I'll find out," he said, and left her alone in the room. And then, "What kind of mother are you?"

Ten days later, on the afternoon of Halloween, in the midst of costume preparations for Lise's Gory Horror at Rideau Hall—a macabre event for younger Rockcliffe Park denizens, trick-or-treaters and Niko—Becky received an e-mail from Pablo's teacher. The teacher wanted to talk, the sooner the better, about changes in Pablo's behaviour at school. Becky understood that to mean *today*. So she put aside Peter's Mountie costume, cobbled together from the crew around Sussex Drive, and Pablo's easy-peasy Zorro, and saddled up and called Ms. Humphries, confirming 3:30 p.m. at the classroom. Peter and Pablo could be dispatched to the librarian and be pressed into service filing books in the stacks.

She considered calling Greg to let him know about this latest development, but it was four days before the U.S. election and he was on the blower to George Bush, and to both John McCain and Sarah Palin too, trying to broker a truce between them, and the Canadian ambassador to the U.S. also seemed to need constant tranquilizing. Greg was so suspicious he even thought the Democratic presidential candidate had authorized euthanasia for his dear old Kansas-via-Oahu grandmother in order to get a sympathy bump, and asked that csis do some quick and dirty undercover in Hawaii toward that end. (Becky had heard about this from Doc.) How about that headline for November 3? OBAMA GRANNY: MURDER OR MERCY KILLING? Greg was talking the ambassador down, promising future glory in a new post as well as pumping him for every nugget of intel. Becky had her own sources for all this, none of whom knew that the PM and his wife weren't currently connubial.

It was going to be Greg and the European neo-cons—he counted Gordon Brown and New Labour as bastard Tories—against lightweight Rudd in Australia and the Columbia University–Harvard Law community organizer and, coincidentally, son of a Kenyan goatherd professor.

So Becky understood why Greg was upset: he was pro-life, big time, whole hog, and this was his first-born, his angel daughter, with her name drawn from Biblical nomenclature, and his own wife had not involved him in this crisis. Also, there was somebody out there, a punk with an erection, a jerk who ejaculated, who had violated the virgin daughter of the Prime Minister of Canada. It was incomprehensible to Greg that this could have happened, be happening, at the same time that it was basically him and the European barrel-o'-monkeys versus the ascendancy of Chocolate Jesus versus Ahmadinejad, Kim Jong Il, Chávez et al. Greg didn't know where to turn, and Becky expected he was having long conversations, when he could manage them, with Pastor Grant in Kelowna.

She was giving him space. She was marking time. She was praying for discernment. She was loving the children, who, in her eyes, were becoming rapaciously needy.

At the elementary school, Becky's conversation with Ms. Humphries, a *nouveau* hippie with red polka-dot triangle

stuck to her head, gladiator sandals on her callused feet and
sparkly scarf that kept catching in the queue of sheeted ghosts
hung off a clothesline across her desk, was informative. Pablo
refused to take part in the Skeleton Boogie, a dance number
they'd been working on for weeks, because it made him miss
his mother and extended family. He'd fled the rehearsal and
Ms. H. had found him crying in the cloakroom. Being an
"attuned" teacher—her words—Ms. H. realized Pablo was
talking about his biological family in Colombia.

Becky told Ms. H. how much she appreciated her input.
She said the family inevitably wore a mantle of duty, reflecting the role of the PM, and it could sometimes be overwhelming for the children, as they became more aware of
the media and people's expectations of their father, particularly. She also mentioned the recent death of Pablo's gerbil.

Ms. H. revealed that Pablo had talked about the sudden
demise of Señor Wuzzy. Becky steeled herself.

He'd told her the gerbil had been whacked, but wasn't
willing to confide the identity of the perp. He also wanted his
own room away from Peter and refused to discuss it further.

Becky could tell that Ms. H. thought Peter had committed
the crime of gerbil passion, and Becky herself hyper-reacted
into fight-or-flight mode. She thanked Ms. H. again, looked at
her watch, coughed and said, "To be continued," as she fled
into the hall. She dropped over the water fountain, pushing
her mouth up against the spigot, where a dribble appeared.
Before heading into the library, now virtually empty of kids,
with only one large overhead light still left on, she watched

through the window in the door. Peter manhandled a trolley of books and was ramming it repeatedly into a reading table, knocking those tall picture books out like big cement greeting cards onto the floor. Under that same table, Pablo was folded up, butt tucked in, covering his head.

Becky shoved open the door. "Peter!" she yelled. "Cease and desist." She scooped Pablo up and ruffled his hair.

By the time Becky landed back at 24 Sussex with the boys, they had to rush into early supper and costume-prep for Gory Horror. Martha was watching Sarah Palin and her family on CNN. The very pregnant Bristol was in her final trimester and Levi, the adolescent common-law progenitor who resembled a young Donny Osmond, rested his hand on her stomach and shared a giggle with her. Peter dug into his spaghetti and Becky took Pablo aside to spend some quality time with him.

"I don't want to go over to Niko's," he said, his accent rendering his apprehension more dire to Becky's maternal ears.

Martha abruptly left the room.

"Why, darlin'?"

"Don't."

"Why, amigo?"

"Scary it will be."

"Maybe you should go as Yoda."

No response.

Becky found herself submerged in a domestic emo sinkhole. Could nothing just proceed normally? Such as: children eat nutritious meal, do homework, say prayers, disappear for twelve hours?

Becky headed upstairs to check on Martha. She was in her bedroom watching Greg on her laptop screen. He played guitar and earnestly sang "Hey Eve," which sounded like a Beatles tune. "What's up, honeybee?" Becky asked.

"I don't know if I did the right thing," Martha said, not looking at her.

"About what?" Becky said, although she knew. "I saw you were watching Sarah Palin's girl."

"They seem happy, Mom. Bristol takes care of baby Trig. Levi supports her in having their own baby."

Becky bent down beside her and gave Martha a long hug. She reeked of Angel, a perfume Greg had sent a minion to buy from the Bay to score paternal points. Becky knew Martha hadn't been in touch with Corporal Shymanski because Becky was now monitoring her phone and all Internet communications. Martha had willingly allowed this. "It's natural to have regrets, Martha. Truly."

Martha said, "Why didn't you help me, Mom?" On screen, she paused her father, mouth frozen wide. "Why did you let me lose the baby?"

"We made the best decision on the day, Martha." Becky was flummoxed.

"But it wasn't the best for me. That's what Dad says." Although Martha and Greg now appeared to be in agreement on this, Martha hadn't ever disclosed Shymanski's identity to her father. She knew better than to do that.

"It may not feel like it right now—"

"I hate myself."

"Martha—"

"And if I go over to Rideau Hall, I'll see *him*—"

"Then stay home," Becky said, exhausted. "Hang with Pablo. Help Daddy with the Republicans. I'll take Peter over to the Gory Horror."

Becky herself was apprehensive about running into Corporal Shymanski, whom she hadn't seen since the showdown in the Challenger when he made his peculiar remarks about the government. But she knew that her best strategy on every front was to behave as if everything was *normal*. She'd advised Martha to let things simmer down, for sure. She knew instinctively that if she intervened, or forbade her daughter to see him, or, God forbid, revealed his identity to Greg, then a crisis would be incited that knew no boundary.

"Okay, Mom," Martha said pensively. "You can wear my costume if you want. It's roomy."

Becky heard Greg strumming again and singing the refrain, "Faa La Fa La Fa La Faa Fa La Fa La Hey Eve."

As soon as Becky and Peter stepped out of the car, Peter, in his petite red serge, took off with a howling Niko, in werewolf fur. Becky, in Martha's Maid Marian costume—dark green dress and long blond wig—wandered through the torchlit grounds, sniffing burnt pumpkin. Security melted away. It was a reprieve to be wearing a costume; she was saluted as Sleeping Beauty, Cinderella and Pamela Anderson Wench—hello!

The entrance to Rideau Hall, which of itself reminded Becky of a squat tomb, was bathed in orange light, and flying ghost silhouettes were projected skittering in a frenzy across the facade. "Monster Mash" played over and over from speakers suspended in the Norah Michener perennial garden. Lise, in her cat suit and whiskers, meowed in French and Becky wouldn't have been surprised if her personal witch's brew had been upgraded by the in-house sommelier. A vampire on stilts stalked by, and the neighbourhood children, lugging shopping bags and king-size pillowcases of candy, ran screaming after him. Lise announced that a séance would be held in Lady Byng's rockery in fifteen minutes.

The nocturnal carnival slowly overwhelmed Becky: the masked hordes, the feral kids in *Lord of the Flies* makeup, the nerve-fraying explosions of distant Mighty Mites. She was also wearing Maid Marian's thin eco-green gloves, and her own hands, in the flickering lights, resembled interplanetary appendages, flesh grafted onto her earthly form. There was the chill spilling out from the sugar bush, and she walked back down the length of the main entrance, away from Rideau Hall, toward Rockcliffe Parkway and the Prime Minister's residence, a stone's throw, really.

"Maid Martha," he said, and grabbed her from behind, pulling her into the dark woods, and perhaps because she was confused by the correct use of "Maid," coupled with the insight that Corporal Shymanski anticipated Martha would be wearing this evergreen frock, these golden locks, she didn't fight him because she was putting everything together. His kiss, a hungry exploration which involved a sweet sucking chew of her lower lip, a dance of tongue and a groin grind that rendered her moist in seconds, transported her through time and geography to her honeymoon in San José del Cabo, to Playa Santa Maria to be exact, a beach in the shape of a horseshoe, with pink sand, secluded, with Dos Equis bought out of a truck in a parking lot, and an afternoon dalliance with Aidan, her first husband, far enough away from the local families to not arouse suspicion, where it seemed they would never arrive at enough, and her nipples stung in her bikini, and the involved anatomy was titillatingly raw for the rest of the day, and the kiss was a painful reminder of the glory of surrender.

She'd started to kiss him back just as he was brutally pulling away.

"*Mon Dieu!*" he said, the light illuminating her face, with only its vague resemblance to Martha.

And then his head was covered with a hood, he was kicked in the balls, and knocked off his real foot and prosthetic sneaker by operatives, in balaclavas no less, whom Becky couldn't recognize, and didn't. Although wasn't that the Olympics-watching, nachos-chomping Corporal Robard from Harrington Lake?

"It's a mistake," she shouted. "Stop!"

They didn't acknowledge her.

Shymanski shouted, "Madame Leggatt! Madame Leggatt! I didn't know it was you. I didn't know!"

Shymanski was cuffed at the wrists and ankles.

"Stop this!" Becky said to the operatives. "Don't you know who I am? ID! Where's your ID?!"

An unmarked vehicle, a black SUV for Black Ops, Becky decided, careened up the drive from the little enclave of gift shop, guard's gate and guesthouse. Becky realized nobody was around them; the kids and grown-ups must all be at Lady Byng's séance. Where was her own security, anyway? And Shymanski, writhing, shouting, was thrown into the rear of the van by the four balaclavas, and the SUV sped away, lights turned off, through the Rideau Hall gate out to Sussex Drive.

Becky ran after to see which way they turned. East, away from the city.

"Becky?" Niko was panting. "Where's Taylor?"

Becky turned to see him, his werewolf head dangling from his hand. Coming up behind, Peter, her junior Mountie, his fake taser drawn, pointing at her. And then her security arrived, their gazes insolent in the October night, their breath a ghostly fog.

"I haven't seen him, guys," Becky said in a maternal register.

Niko clearly wasn't sold. He stared at the security.

"Brrrr, it's cold. Should we fetch some cocoa before it's all gone?" Becky grabbed Peter's taser to pull him back to the party. "Niko, come on."

He ignored her, and took off out the gate.

novembre 2008

9
—

ON THE MORNING OF THE SPEECH FROM THE THRONE, Lise discovered the note. There, in her underwear drawer, on top of the silks, a circus of scissored letters, upper case and lower, glued onto *la petite carte postale*, heavy-weight bond.

Traître.

What a feeling it was to know that a person with such ill will had full access to the frills of fabric, the thin sheer strips of civilization, that lived next to her very flesh. She dragged René—back in Canada for a viceregal cameo—from the shower, dripping wet, around the suitcases accruing for her African junket, to show him.

"N'y touche pas!" he snapped. He'd acted in enough thrillers to understand the forensics, or believed he did. "Who would do this, Lise?"

"Je ne sais pas."

"Call Margaret Lee."

"*Non!*" Lise wouldn't stand for that—she wasn't about to beckon *her* into their bedroom.

"Security then." He grabbed a robe and covered his damp butt.

"*Pas maintenant.*"

"Why not?"

"I don't want to call them," she said. She wasn't about to tell him she suspected the note might have been left by Niko. Ever since Corporal Shymanski had abruptly left in the middle of his shift (for emergency medical reasons, according to his superiors), on Halloween no less, and been replaced by Corporal Robard, Niko had become suspicious about the RCMP, even accusing her of complicity in fronting for a government that had turned to the "dark side." All of this was extremely worrisome, with Dr. Pelletier, Niko's psychiatrist, out of town and no appropriate time for a longer conversation with René.

"This is a threat," René said. "I'll call them."

"First let me get through this Speech," she said. "Where in hell is it?"

One hour later, the PMO still hadn't provided the text, and Lise, dressed in her Montreal designer suit, in the stylish tar-sands carbon shade, with Labrador seal collar and cuffs, was now not only upset, she was rattled. She fretted in her foyer; they were to depart any second for the Senate. She'd asked Margaret Lee to deliver a rough draft so that she'd at least be able to skim the big ideas *(la perspective d'ensemble, pardon)* she'd be selling to the baker's dozen of Canadians actually viewing the proceedings.

Margaret Lee finally appeared in her predictable Talbots Throne Speech suit, teal.

"Where is it?" Lise demanded.

"Embargoed."

The stylist adjusting the military epaulettes on Lise's gorgeous coat moved away from her, reading Lise's energy.

"Not for me," Lise said. "Impossible."

"Trust me. It's possible."

"I am actually giving this Speech. I am speaking it. I am the messenger."

Margaret Lee blinked mascara-starved eyes, then a call came in on her cell. She took it.

René, resplendent in his tuxedo, cute sash and badges, firmly guided Lise outside into the bleakly cold, minus-ten-Celsius morning. "Do you think the note was planted by one of the domestic staff?"

"*Non.*"

"An *aide-de-camp*?"

"*Non.*"

There was silence in their limousine as they passed 24 Sussex. Neither of them had got over *Jeune Levesque*.

"*Aagh, ça m'fait vomir,*" René spat.

It had now been five weeks since the Prime Minister's incredibly ridiculous election, for which he'd contravened his own limp four-year law, blown 30 million in tax dollars (excluding attack ads sent by his MPs to ridings held by the opposition), alienated her province and most of the cities, and ended up back where he'd first blundered.

Minority, with a majuscule M, monsieur.

In the interim, the new MPs had spent the last few weeks trekking to Ottawa, subletting the stale flats of the defeated, while Greg had chewed the fat with the outward-bound U.S. president Bush and his vice—what to do with Angela Merkel and her coalition? how to shrink-wrap Brown at warp speed until they crowned David Cameron? how to sink Brazil's Lula? Or so Lise had speculated.

In the limo, René stared straight ahead. She knew it sometimes took him weeks to shed his film character. That, of course, could be quite exciting in bed, particularly when he was playing a conquering-libido sort—a Mark Wahlberg meets Gérard Depardieu—but Father Benedict wasn't. *Quel dommage.* She wasn't sure if he was still worrying about the note or if it was something else.

He'd really not been himself since leaving the second unit (and co-star Penélope Cruz) in Cluj-Napoca. He'd returned on the day of the U.S. election and he and Lise had cloistered themselves in their quarters, leashed to the television. They'd watched Senator Obama holding the hand of his gravely silent mother-in-law in the Marriott Hotel suite in Chicago, the *splendide* Madame Obama unable to sit or pace, and wept as he accepted the will of the American people, embracing his destiny with un-Greg-like eloquence in Grant Park. René had whispered to her that Obama would "get" Quebec, would see that Quebec was the nigger of Canada. Lise said, speaking as an African-Canadian, that Quebec was not necessarily the blackest in the land. She gave that distinction—as she could, given the full complexity of her marriage to Brett Neeposh and as mother of a half-Cree youth—to the First Peoples. And then she and René had fallen asleep, without kiss or connubial celebration, with CNN replaying speech snippets, and Anderson, and Wolf, and Candy, and Donna, and James, and Anderson, and Wolf, ad infinitum. And since then, between them, she'd sensed a distance.

Two skateboarding boys blew kisses as the limo skimmed the U.S. embassy. Lise robo-waved back.

As they arrived at the Hill and turned right, proceeding past the Eternal Flame, where a group of evangelicals prayed daily with a beatific wickedness, an extraordinary gathering of police cars, lights flashing, sat parked with the troops before the door of the Centre Block, along with the broadcasters' trucks. Lise looked up. On the roofs of Centre and West Block were a number of snipers, more than usual.

"Lise," René said, leaning over and snagging her baby seal fur cuff, "I have to tell you."

She shifted to take his hand in hers. It was rough, callused, not the hand of a thespian priest. She really hoped this confession wasn't going to involve Ms. Cruz.

"I did some work for Foreign Affairs."

"What?"

"Some meetings for them. In Romania. Days I wasn't needed on the shoot."

Past spouses of the Governor General had often been enlisted by Foreign Affairs; the public didn't pick up on this because they were misdirected by the government press or, more often, preoccupied with pomp and puffery. Meanwhile, the consort with the deep oil profile pitched pipelines in overseas embassies or deconstructed NATO, in fluent Farsi, at a seminar in Tehran. That was how the government secured two intelligence assets that were, at the same time, considered expendable, frivolous, anachronistic extras by the public.

Lise's consort, however, was an artist, a civilian, and one who'd been treacherously manhandled by the PMO.

"René, what were you thinking? Why would you do that?"

"I was thinking only of you in your job. The atmosphere here." He waved his arms. "I thought I should build a bridge."

"After what they did with your *Lévesque* cleep?"

"Yes." René shrugged. "But they let me go do the film."

"And I agreed to pull the plug on the government."

"But that note in your drawer—"

"What about it?"

"Now I wonder if my meetings in Romania are connected to that note . . ."

He turned away from her, his left shoulder slightly raised.

The limo pulled up to their precise debarking spot. Lise was dry-mouthed and weak-kneed. The door opened and a stubby hand was proffered. *À bout portant,* it was Greg's. René vanished out the opposite door. She could barely look at Greg. She'd last seen him on Remembrance Day, when he jostled with her for prime position on the podium and even stole her designated wreath, which was larger than his, to place on the memorial. Since the election, he'd gained weight and his eyes were hooded. When he said "Lise" with his vein-shaded lips, it sounded to her like "Please."

Lise spoke between clenched lips. "Speech."

"Sorry about that. Between Chief and Doc, commas go nuclear."

"Still," Lise said, "an advance copy is common courtesy."

"I'm sure the NGO Channel had its moments," Greg said.

"Jamais." Lise lied. "Professionals."

Briskly, because it was cold, the anthem was played, the flag raised, and Lise inspected her troops, the King's Own Regiment. René filed behind her. The soldiers were only hiccups older than her own Niko, and the sight of them drained her. This was the hardest part of her job, the role of Commander-in-Chief, when she was essentially a pacifist, a believer in dialogue and consensus; and why wouldn't she be after what had happened long ago and recently in St. Bertrand? The coup, the slaughter. The 21-gun salute, although expected, *lui a serré le coeur.* And then, with her secretive husband at her side, flanked by Greg and his cub-pack Cabinet, she climbed the red carpet with her winning smile, just after the Keeper of the Carpet finished his final whisk.

Lise led the way into the Red Chamber, past the oak doors displaying the insignia of the provinces and territories, with Nunavut a last-minute, oddly shaped addition, hanging in its own row. The walls of Tyndall limestone from Manitoba, embedded with the fossils of an ancient sea, closed in, as did the fossils occupying the seats. The Senate was also known as the home of sober second thought, a phrase she found thrillingly ironic.

She sat down, and René followed suit, and then Greg, occupying the dunce chair: approximately two feet lower than her 1916 reupholstered throne and three feet away to her right. The Supreme Court judges, ciphers in their Christmas regalia, were also present. The Gentleman Usher of the Black Rod bustled off to knock on the door of the House of Commons and advise the MPs that it was time to face the music of the umpteenth parliamentary session.

Greg tried to get René's attention. *Bonne chance.*

Still no Throne Speech. In the distance, she thought she saw teal-shaded Margaret Lee talking to Greg's Chief of Staff and Director of Communications at the entrance. She never retained their names; they came, they went, and René just referred to them collectively as Jekylls and Hydes. Margaret Lee was *très* cozy with those boys.

Lise leaned over toward Greg, pointedly staring down on his buffed and powdered bald spot. "Maybe I'll make up the Speech."

"Ha," he said. "Good one."

Lise looked up, way up, at the paintings hung on the walls. Eight sober images from World War I, when Canada militarily came of age and wholeheartedly spilled the blood of its young. Supposedly, as the political grandchild of the House of Lords in the English Parliament, the Senate's carpets and seats were red to symbolize the colour of royalty. For Lise, the ruined cathedral at Arras, the demolished Cloth Hall in Belgium, the troops at the railway station and even the smoke in the air served to remind her that the Red Chamber was drenched in the brotherhood of common blood.

"Prime Minister, is Becky—" Lise cast her eye toward the private gallery. Usually Becky brought Martha and listened, smiling with her lips closed, in the front row.

"*Pas aujourd'hui,*" Greg barked.

"For God's sake, give me the Speech." Lise was desperate.

At the entrance to the Senate, Margaret Lee seemed to be shouting.

Suddenly a Senate page delivered twenty-five sheets of paper so hot off the King's Own Printer press that they scorched Lise's palms. "Your Excellency," she said.

"*Merci beaucoup,*" said Lise.

But when Lise turned the cover sheet, she found a dense, single-spaced document from the Department of National Defence with a series of acronyms: ANP, NATO, RCMP. Words randomly drew her eye: *Kandahar, prostitution ring, drug lord, murder.* This wasn't the Speech from the Throne. She raised her eyes in horror as Margaret Lee bore down upon her.

"*Désolée,*" Margaret Lee whispered, and slipped her a thinner, cooler stapled packet. "*Donnez-moi l'autre.*"

"No." Lise wouldn't let go of it. "*Ça va, merci.*" Lise tucked it behind the Speech.

Margaret Lee shot one glance toward the rear of the Senate and then raced in her sturdy pumps past the cameras.

"Honourable Senators, Members of the House of Commons, Ladies and Gentlemen . . ." Lise began, with Oscar-worthy conviction and warmth. She shifted to the edge of her throne, where her shapely legs could inspire national lust. Whatever it took. She faced down the assembled non-blinkers.

"And reconsider our fiscal duties . . ."

Nobody saw these political elites from her singular perspective—not the cameras trained upon her benevolently non-partisan facade, not the press, fascinated with their technological toys and holstered by their corporate sheriffs, not the citizens of this blindfolded gentle giant, this ventriloquist's dummy of a country, with the middle-class populace in a systemic funk about their mortgages, pensions, kids' educations, cruises and replacement hips.

"Renforcer le gouvernement . . ."

She'd met the Canadians in their mosques and colleges, at their theatres and barracks and gyms. Talked the talk with the senior citizens, Canada born, who were watching the Arctic ice melt and trickle down to their suburban postage-stamp lawns, flooding the forty-ninth parallel; they'd confided in her about the dilution of the Canadian brand, a public broadcaster now showing *Jeopardy* reruns. Hugged the new Canadians, her fellow immigrants, who'd happily sworn allegiance, those who shrugged on their earmuffs and carried on as if they were in the Punjab, only it was much cooler here, and bought boots that sounded as if they were named after a curry: *mukluks.*

"Guard our citizens . . .

"Beaucoup d'emplois . . .

"Also, we will aim . . ."

She saw the weary face of the separatist leader; he was such a good dancer. Ditto, the trim socialist dude. Such a sweet ass. The Chief Justice of the Supreme Court stared at the ceiling; he was Asian, Alberta born, the rebel son of a famous dim sum chef. Lise couldn't bring herself to steal a glance at the rigid RCMP commissioner. Or Greg's Cabinet: the left-wing media called them Old Testament golfers, moose stalkers and misogynists.

She met the eyes of the Leader of the Official Opposition, Monsieur Triste. He regarded her with an unwavering sort of unrequited trust.

What would happen if she switched the documents?

The thought lounged upon her *langue de bois.*

She faltered.

Greg scratched his calf, a brow, the other calf. Her pause made him nervous. "Give me," he said.

"Pardon?" Lise turned.

"The Speech." Greg grabbed for it.

A sudden commotion overhead. Shouts from the gallery.

"Murderers!"

Lise craned her head to see. MPs ducked. Senators jerked awake, wondering where they were.

Security scrambled and a phalanx of RCMP and other operatives charged toward Lise and the PM, ready to escort them to the safe room.

"Murderers!" A gut-wrenchingly familiar tone of voice.

Then she spotted Niko. In the front row, wearing a black toque with skull and crossbones, and he was not supposed to be there, he was supposed to be in pre-Calculus II. In a quick second he was apprehended and hustled out the side door by security. She couldn't believe what she'd just seen. And neither could anyone else in the Chamber.

René stood on his throne, ready to run out after his stepson.

"*Assieds-toi.*" Lise waved him back down. "René."

The Speaker of the Senate rose to take charge. Lise waved at her to sit too.

"*Silence, s'il vous plaît,*" Lise said to the gathering. "Silence, please."

She was shocked when they obeyed.

She'd never felt so strategically African, so black, so *other*, and it had to do with being the mother of the outspoken boy now being manhandled off-camera and, oddly, the improbable death of his Cree father, who'd been in his intellectual and legal prime when his canoe capsized in shallow water on the calmest day of the year.

And everyone in front of her was so very very shocked and *blanc*.

She took a deep breath.

Then, from the sidelines, where she'd repositioned herself in the ruckus, Margaret Lee flagged a special parliamentary page, who ran like a nimble ballgirl at Wimbledon to shove a glass of water into Lise's hand. Lise reacted, taking a sip only to save face for the girl. As she watched the CPAC camera tilt to focus in on the brass and gold mace, the page artfully reclaimed the Defence document and bounded away.

"Holy shit," Lise said nationwide.

René secured Lise's arm as they descended in a private elevator to the bowels of Centre Block. It crossed her mind that it was likely no Governor General had ever visited the jail in the basement of the House of Parliament, at least not to spring his or her child from custody after a Senate meltdown.

It was tooth-achingly cold. The halls were a fluorescent labyrinth with the layered scent of decades of aftershave and possibly French fries. Lise's legs were those of a newborn Bambi, bendable drinking straws, not suitable for charging behind this very apologetic RCMP liaison.

"*Ici,*" he said, and carded them through into a locked-down zone, a room crammed with men staring at live Hill images on their computer screens, and on into a tinier office where a plainclothesman sat vigil with Niko. He left when René swept her in.

Lise bundled her boy. She couldn't say anything to him; she just hung on to him and dry-heaved.

René patted her on the shoulder.

"Don't," she said. "What about him? What about Niko?"

When she stopped, she sat up in the plainclothesman's chair and took in her son.

He looked exhausted and wired at the same time. In his thug's clothing, with the acne, the grimace and the furtive turn to his eyes, she didn't know what to make of him or this situation. Where had he found that toque? She prayed that Margaret Lee and the PMO were burying the incident. If she had to, she was going to use the fricking government Challenger to bring back Dr. Pelletier, Niko's shrink, from wherever he was burrowed away. Ministers often used the jet like a cab, so there was precedent.

René sat down, cross-legged, on the floor. He seemed to have forgotten he was wearing Excellency haberdashery. He had to look up at Niko.

"What is going on with you?" Lise asked Niko. "You need to tell us."

"I've told you, *Maman*," Niko said. "You don't believe me."

"What's this about?" René asked.

"It's Shymanski, isn't it? I don't know what you think you thought you saw, but you didn't," Lise said.

"Let Niko talk, Lise."

Niko looked René directly in the eyes. "At Rideau Hall on Halloween, I saw four men in masks come out of the bush and attack Corporal Shymanski. He was handcuffed, ankle-cuffed, if that's what you call it, and thrown into a van." Niko mumbled, "Becky saw too."

"You didn't mention that before," Lise said accusingly.

"Maybe you should talk to Becky about it, Lise," René said.

"I'm not talking to her right now."

"Isn't Niko staying with her when you're in Africa?"

"I plan to talk to her before I leave and not a moment before."

"Perhaps Niko shouldn't be staying at 24 Sussex then?" René said.

"*Je n'ai pas d'autre choix!* I want a pair of maternal eyes watching him! I want security! *Vingt-quatre heures sur vingt-quatre!*"

Niko's shoulders slumped.

Lise felt like *merde*. "I'll talk to Becky, then. *Tout de suite.*"

Niko and René didn't respond.

"I'll get to the bottom of it," Lise declared.

René contemplated all of this; Lise could see his mind somersaulting as he passively stared at the limestone wall. "Niko," he finally said, "it doesn't make sense that you witnessed this and yell at your mother when she's giving the Speech from the Throne, in the Senate, on television."

"René. She didn't take me at my word."

"This is serious, Niko. *C'était fou.*"

"René. I am not crazy. I'm mad."

"You mean angry," Lise said.

Niko nodded.

"So angry you'd leave a note in my underwear drawer?"

"Lise." René was shocked.

"What are you talking about?" Niko said. "What note?" It was clear he didn't know what she was referring to.

"I have to go and be the Governor General," Lise said. "And fix this. Then René will take you home. I'm going to locate Dr. Pelletier and we will deal with—how you're feeling. And I promise you I will talk to Becky about Corporal Shymanski and find out what happened. I love you, Niko, more than anybody in the world, and René and I stand with you. We're with you." She pincered him in her embrace.

When she released him, he looked ruined.

Then she left him with his stepfather, who wouldn't look her in the eyes.

At the reception in the Speaker's salon to celebrate the opening of the parliamentary session, there was contagious relief that it was only the GG's half-Indian son snapping like a pine-beetled twig and not al Qaeda. Scotch flowed.

Lise was held hostage by the Chief Justice, George, who lived in fear that Greg would stack the Supreme Court with pro-life/capital punishment justices. He was one of Lise's biggest boosters by default, given that they were the two top non-Caucasians in Ottawa. He also very sweetly dismissed Niko's bizarre behaviour as adolescent attention-seeking.

"Kids," he said, which he could safely say because his offspring were filed at Johns Hopkins, Brown and McMaster in postgraduate programs.

Greg appeared at Lise's elbow. She mustered her courage.

"Excuse her," he said to George. "I need to speak privately with Her Excellency."

George disappeared immediately.

"How's Nick?" Greg asked.

"Functional," Lise lied. "What was that classified document I almost read to the country?"

"Listen, Lise—your shots up to date?"

"*Oui, oui, toujours.*"

"*Très bien.*"

"*Pourquoi?*"

"You're going to Afghanistan."

"When?" said Lise.

Greg looked at his watch. "Thirty-six hours," he said with a bow. "*Inshallah.*"

10

INDIRA JOPAL, older sister of the president of Pakistan, meandered through A Thousand Years of History, the primo exhibit at the Canadian Museum of Civilization. At this rate, it would take Indira longer than a thousand years to appreciate the capitalist evolution of her host country.

It was at times like these that Becky cursed the duties of her unofficial job description; rather than touring boring exhibits, she preferred a session of sit-down beadwork with First Nations women. Less time-consuming for her, and some of those Third World wives were actually very good at the craft and felt a sense of accomplishment, which transferred into positive feelings for Canada. For God's sake, they were naturals—*natives*, even, themselves. However, the regular First Nations beaders were away on another traditional holiday and as a result Becky was midway between the Hudson's Bay Company mink pelts and Pacific logging.

She'd been through this maze many times, not only with the spousal corps and their sherpas, who always found that the settler hovels, cobbled together from timber and tin, reminded them of a certain village at home in the southern hemisphere, but also with all her children and their Ritalin-and-juice-addicted classmates, which included hosting sleepovers in the Raven's Village.

Today, Becky found Canada Hall, without the brigades of students, queasily empty and silent.

Indira stroked the mink and addressed the translator, who asked Becky, "You own this?"

"I wish," Becky said. "Maybe for my twenty-fifth wedding anniversary."

Indira smiled at the translation, then nattered on in whatever language she spoke.

"Too hot for Islamabad," the translator said, holding the pelt.

Becky imagined every strawberry strand of hair on her head tarnishing into rusty silver as tour time dripped to a standstill.

When there were no immediate prospects of ideological conquest or conversion in a social situation, Becky's intimate knowledge of the most proximate restroom in any government or public edifice was pressed into service. She pulled aside a security aide and sped-walked away on her spike LuLu's, past the miners panning for gold and the Doukhobor church, toward the closest respite. It was a holiday to get away from the perpetual twilight of the history exhibit, to pee vociferously, and to take a long time washing her hands and reviving her lipstick. They were going to have to speed it up if Ms. Islamabad was going to be on time for a luncheon reception at the Supreme Court.

"Becky."

She turned to find Doc, inside the door—and his maleness seemed incredibly inappropriate in the women's washroom. He was pinning the door shut, keeping security and Third World bladders at bay. He was dressed for the Hill, in an Armani wannabe suit, probably zigzag-stitched by a Hong Kong tailor hired by his girlfriend. Bespoke, bothered and breathless.

"Just FYI," Becky said, dropping her tube back into the clutch, "this is the women's."

"You haven't returned my calls."

"*Quid pro quo.* Heard of it?"

"Come on, Becky."

"What goes around comes around."

"I'm not here to talk karma."

"Good." She moved to go past him out the door.

He didn't budge. "But we're facing Karmageddon here."

"Doc," she said, "I have a foreign dignitary under my arm, you're completely out of line, and DFAIT will have a stroke."

"We've got a problem."

"What?"

"We need your help."

"What?" she said, already sensing what was coming.

"Greg. He's losing it."

"What makes you say that?"

"In a few minutes, we're going into an update and—"

"I already know this."

"You know the details?"

"No."

"We're stripping federal public servants of the right to strike. We're abolishing pay equity for women." He paused.

Becky didn't comment. Yes, women should be in the home, raising their own children. While we're at it, send the Filipinas back home to raise their own. And, yes, all those secret socialist feminists should tie on their Hush Puppies and heave-ho off Parliament Hill. Of course, the *urbanistas* would kvetch.

"And he's decided to cancel per-voter public financing of the political parties."

That got her attention. "Not good," Becky said. "Not now."

"That's what we're telling him. And Finance is telling him. It's the time to appear conciliatory. He and Chief, they won't listen."

"What about the stimulus?"

"No." Doc slumped against the door. "Not even a sliver."

That was grim indeed. Becky pulled out her phone, but there was no signal. The Museum of Civilization was the equivalent of a mummy's concrete bunker. "How much time?"

"The press is already in lock-up with the fiscal update."

"What? Are you kidding me?"

"We're in motion."

"I can't change this!"

"You must," Doc said. "Pull a rabbit out of a hat."

"I'd like to pull," Becky said, "a wireless signal."

"You have to talk to him."

"Follow me."

Becky blasted out of the washroom with Doc in tow and told a bored aide to escort Indira through the rest of Civilization and on to lunch. She ducked past the Canadian postal museum and down the escalator to the Great Hall, dwarfed by the Pacific Coast totem poles. Standing in front of a Tsimshian manor, with a monotone drumbeat in the background, she stared across at the shining rump of the Parliamentary Library and a statue of poor murdered D'Arcy McGee, advocate for Confederation, stashed at the rear of Parliament Hill, as she hit the button.

Doc watched her hopefully and stroked a few rogue chest hairs.

"Yes." Greg actually answered his personal line.

"Greg," said Becky. "A minute." She could tell he was being groomed; when his stylist subdued his remaining hair he went into a trance.

"Is this to do with the kids?"

"No."

Greg hung up.

Doc got it. "Oh my God. Oh my God. He's night and day since Obama got in. Oh my God. Oh my God. Night and day. Night and day." ·

Becky refused to respond. Her husband wasn't affected

SUSSEX DRIVE

by the threat to global conservatism posed by Obama's election. It wasn't the crash of the planet's financial markets. It was much more than that. She wouldn't tell Doc if she could, and he was already on the run—jumping over a Haida canoe and bolting up the escalator, saying into his phone, "Mayday."

Becky squeezed into the back row of the visitors' gallery of the House as Greg, below, in the Prime Minister's seat, turned his gaze back to Finance, who was about to deliver the long-awaited economic update. Finance, a Newfie Barbie of Norwegian descent, was fired up, placing the Hill and a nation of citizens on high alert: "financial degradation," "difficult financial deterioration," "financial decimation," "severe financial devaluation" and "financial deliverance." The final utterance sounded to Becky like reservations for the Big Five banks at the Rapture. She sensed the discomfort of the opposition, most of whom had already premasticated the speech in the lock-up, parsing its guts at the same time as the press. Tai Chi squinted in the dim light and squirmed in his skin as Finance dirged, in a liturgical litany, the fallen saints in the American financial firmament: *Santa AIG, Santa Bear Stearns, Santa Citigroup, Santa Fannie Mae, Santa Freddie Mac.*

"We cannot ask Canadians to tighten their belts without looking in the mirror," Finance declared, sticking out her Norwegian cleavage. She went on to make the announcement Becky dreaded: the $1.95 per vote paid by Canadians

[165]

to each political party, which prevented the unions and corporations from playing ringmaster at the electoral circus, would be terminated. The opposition heard this in the same way they would an order to march out of the House, turn their backs on the Eternal Flame and face a firing squad. This was endgame. Bankruptcy. No funds for travel, party building, policy conventions, internal polling, nada.

Becky noticed that everyone across from her husband in the Commons was looking directly at him, or perhaps at Chief, a shadow lurking. Becky allowed her mind to travel freely for a second and imagined what would happen if the Liberals, Bloc and NDP went bankrupt. The Conservatives would morph, like a nicer Gollum with the ring, into one über-tribe to lead them all.

While Finance ended with an earnest, "We'll get through this," Becky did the math. Her husband's government would transfer approximately 89 cents per man, woman and child from the voter subsidy back to the public piggy bank as stimulus spending. She compared this $30 million with Germany's $213 billion, Japan's $275 billion, Britain's $418 billion, China's $600 billion and the U.S.A.'s staggering $1.5 trillion. Greg's belt-tightening, ball-freezing parody wasn't any form of stimulus—not with the Employment Insurance claims increase of 96.4 percent over the last year and the auto industry tarred, feathered and hitchhiking. What was Greg thinking? *Was* he thinking?

Finance, with a flip of mermaid hair, thanked the Speaker. This was usually the cue for riotous appreciation from the government benches. The Tories, however, were restrained; there was an extreme nervousness in their team demeanour, particularly after the announcement of fiscal genocide for the opposition. She smelled fear.

The socialist leader, ever sentimental, had the floor. "Instead of an immediate stimulus package to attack the recession, the government is apparently going to attack democracy."

He received a minority standing ovation. And then the session was over.

Greg and his posse—Chief, Doc, Finance Barbie and a few other loyals—exploded from the House.

As Becky took her leave, she caught sight of the MPs in the opposition lobby. It was disturbing. A Bloc Member from Montreal hugged a Grit from Ontario. A female NDP MP hugged a former Liberal Cabinet minister, also female, a doctor, a person Becky had personally courted for the Tory cause, a prestigious catch. The fiscal update required a confidence vote, and Greg was obviously betting that the opposition wouldn't vote against it; it was too soon to trigger yet another unnecessary $30 million election. And when they supported the update—by not showing up to vote against it—he'd have the pleasure of watching them cut off their own political welfare.

She was en route to Greg's second-floor office in Centre Block when she was accosted by Greg's former mentor and a current member of the King's Privy Council for Canada, Alice Nanton. Greg had eventually betrayed her, in a good way, by running against her, trouncing her, and then appointed her to the KPC, for which she wasn't appropriately grateful as far as Greg was concerned.

"Did you hear what he said?" Alice asked.

"Who?" Becky said.

"The Socialist. 'The government is apparently going to attack democracy.' Christ! It's the first time I've ever agreed with that man." Alice was spooked. "You look like we need a drink," she said, taking her arm.

"I'd love to," Becky said, "but I'm popping in on the PM, and then the Pakistani delegation's over with George at the Supreme Court."

Alice shrugged in closer to Becky; she'd already been dipping into the well. "What's going on with him?" she whispered. "What's the matter with that man?"

Becky wanted to shut that down. "Greg's fine, just tired. We've got the Governor General's kid staying with us while she's away."

"He's a caution, that one," Alice said.

Becky stickhandled. "It's hard to do the good work Greg wants to do. With the minority."

Alice rubbed Becky's shoulder, commiserated. "Yes. It's hard to cut the Leviathan down to size. Like trying to butcher a whale in the middle of the ocean."

"Something like that."

"And they're slippery."

"Yes."

"Pull you under."

"Possibly."

"But you know, Becky, I haven't seen him like this—so, so dark—since the Nina Episode."

The Nina Episode. It took her a few seconds to realize that Alice wasn't talking about a key political operative beheaded in the Horn of Africa, but about Greg's depressed pre-Becky *amour*. "Yes, I know that was a tough time."

"Above and beyond tough."

Becky was silent. When she was unsure about where an ally was heading, she waited for her own inner direction.

"He was head over heels about her. But, and I quote, after a few years she came to distinctly 'dislike his vibe.' And then she dumped him," Alice said.

"Pardon me?" Becky had always understood that Greg had done the deed.

"Of course, he's impossible. You know that first-hand. Nobody denies the will of the Great Leggatt, not least a young rural lass with no apparent mind of her own."

Becky quickly reshuffled her mental deck and dealt. "And such a tragedy, too, that she went off the deep end and was institutionalized, all that."

Alice looked at her as if she'd gone barking mad. "What are you talking about? Nina wasn't institutionalized."

"Uh—"

"She up and disappeared. Don't you remember?"

"It's coming back to me now you mention it."

"She dumped him, he went nuts, *berserk*, quite frankly, and she had to get the order, so many metres distant, and he still didn't observe it. So she disappeared. Halifax, Vancouver, someplace she could fade into the weather."

Becky was suddenly disoriented, crossing a high bridge in the pitch dark. "That's right," she ventured.

"I encouraged her to give him a second chance—Greg begged me to ask her—but no cigar."

They were standing in the Hall of Honour and the portraits of the prime ministers, lining the hall, all stared at her, including benign Avril Phaedra (Kim!) Campbell, now living in Paris with Canada far to the east of her, and Charles Joseph Clark. A Hill decorator and flunky passed by, transporting one of the giant Sitka spruces intended to grace the Hall. She had to brace herself against a shining water fountain that nobody drank from.

"Wait a minute," Becky said.

"You didn't know this," Alice said. "God. How could you not know this?"

Becky wondered the same thing. Umpteen years, after the two or three kids, it should have come up, or Greg's stepbrother, gregarious Paul, now steering a ministry in the Australian government, could have offered a diplomatically intimate aside—if he knew. Of course, when she'd been seducing Greg after the riding meeting, it was before the glory of Google, back in the nineties when one had to rely on old-fashioned gossip, and back when their grassroots organization was essentially manure for other more mature political parties, and back when the leader-in-waiting had to be groomed, nurtured, garlanded. But, given that this was the Prime Minister of a nation with a supposedly free press, wouldn't some enterprising journalist have stuck his nib deep into this dirt? By now?

"It might be an idea to talk to Greg about this, Becky, when he's back." Alice patted her arm.

"Back?"

"In the land of the sensible." She spotted another old warhorse then, a skinny Grit senator with a briefcase of causes, and trotted away in the opposite direction before he could spring an arm-twister.

The clock in the Peace Tower chimed the hour. On the floor above, in the Memorial Chamber, a page had been turned in one of the six Books of the Dead, a ritual that allowed every Canadian soldier who had fallen in a war, from South Africa to Afghanistan, to be honoured by the country one single day of the year. *Where's the book for girl-friends?* Becky wondered. *Where is the book for wives?*

A few minutes after Alice's evaporation, Becky expedited herself to Greg's office. The corridor outside, usually bustling with Cabinet ministers and their extraordinarily busy staffs, was roped off with velvet cables and quiet as a crematorium. In the antechamber, chock-a-block with stacks of the *Economist*, policy publications from the Rand Corporation and the *Wall Street Journal*, Becky listened as the executive assistant, Firstname Surname-Hyphenate—they changed so often—informed Greg that she was there.

Her cellphone beeped. A text message from Glenn, which she read because she was practising self-hatred. *My son-in-law is God.* She deleted this. There were limits.

Greg's heavy oak door swung open and there was a miserable exodus of the faithful meek such as Chief, Doc, who held up a paw, Clark the Privy Clerk, and the heavy hitters Greg hauled out when he wanted to barbecue the opposition, the ministers commonly known as Cabinuts.

The executive assistant nearly bowed to Becky. "The Prime Minister will see you now."

Becky had had the biscuit. "Oh, la de-f-ing-da," she said. "This isn't Westminster."

The assistant closed his eyes. If an offhand remark like that had zapped him, he'd definitely be gone by dawn. She could read the tea leaves as clearly as *Maclean's*.

Greg's office was dark, drapes pulled tight. It had always struck her as about as comfortable as a dentist's waiting room. Greg wasn't behind his desk. She turned around. He was slouched in one of those nondescript eighties office chairs, something she'd stretch her calves on while waiting for a prescription at the pharmacy. He cradled his largish head, with its distinctive dark fringe, in his two hands.

"Greg."

"What?"

"I'd like to talk."

"About?"

"About what's going on here."

"There's nothing going on. Nothing. Nothing! Nothing to talk about. Got it?"

"There's a lot going on, Greg."

"Right." And then he just lost it. "Becky. Becky. Oh, fuck me. We're going down."

Becky was shocked. He'd never admitted defeat, not ever.

"They're going to form a coalition. Those fucking assholes."

Her throat tightened. She chose not to remind him that he'd basically attempted the very same move when he was in opposition. Don't go there. She was nauseous, and then slowly the anger surged and was sucked up to her brain through a short straw.

"Those fucking assholes couldn't form Jell-O in a mould," she said.

Greg wouldn't look at her. "They'll draft a non-confidence motion."

It was very difficult for her not to say "I told you so," but then, technically, she hadn't been consulted. And he knew her well enough to know she would have vetoed, or at least tempered, his stupid suicidal move if they'd been in robust daily dialogue.

He broke down. "I can't do this by myself. I can't. My government's going to fall."

She handed him a tissue and he honked his nose, snot soaking through and onto his hand, which he wiped onto his other hand. She advanced a few more tissues, aggressively, and he wiped his fleshy appendage clean. Strangely, she felt no pity for him at all, but experienced a surge of venomous antipathy toward Chief.

"I am so sorry, Becky." He took hold of her skirt. "Our poor little girl."

By this, he meant Martha.

Becky knew she was a lamb, a sponge, a victim for contrition in any form. She knew he knew this too. He was a tactician. Most of the time.

She extended her hand until she reached his knuckles, where he was pinching her skirt. "Greg. I have to know."

He met her gaze.

"What happened to Taylor Shymanski?"

Because the Governor General had held a summit with her before dropping off antidepressant medication and Niko at 24 Sussex. Lise had demanded to know what had happened at the Gory Horror; the sanity of her crazy son depended upon this. Becky hadn't come clean, of course. She'd said it was a training drill staged by Shymanski's unit.

There was a long pause and he did not blink or look away. "He's on a mission."

"Really? I was with him. When they—took him."

"I know." Greg's other hand crushed a fistful of her skirt.

"You swear on the life of your son?"

He knew which one she meant. "I do."

The last few weeks she had been in nocturnal lockdown, sleeping on the top floor of Sussex in a mercifully quiet guest bedroom. She'd been a refugee in her own mansion, ducking somnolent Niko, misleading distant Martha, counting on the willed ignorance of the servants, while she avoided her spouse. But in the next few lengthened seconds of skirt-raising, jacket-shrugging and trouser-shedding, she ultimately perched herself on top in his Centre Block office with her eyes closed *tight, tight, tight* and thought of *Canada, Canada, Canada,* not *Nina, Nina, Nina, Nina,* but *Canada, Canada, Canada, Canada, Canada, Canada, Canada, Canada.* She would rule this roost.

11
—

IT WAS A FIFTEEN-HOUR TRIP from Ottawa's Macdonald–
Cartier International Airport, or YOW, to Camp Mirage,
Canada's openly flaunted secret base in the United Arab
Emirates, with a two-hour stop for refuelling and mechani-
cal putzing in Frankfurt. Lise found the Challenger 601 cabin
about as comfortable as one of René's trailers on set,
le milieu camping-car saturated with Febreze, Windex and
the stench of jitters, and also somewhat claustrophobic
because she was cloistered with her thin-lipped underling, the
omnipresent and ever-watchful Margaret Lee.

Also, the Afghan ambassador to Canada, Jabar Khan, ex-
mujahedeen and former Khost loans officer, sat across the
aisle from her, skimming through *People*—the U.S. election
special issue. *Très étrange.* They'd previously hovered
together when repatriating dead daughters and sons at CFB
Trenton, in solemn advance of the family convoy along the
Highway of Heroes to forensics in Toronto. Jabar also threw

a terrific levee every Eid, featuring a spread of kebabs with coriander, ketchup, cumin and mayo.

After Greg had dropped his *petit* bomb at the Speech from the Throne, Defence had crossed the threshold at Rideau Hall later that afternoon, while she was in the panicked throes of packing for the trek through the stew of Africa, the sudden mini-parachute into the Afghan theatre and soothing jostled feathers at Senate security after Niko's mini-scene. Defence, without his second, barred Margaret Lee from the meeting. The customary policy and procedure for a sensitive mission involved portentously slim briefing documents in svelte numbered binders, with code-issued pages and secure distribution lists, all kept under lock and key by a fastidious, constantly vetted clerk. In this case, Defence, a University of Waterloo engineer and Brahms buff, had said the mission was too Top Secret even to be committed to print. He'd been convinced to opt for a viceregal "verbal" and to discern her disposition toward the matter on the spot; she was to let him know immediately whether she was "in or out."

"I have a choice?" Lise had asked.

"Really, no," he said.

"Will I be in danger?"

He didn't mince words. "Hell, yeah."

As she reflected on the scale of this op, Defence turned away and said, "So I take this as a *oui*."

Outside the plane window, the stars barely registered in the sky, like useless numbers scraped on an unlucky lotto ticket.

Mon Dieu, she was depressed. René was below her, sleeping on Earth, back in Romania. Right then she could have been over the Caspian Sea, or the Black, and it didn't matter. The pilot, an air force base commander, had invited her to the cockpit, but even his respectful conversation hadn't distracted her from her concerns.

And Niko. Becky had promised to treat him like her very own, even touting Exhibit Pablo and his experience with trauma. Dr. Pelletier was back in the Glebe, with twice-weekly sessions on the books. And Lise had sat down with Niko, after René headed back to Europe, and disclosed her conversation about the Corporal with Becky.

Niko didn't question anything. Either the meds were already subduing him or he bought the explanation, Lise wasn't sure which.

It was truly awful to leave him.

To avoid small talk with the Kebab King across the aisle, she absorbed the backgrounder—updating herself on whatever the hell NATO, Canada and the gang of goons was doing in Afghanistan. She was unburdened, in a way, since René wasn't with her; he scoffed at the simple military sentences marching to their self-congratulatory conclusions, at the graphs documenting successful CIMIC operations out of Camp Nathan Smith, the work of the Provincial Reconstruction Team, the ISAF updates about the number of Afghan girls attending elementary, middle and high school, the unemployed youth joining the ANA or ANP, the upsurge in organic pomegranate grow-ops, and the progress on the construction of the Dahla Dam, which would irrigate the entire province and revitalize the fields framing the Arghandab River—yielding peace, prosperity, microbreweries, vineyards, and so on and so forth. René claimed it wasn't about al Qaeda or even the Taliban. If it was about al Qaeda, he said NATO would already be across the border in the province of Baluchistan, Pakistan, or drone-bombing downtown Waziristan.

It was about resources, he always said. Which was what Brett Neeposh had always said too. A pipeline from Turkmenistan, oil from Angot in northern Afghanistan, iron and copper deposits, even opium. And she had to agree, because after her photo ops with the Princess Pats, or standing shawled and sandwiched, hip to hip, between Meena and Hamid Karzai, and hugging the three-year-old Pashtun cherub who had lost half her face to an IED, with opium suppositories shoved up her tiny useless anus by an aunt who couldn't afford 100 AFNs for proper pain meds, the bulk of the missions were devoted to governmental accords with private corporations, land appropriation, deals that would line the deep pockets of Canadian resource extraction and reconstruction firms, and private security concerns.

Margaret Lee emerged from the washroom at the front of the jet and ruddered herself toward Lise. She held a metal portfolio case and Lise knew what this meant.

"Open it on the Herc," Margaret Lee advised, handing her the case.

"Bien sûr." Lise saluted her.

Margaret Lee passed a fob key in a tacky plastic case.

Then they were into the descent. It was too dark to see the exoskeleton of the Burj Dubai, the tallest building in the world, still studded with building cranes. The sixteen-lane highways rose invisibly out of the desert and drove straight into the sea. The Afghan ambassador lifted his hands, two puppets engaged in silent dialogue, and she saw he was praying.

And then it was the middle of the night, two a.m., three, and she, *son équipe* and Jabar bade *au revoir* to the palm-pressing captain and his crew, to debark at the Camp Mirage supply depot and climb into full battle rattle, combat fatigues—eight-pound helmets and body armour weighing thirty-five pounds. She'd forgotten how heavy, literally, war could be. *La guerre, c'est lourd.* In the distance, while Dubai sparkled—a business dream, a Disneyland for the primarily blue-collar expat Indians—they were reminded by the base commander about military etiquette and told to follow their leader. Everyone stampeded the bathrooms, because the loos on the Herc were boot camp, a metal seat pronging out of a curtained semicircle. She used the sat-phone to call Niko and let him know she'd almost made it all the way to her final destination, but he didn't answer his cell. She called Becky's cell and Becky couldn't talk because she was at the boys' violin recital. This added to Lise's cumulative list of concerns. They climbed into the looming ass of a C-130 Hercules; they were told that the same plane would be used for a ramp ceremony almost as soon as they landed at KAF.

They hit Afghan airspace in a couple of hours and were put on high alert. It was daylight, but Lise couldn't see anything because there were no windows. She was suspended in the web-seating, forward section of the cargo hold, and her feet tapped at the rollers. From time to time she stared at the bulkhead as if there might be good news from that area, an in-flight film featuring Audrey Tautou, *s'il vous plaît*.

That was when she opened the portfolio, read the document and then put it back in its case.

A triggered memory from the Throne Speech: Margaret Lee thrusting the classified document into her hands and then dispatching the page to steal it. The PM had insisted the delay of the Speech had to do with a comma.

From 35,000 feet they started the steep corkscrew descent into Kandahar Airfield; she'd done this before and it didn't get easier. No prefrontal gymnastics or spiritual kinesiology prepared her for this counterintuitive and topsy-turvy plunge toward a thin rib of cement in the Kalashnikov-cultivated desert. She heard a woman crooning the soothing "La Vie en Rose." It was her own sweet voice. When they'd been civilians, the song was René's go-to ring tone.

When she finally stepped out into the cold, brilliant, judgmental sunlight and the intoxicating reek of diesel, surrounded by planes, soldiers, trucks, ammo, weapons and military *merde* from 118 countries, and onto the jet-juddering and emasculated groin of the fifth-poorest country in the world, Jabar Khan even hit the ground; the soles of the ambassador's Mephistos shone.

She hoisted herself into the rear of an armoured Toyota for the drive to Canadian HQ, where she could look forward to a brief shower and a quicker meal amidst HESCO architecture. Unlike her other sorties, this time there was no heraldry, pageantry, flag-raising, speech-making, oath-taking, wreath-laying, puck-throwing, medal-pinning, chai-sipping, *shura*-squatting, no meet-and-greet along the KAF boardwalk.

She'd read the mission plan, twice, so wasn't surprised to see Shymanski riding shotgun in her vehicle. In profile, he was still the on-duty RCMP she'd last high-fived at the Gory Horror, spooking the entitled *enfants* of Rockcliffe Park on Halloween, but she realized that he was *sans* his signature seventies *Canadiens* sideburns. He wore a Jarhead buzz cut and seemed hardened, older than she remembered, and she was glad Niko couldn't see him.

"*Bonjour*, Taylor." Her hand waited.

He clasped it. "*Bonjour*, Excellency." His pupils were pin-pricks in the violent sunlight. His eyes moistened.

The Brigadier General overseeing CAF in Kandahar did not suffer Defence or women or other fools gladly, but Lise had outdrunk him in Prague and he'd never forgotten.

"We have less than two hours," he huffed as Lise and Corporal Shymanski settled into standard-issue conference chairs in front of a naked whiteboard. He shut the door on the inquisitive snoot of Margaret Lee and then cut to the chase. "Operation Fatima commences at 1300. I will be plain-spoken as a Winnipegger because time is short."

In late 2007, he told them, allegations arose regarding Afghan National Police aiding and abetting a prostitution ring exploiting underage girls in and around Kandahar. These ANP protected a certain drug lord's operation, accepted bribes and also took payment in sessions with the girls—who were under the influence of substances, often coerced, and who should have been in the fricking schools Canadians were dying to build for them. The ANP, with RCMP support, had even conducted an investigation, which was when Lieutenant-Colonel Aisha K. became involved. She'd infiltrated the ring, worked undercover with the prostitutes, earned their confidence, and when she blew the whistle on the operation—essentially revealing to a sketchy superior that recruits she'd trained and worked with had been corrupted—the drug lord was tipped off, and he told the Taliban, who were recipients of tidy kickbacks, and the RCMP convoy was duly bombed.

The Brigadier General nodded toward Shymanski. "That part you knew."

Lieutenant-Colonel Aisha K. was abducted, and assumed murdered somewhere west in Panjwai, far east in Spin or north in Shah Wali Kot—who the fuck knew. She'd never been found, nor had her remains been recovered, and she hadn't ever contacted home. However, information had come to light that she wasn't abducted by the Talib at all, but detained by Afghan government security. Her Excellency had already been apprised of this.

The Brigadier General waited for Shymanski to process.

"My God." He sank into his chair. "Aisha's alive."

"That's what they claim."

"They?" said Lise.

"Our friends in Kabul."

Lise spoke flatly, unemotional. "So Karzai *is* involved."

"No, Your Excellency—"

Lise felt punched in the gut. "I held Hamid's twins when they were seven days old. Meena, Hamid's wife, phoned me after their births. I held Zahra and Babur in my arms in a suite at the Serena Hotel." She looked away.

"Your Excellency—"

"This young man's leg."

"Excellency—"

"Aisha, mother of four—"

"Excellency . . . No, no, no, not the President, definitely not," the Brigadier General said.

Lise glanced at Shymanski but couldn't read his eyes. His silence spooked her. "Perhaps detention was a form of protection for the Lieutenant-Colonel," she said.

"As I've said, Your Excellency, we have no squeaky clean intelligence implicating President Karzai. We were briefed by an ally as to Lieutenant-Colonel K.'s status and approached Kabul about her release."

"It's still possible Kabul executed the IED," Shymanski said. "Planted the explosives."

"Negative. Forensics pointed to the usual suspect."

"She can never return to Kandahar," Lise said. "The Taliban are everywhere."

"No way, nohow," the BG said.

"So?" Lise said.

"Saskatchewan."

"An empty province," declared Lise. "Oil."

"You can say that again," said the BG.

"And her children?" Lise asked.

"Part of Operation Fatima. She'll connect with them at Ramstein at 0100 tomorrow."

Lise absorbed this. "Why now? Is this housekeeping before President-elect Obama's inauguration? Rallying the troops back in Canada for Obama's anticipated surge?" Lise tried to control her anger. "Or Hamid's doing whatever it takes to please the Western masters because he seeks more NATO troops? What do you think, BG?"

He shrugged. "They don't tell me nothing, GG."

"Canadians already know that the country is 'cutting and running' from Afghanistan on whatever date Greg has devised." Lise couldn't stop herself. "It stinks of the photo op, sir."

"There will be none of that nonsense on my watch." The Brigadier General banged the desk. "Zippo." He pointed at the clock.

Lise wasn't finished. "Also, it hasn't been fully explained why the Corporal and I are needed here. This is a transfer with friendlies, *oui*?"

"At the discretion of Defence. Corporal Shymanski here worked with Lieutenant-Colonel K. They trained recruits together, toured Canada, and he was travelling with her as a bodyguard on the day they were attacked at the governor's palace. He lost his leg and almost sacrificed his own life. It's about her comfort in coming to Canada." The Brigadier General paused. "And the Lieutenant-Colonel personally asked for him."

Shymanski betrayed no response.

"*En effet*, Corporal Shymanski was seconded from my service without any notice. In the middle of a public event. Snatched, according to my son, against his will."

Lise noticed that Shymanski stayed absolutely still.

"Defence."

Lise said, "*Et moi*. The Commander-in-Chief, representative of the King, here in the AO, heading with Special Forces and JTF2 into a shooting gallery. *Vraiment, c'est un cauchemar*."

"The PMO believes you can identify the high-value asset."

"Sure, but send me a photo from your phone already. I'm not the only person who has seen her face. Corporal, you've seen her?"

Shymanski shook his head.

"You are the one the PMO trusts to verify her identity. *Aujourd'hui*," said the Brigadier General. "*Maintenant. Ici.* Period."

Corporal Shymanski said, "May I ask which ally reported that Lieutenant-Colonel K. was in Afghan detention?"

The Brigadier General said, "A certain drug lord."

A silence of ironic befuddlement.

"Fatima's already in play. Our turf, our terms. Lieutenant-Colonel K. is en route as we speak. It's a very tight window. There'll be two Chinooks, fully loaded, a flock of Black Hawks with Special Forces and our own JTF2. We're ten clicks off Ambush Alley, in territory that has been recced up its asshole so many times it's sweeter than my armpit, courtesy of our Forward Operating Bases. Any final questions?"

"Is the PM going to tell the media what really happened to her?"

The Brigadier General was already out the door.

Lise and Margaret Lee were the last to board the Chinook, sardined with soldiers, RCMP, CSE, Defence and DFAIT personnel, some female, and even a rep from the UN Agency for Women, who happened to be male. All the young men reminded her of Niko. They were damp and emotionally flattened from the ramp ceremony for a beloved medic, aged twenty-seven, a Pac-Man fanatic with a fiancée vying for the Canadian Olympic speed-skating relay team. Lise sat in her designated spot, one of thirty red, tongue-like seats pinned to the interior wall, and strapped in next to Shymanski. Margaret Lee slotted herself in nearby. Lise inhaled the frigid urine-tinged air.

The ride was short, which Lise expected as they were travelling as far as she could spit, at 150 clicks per hour, twenty-five feet above Afghan World. She looked out the gaping rear of the two-rotor, where the machine gunners crouched, as they flew over razor wire, a hodgepodge of checkpoints and HESCO bastions, camel breath, a traffic circle in lockdown, brief clotheslines, poppy palace satellite dishes, frozen pomegranate and wheat fields, and wadis and more wadis, as well as invisible rocket launchers, of course, with the snow-spritzed mountain range like an inspirational mental handrail in the distance.

The rotors: cacophonous, duelling lawn mowers that cut down every thought sticking up in her brain. Her nervous system synchronized itself to the rhythmic roar. This was her opportunity; this was the only chance she'd have before they took their separate paths and possibly never connected again. She nudged Shymanski and bellowed in his ear, *"Qu'est-ce qui t'est arrivé?"* At that point, everything had become so bizarre, with colour bleeding beyond the lines, that she didn't care who saw.

He just looked at her.

"Tabarnac! Niko saw what happened to you!"

But he behaved as if he'd been waterboarded, psy-opped and had the shit beaten out of him.

She actually seized his pointy chin and jerked his face toward her.

He still didn't respond, just looked around at the faces gazing at them and stared at the floor again.

The Chinook decelerated and the noise emulated a shrieking dental implement. Hovered, hovered, and landed beside its twin in the desert, not far from what was obviously Highway 1. Through the opposite window, Lise spotted

Black Hawks circling the perimeter like an NHL team warming up on the visitor's rink, and she heard more of them buzzing above. They were out in the wide wide open.

Everybody but Lise and Margaret Lee, who had been instructed to remain with the Chinook, along with a few security, debarked. Corporal Shymanski bent to her shoulder. "The Prime Minister plans—"

"*Quoi, Taylor?*"

But he was gone—shoved by that CSIS agent?—and filed out the side door.

"Taylor!" The agent stared back at her, but Shymanski strode ahead with the inimitable hitch and then climbed into the G-Wagen, which had been disembowelled from the other Chinook. It sped away.

Lise moved up to the cockpit, where the pilot and co-pilot listened to militaristic babble.

"CENTCOM?" she asked.

"Affirmative," the pilot said. "Stand by." U.S. Central Command in Florida ran the whole show, with even NATO reporting to them.

In the distance, up the highway, three standard-issue white Toyota SUVs appeared on the horizon, followed by a rickety, weaving helicopter, which seemed attached to the vehicles like an orphan kite. They braked a kilometre from a checkpoint manned by a platoon. The Toyotas shut down, and a slight goatherd, for that's what he looked like, climbed uncertainly from the back of the middle SUV. He wore Pashtun peasant gear, his hair in a bowl cut, and shuffled in flip-flops toward the ad hoc utility tent, literally in the middle of nowhere. The Toyotas backed up another kilometre, cut tight and synchronized U-turns, and bombed back toward the north.

"Are we looking at the asset?" the pilot said almost to himself. "Or the asset's goatherd?"

Lise asked herself the same question.

The welcoming committee of EOD and haz-mat teams approached her. The asset waved eagerly. She was not waving at *them*, the EOD crew, Lise saw that; Shymanski was right behind them and held his hand up at her. Then the asset politely greeted the invasive procedures crew and was swept into the tent with them. Shymanski waited with his handlers.

The Black Hawks vigilantly circled. CENTCOM was quiet.

Then an order came for Corporal Shymanski to enter the tent. Lise watched him almost run—his one-legged lope. Margaret Lee excused herself to take a message on her satphone.

"We're getting the all-clear," CENTCOM said. "Stand by."

It was Lise's turn, and she followed the combo pack of RCMP, CSE, CSIS, Defence and DFAIT minions to the caboose of the Chinook. The G-Wagen sped from the utility tent toward the two Chinooks and parked between them. Lise stepped out into the still clear and cold afternoon sun onto the unrolled woven Afghan carpet that had mysteriously appeared. She watched the person she prayed was Lieutenant-Colonel Aisha K. walk toward her. For some reason she thought of *Mulan*, the Disney feature in which the heroine disguised herself as a boy to go to war.

"Lieutenant-Colonel K.," Lise said, but she wasn't sure. Oddly, it was harder to tell if it was Aisha because Lise could actually see her face.

"Your Excellency." Lieutenant-Colonel K. curtseyed and held out her hand. Not as smooth as it used to be; the cuticles were nibbled raw.

"We meet under extraordinary circumstances," Lise said.

"Yes," said Lieutenant-Colonel K. "Last time it was your beautiful Riddled Hall and now—" She looked back at the utility tent, where she'd obviously been strip-searched.

"I understand that you have been through a challenging situation," Lise said.

Lieutenant-Colonel K. bobbed her head. "We will talk sometime about that. *Inshallah.*"

Lise studied the shape of her skull, her hair, and imagined pouring a burka over her shoulders. "Very soon you'll be reunited with your children."

"Yes!" Lieutenant-Colonel K. lit up, and Lise thought she could see something familiar in the demeanour—that warm spark.

Time and sequence suddenly became a blur of rushed formality. Ambassador Jabar Khan appeared at the side door of the other Chinook, and Corporal Shymanski and Lieutenant-Colonel K. were escorted to him before Lise could even say goodbye. Lise saw Lieutenant-Colonel K. bend and touch Shymanski's pylon leg. She was asking him a question. She probably never knew what had happened to him the day she was apprehended.

Suddenly Lise started to panic. Was it Aisha or not?

The tent out by Highway 1 had been folded and the G-Wagen disappeared inside the other Chinook. Lise was bundled back into her helicopter as the carpet was rolled and planted under the machine gunners. Margaret Lee shoved the satphone into her face.

"Lise, is it the Lieutenant-Colonel?" It was Defence back in Ottawa.

"Yes," said Lise, overly decisive. "I think so."

"Think so?"

"What did Corporal Shymanski say?" She knew CENTCOM was with them on the line.

"Shymanski! Lise, he wasn't even asked."

Lise watched the other Chinook shut up tight, lock and load. She pressed her right hand to her forehead and inhaled the scent—the plumeria so wondrously hopeful and lush in the Kandahar wilderness.

"Yes, it's her. It's Aisha."

12

———

BECKY TOOK CHARGE OF THE Tory war room, where everything jittered in an agonizing state of play.

She dispatched party spies *en force* on Banks and Sparks, the bars on or near Wellington—D'Arcy McGee's, Parliament Pub, Zoe's Lounge, Milestones, and the Metropolitan—slipping down the hill into the densely gossip-choked ByWard Market. Even a retired and decrepit Conservative senator was practically yanked from his comfortably lined casket and propped up in the Rideau Club.

Bulletins buzzed in: former Liberal PM Jean Chrétien, Trudeau's pussycat, was reportedly bending the ear of Ed Broadbent, the stalwart ex-leader of the NDP, and flying back on the red-eye from Paris. Becky's contact at the Château Laurier was so dependable that even decaf urns had ears. Reports filtered in that the Grits were huddling there over an all-veg pizza with goat cheese marathon. The NDP, salivating at the possibility of Cabinet posts, were stationed at the Marriott in Salon B with a stream of pricey Stash tea, and the king-making Bloc were toasting over Dieu du Ciel microbrews at the Elgin.

Meanwhile, Greg forced his seasonal smile and lit up the capital's Christmas tree with Martha, Pablo, Peter and LEDs. He then retreated to the Langevin and collapsed in a deep sleep on the leather couch. Becky locked the door to keep out Chief and Doc.

"Becky," Chief begged. "Please."

She loved hearing him wheedle.

"Let us in," said Doc.

Wheedledee and Wheedledum. She stepped toward the door and spoke very clearly. "Boys. Stay TFO."

Then she covered Greg with a Hudson's Bay blanket and kissed his closely shaved cheek. "Honeydog," she said. He hadn't started to snore yet.

The Tory hub blazed all night. Becky made time to personally call Margaret Lee, leashed to Lise overseas, for a confidential heads-up: how soon could Peggy execute a forced march cum flight on the GG, if necessary?

On Saturday, Becky attended the launch of Martha's capstone internship project, after driving between indoor soccer matches (Pablo on the superior Rep team, Peter reluctantly on the level below Bronze—which had its repercussions). The National Gallery exhibit, sculptures of common metallic household objects such as flashlights, foil and pasta claws, included her daughter's copy in the pricey catalogue.

"Praise the Lord!" Martha said, taking in the scene. "It's a big success."

Becky, watching the egotistical artist elites hoover canapés, nodded.

"I'll miss the NGC," Martha added. "My internship."

"For sure." Becky was already planning the fastest route to pick up Niko from his pre-Calculus tutorial.

"But now I can focus on *Temptations*." Martha said this without irony.

"Absolutely," said Becky.

Back at 24 Sussex, Becky found Greg in his study. He was lying on the floor under the Diefenbaker and denying reality. When a political situation became dicey, this was a default position.

"Delay Opposition Day," Becky demanded.

"They're just *toy* sabre-rattling."

"And Ways and Means."

"They're too scared to table it." He was referring to the non-confidence motion, and the way he said this made it sound like a question.

"They've formed the coalition, Greg."

"If we delay, it gives them more time to plan."

"They're going to seize power."

"They'll replace their leader with someone we haven't defamed yet."

"Nip this in the bud, or we're in Stornoway for New Year's."

Greg sat up. "Where the fuck is Chief?"

While her nails dried, Becky speakerphoned the campaign chair, comatose in Saskatchewan. She had the plane chartered, the buses reserved, and a catchy slogan flew out to fire up fundraising: *Democracies are **elected**, stupid*. One never knew the timing of a premature election.

After the PMO cancelled the Opposition and Ways and Means day, Becky called in Chief and Doc. Greg, white as the bad starches, braced himself behind his desk. Chief and Doc were buried in a sentimental import—an Ikea loveseat from Greg's Whitehorse constituency office.

"We need to retract it," Becky said.

"You're overreacting," Chief said.

"There's no reason to eliminate the right to strike for federal servants when they just agreed to a deal and we gave them a gold star for doing so."

"She's right," Doc said. "We look mean."

"We are," Chief said.

Greg said, "Mean is a means to an end. Major—"

"You need to *look* as if you'll listen to reason," Becky said. "Or you'll throw it all away."

Greg glared at her. She wasn't sure if he was losing it or had a high fever. "Retract it," he said to Chief.

—

Finance was dispatched to Global to fret about the automotive industry and to mention "stimulus spending" fourteen times.

The Cabinuts, even though their portfolios were far away from anything to do with the subsidies for political parties, told every program on all platforms at the Corpse that a particular controversial provision about voter funding was doing the disappearing act too.

That night, Greg was so physically ill and intellectually stressed he couldn't rise from their bed. Pastor Grant prayed with him on the phone. Greg stared at the stack of dry toast she brought him and dubbed it his doppelgänger.

If the toast fits, she thought.

Becky carried on with the four children, including Niko, and they decorated the family tree at Gorffwysfa. In their own teenage wasteland, Martha and Niko stuck together in monosyllabic unity. Peter, in holly berry polo shirt, persisted in pushing Pablo, in complementary holly green, into the beautiful fresh-cut noble fir, until Pablo decked him. Even though she was absolutely thrilled that Peter (Greg Jr.) had had a comeuppance, she reprimanded Pablo.

"Why is everyone mad at Daddy?" Pablo whimpered, off topic. "Why are they bullying him? Will we have to move out of Gorff? Where will we go? Can we stay for Christmas? Why is Daddy yelling at *everybody?*"

Peter shoved him into the Nativity. The Leggatt crèche, with shepherds, angels and Three Kings on Mustangs, was curiously life-size and Yukon Territorial. When Pablo landed on top of baby Hay-Seuss, Martha rushed to pick up the doll and gently replace it. As Niko put his arm around her shoulder, Peter grabbed Hay-Seuss and hit Pablo.

"Hey!" Becky yelled. "Peter!"

Becky force-marched Peter off into the dining room for a time out. "Martha?" she said over her shoulder. "Take care of Pablo."

But it was Niko who moved to Becky's adopted son; Martha knelt beside the baby Jesus, no worse for the wear and tear, and pressed her face against His head.

Becky found it meet and right that the Tory Christmas party was being held that night at the Museum of War, 1 Vimy Place, in the icy western armpit of Parliament, off the Ottawa River. They were honouring the new importance of the military, of course; Canada was at war in Afghanistan, and would have been in Iraq if Greg had had his druthers. The crowd was inebriated on Rumour. Conservatives, big C and small, were panicking and staggering around the Voodoo jet, tanks and military vehicles in the LeBreton exhibit. The update from insiders who had text relationships with insiders in the enemy camp: the coalition of Liberals and NDP was making magnificent progress, arriving at cordial agreement on the number of Cabinet seats for the Socialists. They were even tinkering with the nitty-gritty composition of the ABCs— agencies, boards and committees.

A lesbian socialist might become Finance!

Someone had heard a pundit on the Corpse report that Greg was considering prorogation, likening this to pulling the fire alarm before the final exam. The Separatists had said that this was an example of "cut and run."

A lesbian socialist might become Foreign Affairs!

It was Becky's MO to literally rally the troops. She took a call from the Karp-Deem polling firm and scooted upstairs to Regeneration Hall to vet their sample questions. Doc told her that the Toronto *Blob* columnist was hectoring Greg over his three limp electoral kicks at the can, with the ultimate verdict being that 60 percent of the country rejected him.

A lesbian socialist might become deputy PM and, if something happened, by default Prime Minister—Becky whispered all this and more in loyal ears. She kissed blanched cheeks, led them in a tearfully enraged anthem, and smilingly, cheekily, hearteningly, inspiringly and unreservedly pinned buttons on over five hundred lapels at the coat check: SAY NO/NON TO THE COUP.

When she arrived back at Sussex Drive, she found Greg and Martha in the Arctic subzone of the rumpus room, ostensibly watching *A Beachcombers Christmas*. But Greg was also engaged with his BlackBerry. Can Vox news, already singing in four-part harmony from the Tory song sheet, played silently in a corner of the screen. Becky collapsed on the couch, Martha bumping into the middle. Greg said, "How are the troops?"

"Drooping."

He passed her his BlackBerry. A text from her father. *Socialist separatist wankers. Off with their dicks.*

The next morning, Ottawa was a winter wonderland. It was so cold that, on the school ground, Becky's nose hairs seemed to freeze like stiff trees in a mini-forest. She hadn't been aware she had so much new growth. Later, while she exercised and overreacted to the breakfast shows, a speedy anchor checked her Skatecam and marvelled at the seniors steady on their blades, the toddlers toe-tripping, with their pompom toques and pockets full of bonbons, along the frozen Rideau Canal.

Other than the endless fascination Canadians displayed for their weather, and wreath-making tips, the main event was *coalition*. The anchor pronounced it first as *coercion*, then corrected herself and said the opposition was forming a *collision*.

Becky met Greg at his Langevin office and took notes as he conducted ten-minute phoners with Brown, Sarkozy, Merkel and finally with his stepbrother in Australia. Berlusconi didn't call back, which wasn't unusual; Putin, out of the blue, rang up but Greg didn't take it, had Firstname Somebody-Hyphenate tell him that he was in the can. Greg had mentioned that Vladimir often gloated because he was able to use force and corruption transparently. Lucky stiff.

The executive assistant stammered as he announced each caller on the intercom. "Mr. Prime Min-Min-Minister, are you in-in-in for President Bush?" Bush, in his final weeks in office, was sending Alexander Manson, the fixer Becky and Greg had met at Harrington Lake last August, up by private jet. By now, Becky had ensured that Greg had reneged on every threat in the fiscal update, buttressed by plenty of scrummy chit-chat from Cabinet lackeys about opening the vaults.

And then, a surprise opposition press conference on the Hill, covered, unsurprisingly, by all the broadcasters. Greg sent everybody out of the room but Becky, Doc and Chief, and told the assistant to hold all calls. He actually locked the door.

On the TV screen, a tiny, nondescript table and a plethora of Canadian, provincial and territorial flags. A veritable plantation.

"Count the chairs, boys," Becky tasked.

"Three," Greg snapped. "Oh, praise the Lord, *three*. They've brought the Separatist!"

Tai Chi, the earnest Liberal, strode into the shot with stapled papers in his shaking hand. Handily defeated in his run for prime minister just shy of two short months ago, he was joined by the Socialist, with his super posture, and—yes, yes, yes—the grim and self-righteous Separatist. They sat down together and faced the press.

"Thank you, thank you, thank you, God," Greg gushed. "The three musketeers. The three stooges. The three fat ladies fucking sing."

While Tai Chi explained the guts of the agreement—that the Liberals would join a coalition with the Socialists, and the Separatists would support this coalition for two years on any confidence votes—Greg sank to his knees on the Capital Commission carpet and commended God the Father. His arms waved in holy motion, his eyes shut, and Chief hit the floor as well, to show his great respect. It was harder for Doc to do this, because of some injury incurred during a visit from his Vancouver girlfriend, but he was finally down with Greg and Chief, chin punched into his chest.

On screen, the Socialist added his two red cents: that the coalition would vote non-confidence on the fiscal update and then, since the recounts from the last federal election had barely been tabulated and turned into history, they would present themselves to the Governor General, Her Excellency Lise Lavoie, as soon as she returned from abroad, as a worthy alternative to the current ruling party. Greg, Doc and Chief, heads still bowed, now curved around the TV and gripped hands.

Becky rejoiced too, but there was no time to coast on enemy blunders. She stepped around them and picked up the phone to Larry Apoonatuk. It had been a while. He'd in fact been token fired after the "do-over" Opposition leader incident, and was now with the 24-hour cable news outlet Can TALKS. Failing upward!

"Apoonatuk."

"It's Becky."

"I know," he said. "I'm on deadline. Call you back." He hung up in such a way that she knew he wouldn't.

—

"Demagoguery isn't a dirty word," Alexander Manson said.

His private jet had been grounded in Buffalo, a wicked blizzard, and Greg was on the phone with him. Becky was conferenced in.

"Isn't a dirty practice. If it's for the public good. Now take you Canucks. Take your own Declaration or Constitution or whatever. How familiar with it are your Joe Blows? Your Sikhs? Your Chinamen?"

"Not very," Greg stated.

"My point," Manson bit. "What do they know? They get their green card. Evade taxes. Rat on terrorists. Hook up cable. And that's it. The average person doesn't want to be bothered with the shit we deal with. That's why they elect us. Appoint us. Anoint us. 'You deal, and let me get on with *le* sex. *Le* church. *Le* hockey.' We're doing a fucking *favour*—"

"I hear you," Greg said.

"My man's president for a few more weeks. We don't want these Communists. We don't want Hail Mary pass crap." He paused. "Demagoguery's a long word. Because demagoguery takes a long time. And it pays long term."

"I hear you," Greg said again.

"Good man," said Manson. "Now take care of that lovely wife, Greg. Or I will." He chuckled lustily.

Greg glanced at Becky, then away.

"More importantly, tuck that colicky country of yours into bed with some *Happily ever after*. Think Reagan. Works like spit in a pinch."

—

Becky watched Monday's entire Question Period on CPAC. Her husband made it sound as if the socialist hordes were descending upon Ottawa to eviscerate the organs and eat the heart of the country. Or that the coalition was a conspiracy nurtured by Quebec sovereignists who wanted to cut off the testicles of Parliament. He referred to the coalition press conference repeatedly—pointing out that there were no Canadian flags. An election had been held only days earlier, yet they intended to force an unelected Liberal eunuch loser down the throats of Canadians as the new prime minister. That violated federal law. He didn't say *coup d'état*, because it was French and would confuse the lowest common Conservative denominator. He added that citizens would flood the streets. Armies would get involved, closing borders, and perhaps even malls and liquor stores, which would hit citizens where it hurt.

The press jumped on board, of course. The Corpse knew which side its bread was truly buttered on. Can Vox, with its demands for more specialty channels to the CRTC, cast mild Tai Chi as Genghis Khan. Can TALKS, ditto. The party's own Conservative pollster was working overtime, phoning citizens in staunchly loyal ridings in every province, and asking red-flag questions, framed with barely perceptible Becky finesses.

Becky couldn't have been more pleased.

The media, however, couldn't be completely controlled, and she and Greg were becoming very concerned about academic creep. The constitutional scholars at campuses across the country had been dragged by the media out of their tome-ridden research tombs, particularly the emeritus tribe, whose outspokenness wouldn't necessarily impact research dollars awarded to their institutions. Legal beagles, former Governors General, who in their own minds hadn't really left the throne yet, and Privy Council diehards with an axe to grind flooded the op-eds, letters to the editor, call-in shows, or bought half-page ads to print their unreadable petitions. In one voice, they were on the record stating that the Governor General, Lise Lavoie, could not possibly agree to prorogue Parliament simply because a minority government would be voted down on a confidence motion. It went absolutely against the ingrained grain of the Canadian Constitution.

It didn't matter that Greg was brilliant in Question Period, and that his ministers had been coached by American pros, every inflection rehearsed and key words repeated until they were programmed into the national psyche. On every TV channel, in every newspaper, on every radio station and partisan blog, a pundit harped and harked back to basics: A minority government could only rule when it had the backing of the opposition. If it didn't have the confidence of the House, the opposition could approach the Governor General, or vice versa, re the formation of a new government. In fact, Greg Leggatt had asserted the exact same principle himself, one short Governor General ago, when he led the opposition. The principle started to take hold, amidst the Tory hysteria.

"We need to change the conversation," Becky told Greg.

Becky had Greg's aides check with CSIS, CSE and the RCMP to see if any terrorist investigations were ripe for arrests, charges, revelations—any big-ticket headlines. It was a no go; even rogue organizations had been impacted by the financial meltdown. A meteorological boss was pressed for imminent natural disasters such as ice storms, tsunamis, the arousal of a dormant volcano or the mass starvation of wild horses due to blizzard conditions. Only scattered flurries.

The deputy minister at Foreign Affairs insisted that on his turf it was still the economy, economy, economy, and the constitutional crisis had given him a chance to catch his breath.

The prospect of a convenient avian flu epidemic had flown the coop.

Greg took to the airwaves, live, on Tuesday night before east coast hockey. Becky was camped beside the director; the cinematographer's portfolio (he was a special hire) included corporate work for Apple, Ford and Pfizer. Greg began, "Good evening, my fellow Canadians. In the last few days . . ."

Because it was a political speech running in real time, they couldn't cut in a sweeping shot of the family photographs on the fireplace mantel, but they made sure Becky and the kids smiled contentedly in the background, and Greg's *Jesus Christ Superstar* mug was plunked centre stage on his desk, a triple whammy of art, faith and family. Greg's voice was pitched a tad high, and the stylist had used a shade of lipstick that tilted toward drag, but generally Becky was feeling good.

Then Doc slipped her a copy of Tai Chi's speech.

It was a short and direct hit, an immediate connect with the cortex and solar plexus of an ordinary Canadian, with appeals to the glory days of Prime Minister Pearson's Nobel Peace Prize, a reminder that the country wisely stayed out of Iraq due to the extrasensory listening skills of the Liberals, of Greg's amply illustrated totalitarian impulses, and of the legitimate, constitutionally condoned crossroads the country had now arrived at, led by a united, transparent and rational opposition. Tai Chi had the potential to hit this out of the park. Before Greg even concluded his live address to the nation, Becky disappeared from his set-dressed office into the dungeon-like hall and pulled her phone out.

"Larry," she said.

"Becky." She could hear Greg's drone in the background. The country was glued to this; it was almost as big as a Stanley Cup playoff with two Canadian teams.

"You didn't call me back," she said.

"Sorry."

"We're still BFFs, right?"

"Sure."

"Larry?"

"What?"

"You're grumpy."

"Why would I be grumpy?"

"Yes, why?"

"Especially after delivering an election to your doorstep like Domino's."

"Dominoes?"

"Pizza."

"Ah. Like the House special."

"The House of Commons special."

"Funny."

"Not really."

"Larry. To the matter at hand. Can TALKS is handling the Liberal leader's rebuttal, right?"

"Yes. The CBC doesn't have the crew to handle—"

She didn't care about the Corpse's plight. "You've read his speech?"

"Yes."

"What do you think?"

"It's good."

"It *is*, isn't it? That's what I thought."

Pause.

"It needs to be *not*," Becky said. "Just saying."

"I understand," Apoonatuk said.

"You'll be at his speech?"

"I'm on site now."

"You know the crew?"

"They're mine."

When she fell silent, Apoonatuk laughed. "Along with a team of interns from Carleton."

Becky cackled. She never knew she had that in her. "So creative," she said.

Becky arrived back by Greg's side as the moody public broadcasting crew traipsed away, bound for the pub with their inflated paycheques. She gave Greg a peck on the lips—anything to blot that agonizing pink—and he asked if she'd read Tai Chi's speech.

"It's hysterical," she said. "The usual gibberish-fibberish."

Instead of inviting the gang to stay and watch Tai Chi's address in the Langevin office, Greg sent Doc, Chief and Clark away. "And take that prick assistant with you," he demanded.

Becky curled up in a corner of the couch, Greg sat in the armchair, and they watched CTV's subsidized American programming, sixty minutes of tits and autopsies, while waiting for the main event. In the midst of six commercials, Greg cut to Can TALKS. There was a shot of the main door of the House of Commons, now dramatically padlocked, waiting for Greg to officially prorogue the session with Lise's consent. A header—*Special Announcement*—sat upon the screen, then disappeared as a custodian pushed a cart into the frame and the broadcaster returned to a Florida orange juice commercial.

"What's happening?" Greg said.

"I'll get Doc."

"Get Chief."

Chief dashed in. "You're not going to believe it."

"What's happening?"

"The coalition didn't use the right format. It won't synch up with the Can TALKS requirements, and now they're taking it to the Corpse. The Corpse is so retro they can handle it."

"You're kidding me."

"No, it's amateur hour on the Rideau."

"How could Can TALKS not use the right format?"

"Interns! They were using interns! Does somebody there love you or what?"

Becky changed the channel. "Be quiet! He's on!"

Tai Chi, dressed to ascend, was somehow dwarfed by the archivolt of the House of Commons oak and iron door. He was also slightly out of focus, while the British Columbia coat of arms was razor-sharp, sun rays jutting upward. His face was supposed to dominate the screen; they weren't on a Hill tour of the hanging tracery. Was the camera hand-held?

Becky found it almost impossible to concentrate on what he was saying—that beautiful speech, intellectually crafted, humane, and ready to resonate more forcefully than the cacophony of the corporate media and Conservatives com-bined. The effect was of an academic croaking a Canadian Tire catalogue of guerrilla manifesto and call to arms.

"It's over," Chief announced. He polished his cuticles with his shirttail. "DOA."

"Not yet," said Greg. "When does the GG get back?"

Clark, Clerk of the Privy Council, spoke up on cue. "She just hung up on me."

13

—

AFTER THE SENSITIVE OPERATION in the Afghan theatre, Lise headed to the alternate Great Lakes: Victoria, Albert, Edward and Tanganyika. *Six pays en douze jours*: Kenya, Rwanda, Uganda, Tanzania, Burundi and her own St. Bertrand, an irritant, a pimple on the big butt of the Democratic Republic of the Congo.

If it was Monday, it was Nairobi, and while the new energy kid on the block, CanCrude, spun deep offshore exploration in the Indian Ocean to African officials, Lise chugged dark roast, to promote Kenyan caffeine, with the President's first wife (she wasn't to mention his legal second wife) at Isak Dinesen's Coffeehouse and Museum. After which she jetted to Ito refugee camp in Dadaab, close to the northern border with Somalia, to offer newly arrived malnourished child refugees MREs from MSF.

Another day, Rwanda. Lise met privately with President Kagame, who'd arrested the opposition leader and shuttered the pro-opposition newspaper minutes before her arrival, and deflected his complaints about the Canadian PM, who'd dumped Rwanda from a priority list and randomly refused entry to his officials.

While she delivered an official apology for Canada's passivity in the face of the 1994 genocide, in which 800,000 Rwandan people—and she chose *people* instead of *Tutsi minority*—were hacked with machetes in churches, thrown maimed or dead into the Kagera River, and chased and chopped to pieces on the deck of the swimming pool at the Hôtel des Mille Collines (her head rested that night on the feather pillows of the Kigali Serena), the trade mission focused upon partnerships in coltan, an exciting ore critical to mobile phone and video-game console production, and tossed ostrich steaks on the hibachi.

She had to pick her battles.

In between state dinners, symposia and orphanage gift shop stops, where blind children sculpted Hummers out of toxic river mud to ply to tourists, Lise phoned René, winding up his shoot and counting down to the wrap party, and texted Niko, on deep pharma-pilot back at 24 Sussex.

No news was good news.

Another day, and it *was*, because she was counting down *les jours*, she shook nice with another permanently elected president in Kampala, Uganda.

At Makerere University, she drew the attention of the Canadian press to a terrifying new disease with high morbidity in the northern Acholi region, in which young children started nodding at mealtimes, refused food, drooled profusely, and then erupted, over weeks, with *grand mal* seizures. Lise unveiled a research partnership with the University of Montreal that would figure out why these children were violently nodding themselves to death by malnutrition. Was it tainted bush meat? A mystery worm? First World mine tailings?

At the state dinner, she schmoozed with Indian-Ugandan expats who'd returned to the home country to continue becoming even bigger tilapia than they'd been in their pre-Idi days. The first national mineral survey had them tickled black.

And so it went.

Near the omelette nook in the dining room of a five-star hotel somewhere in air-conditioned Dar es Salaam, Lise learned that Margaret Lee was down for the count with a GI. The jaunt to Mwanza, Tanzania, to a hostel for prostitutes beaten up by Russian black marketers, had been cancelled. Lise attacked her frittata while being briefed about the impact of poachers, but not climate change, on the gorillas of the Bwindi Impenetrable Forest.

When Lise asked the aide for the Ottawa sitrep, the top item cited was Finance delivering a fiscal update. No mention of the unveiling of Lieutenant-Colonel Aisha K.

—

Lise's final African stop was St. Bertrand. When she stepped onto the tarmac at the airport in the capital, Jolie Ville, her older sister Solange, tall with a retro Afro, waited while the newish Western-puppet president greeted her. Then Solange enfolded her.

"Little one." Solange squeezed the air out of her.

Lise squealed, caught up in the warm welcome.

"At last you've come back," Solange said.

The women hung on to each other, human bookends pressed together without anything to hold up but themselves.

"Forty years," Lise said. She didn't know how she'd avoided it for this long; the excuse that the country wasn't user-friendly only went so far *en famille*.

"Kiss the ground," Solange ordered.

"Should I?"

"It's your *true* home and native land," Solange said. "You must."

So Lise did, hitting the Hades-hot concrete in her chartreuse Chanel, with the sun reflecting off the grenade-punctured terminal. She pressed her lips against the cement until her bottom lip burned.

The Canadian press snapped.

Margaret Lee, healthy again and fully mobile, fumed.

When Solange pulled Lise back onto her platform shoes, to the wild hoots of the dignitaries and the applause of the Western-puppet president, Lise took a breath and the physical landscape went stunningly HD. The country hit her solar plexus: to the north, the sea of verdant tea plantations, hills of red clay; to the west, the unbelievable blue of Lake Victoria; to the south, the litter of crashed planes, like a bizarre adventure playground beside the runway, and the IMAX volcano, Mount Agogo, rising above the capital, above everything.

In front of her, east, the joyous face of her sister, with her father's close-set eyes and bossy nose. Solange's voice, with the narcotic echo of their mother's cadences: *Eh hehn. Eh hehn.*

That evening, Lise joined Solange and her husband, Dr. Samuel Soleil, an AIDS hospice director, for a private dinner at their home. They lived in an updated bungalow in a gated *quartier* not far from the sisters' parents' former estate, and the courtyard was garnished with banana trees, hibiscus and patio lights that surged on and off with the power. In the night sky, a distant lightning storm provided the alternate light show. Lise's security had taken over the entire *quartier*, and the supper conversation was interrupted by bursts of staticky walkie-talkie chat beyond the adobe garden walls.

"It is wonderful to finally meet you," Lise said to Samuel. Over the years, there had been promises of visits but life intervened: Samuel was setting up a practice, or Lise was pregnant, or in mourning, or in production. "I heard so much about your good work when I was with *oui*CARE. Your pediatric palliative initiative."

Samuel nodded, without adding that Lise's work too had been frankly quite terrific. Her sister had married their own kind; Lise had never done that, and she suddenly wondered why.

"Listen, Lise," Solange said, leaning across the table. "We have to level with you."

"Sure," Lise said. She didn't know what to expect. Did they need money? For the hospice? Was Solange ill?

"Samuel and I have brought back the President."

"What do you mean?"

"Jean-Louis Raymond. We've smuggled him back into the country."

Lise held her head in her hands over the couscous. "Tell me you didn't."

"He's not far from here," Samuel said.

"*Et bien protégé,*" Solange added.

"He'd need that," said Lise, "along with the personal militia." She turned to her sister. "*Es-tu malade?*"

"No," Solange said.

"Sheltering a deposed leader in your backyard. Taking on the Western powers. The U.S."

"*Et toi,*" said Solange. "*You* represent America's petrostate. Bowing to the corporations. The ones who've raped your real country with structural adjustment."

"Oh my God," said Lise.

"Who've stolen our mineral rights," Samuel added.

"You know Canada was part of the coalition, with France and the U.S., who threatened and coerced him to get on that plane to Joburg. Who abducted our democratically elected president."

"Don't go there," Lise said.

"If you don't have a seat *à la table,*" Samuel said, "*alors, tu es au menu.*"

Lise sat silenced. She wasn't sure, but it seemed as if the walkie-talkies outside the walls had gone mute. Everyone at the table noticed at the same time. Then there was a crackle and a choppy monosyllabic spatter.

"Okay." Lise shrugged. "I give up. Okay. I have to agree with you."

Solange reached across and clasped Lise's hand.

"How could I not, big sister? As I visit on a trade mission wearing humanitarian sunscreen. SPF 200."

Lise and Solange hugged. Samuel went into the kitchen. The radio came on—a Paul Simon song from *Graceland*, for God's sake—and he came back with colder beers for all.

"What is the plan?" Lise said. "Besides getting yourselves killed in a coup? Oh, Jesus, don't tell me your plan, or I'll have to—"

"We want your help," Samuel said.

"My powers are limited," Lise said. "Reserve. Really."

"You can influence your government," Samuel said.

"Sway public opinion." Solange tucked an arm around Lise's shoulder.

"*Mon Dieu,*" Lise said.

"We need debt relief," Samuel said. "And we want to retain our telecommunications."

"As we sit here speaking treason and plotting," Lise said, removing her sister's arm, "that's what DFAIT's working on. Right now! Privatization."

They stared at her. Like, get with the program.

"You have more power than you know, Lise," Solange said.

On cue, Samuel pressed a button on the laptop by the table and a YouTube video of Lise kissing the tarmac at Jolie Ville airport appeared. "Two hundred thousand hits," he said. "Already."

"Not every black girl gets to be the King of England," Solange said.

The next morning, Lise was towed away by the Western-puppet president to the local UNESCO Heritage Site, the Former Slave Depot, on the shore of Lake Victoria. It also bordered the Arab *quartier* with its narrow streets, lime-washed walls and houses built as postscripts to the huge, dark bolted doors.

The Former Slave Depot was cramped: a few remaining underground chambers preserved near a Catholic church. There were no queues. Lise slouched in the cavern; she couldn't stand at full height. A shallow canal cut into the floor opened directly onto the lake. Africans from lesser tribes were captured and stashed underground, waiting for passage east. All slaves were chained to the floor, not even allowed a squat to excrete, and sanitation was left to the lapping lake— washing bodies and whisking away feces. Of course, people drowned, children too, lying prone and chained below rising storm waters or floods. The survivors were finally crammed on magnificent dhows bound for Mwanza, and then beyond to Zanzibar, Oman, Yemen, Persia.

Through a window as wide as her hand, she could see the lake. For some reason, the sacred shade of blue, the sheen of the surface, took her back to the farewell for her first husband.

His body had never been found, of course.

But they'd restocked his canoe. His Nokum had packed smoked rabbit, beaver and bear, and fresh-baked bannock stacked on combustible paper plates, so he would never go hungry. Lise had folded and packed his winter clothing, so he would never be cold. Their marriage blanket stained with menstrual blood and blessed afterbirth. His toiletries kit with nail clippers and Q-tips and condoms and Mennen. Then she'd poured gasoline so generously from bow to stern. She would never forget the heat from the fire on the water.

There was to be no relief for Lise in her birthplace.

A few minutes, later, outdoors again, free, she turned and almost fell into the pit: three statues, an African family, mother, father and adolescent son, planted four feet deep. They were collared. They were chained to each other with the original iron shackles. The parents—without power. The boy was looking toward his mother, and it was then Lise saw that they were legless, sculpted from the waist down in feces and seaweed. Their long arms coalesced and grew into their torsos. They weren't going anywhere.

The Western-puppet president nattered on. Lise didn't hear him.

Lise had stood upon sacrosanct ground in her role as Governor General and as an African-Canadian: Auschwitz; Pol Pot's killing fields; the Mémorial des Martyrs de la Déportation, in Paris, on her honeymoon with Brett; and the rather plain stump of a rare Sitka spruce on Haida Gwaii. She knew how to take on humanity's real hit parade, as René called it. It was her job: forbearance, forgiveness, these F-words. But all of her training in protocol, her self-regulation, reserve, the quantum control of her demeanour, was out the window.

She thought of Niko.

She whimpered as she stood on the iron-red earth of her birthplace, with the scent of frangipani frying her brain. And then she crumpled on the ground; she wouldn't get up. The President beseeched her. Lise heard Margaret Lee curtly advise the press to delete any video of the Governor General keening in the dust.

That night, Lise proceeded through the VIP area at the Jolie Ville airport and passed a serious-looking posse of men, African and U.S. operatives, hurrying a skinny, newly middle-aged African man in a flapping suit and horn-rimmed glasses. Margaret Lee was distracted and on a high-priority distress call from the PMO and didn't see him at first. He was being muscled toward departure and Lise and Co. were heading in the opposite direction. He turned around and said, "Lise Lavoie."

Margaret Lee was suddenly coaching, "Keep moving, keep moving," but Lise stopped because she recognized him. It was Jean-Louis Raymond, former president of St. Bertrand and her sister's smuggled fugitive, who shouldn't have been in public or in the country.

She had always, truly, admired him.

"President Raymond," she said.

"Look at what they are doing to your country." He meant St. Bertrand, she thought. "We need your voice."

She was shocked that he knew who she was.

A hand was clamped over the President's mouth, then Raymond did something that made the guard remove it— did he lick it? They hustled him away down the pest-stripped corridor.

Then Lise was levitated, lifted and carried by her own security. The sensation of being captive and legless while realizing she'd probably never see her sister alive again.

Margaret Lee was in her face, telling her they had to fly back to Ottawa immediately, there was a crisis, no it wasn't Niko, Niko was fine, but they must leave, it wasn't negotiable. She foisted her cellphone on Lise. "It's Clark," she said. "The Privy clerk." As if Lise might have forgotten.

Lise hit disconnect as her own cell rang.

"Put me down," she said to her security. "I'm answering my fucking phone."

They complied.

She punched the button. *"Allo."*

There was a long pause because cellphones worked that way in Africa.

"Traitor," Solange said.

décembre 2008

14

—

Bien sûr, she returned. By the time the Challenger had
looped the Central Experimental Farm, swanning over
Promenade Paul Anka near the Ottawa Hunt and Golf Club,
following the dirty white zipper of the Rideau Canal, banking
at Beechwood, the country's largest military cemetery in the
backyard of Her very own Hall, it was high noon in Ottawa,
minus-four Celsius, overcast. The fairy-tale Château appeared
to be, like the city itself, frozen in time. Except for the mob
that ranted and chanted, morphing on the Hill.

Lise had not even dozed on the flight from Africa. After a
long meditation above the Sahara, she'd finally flung herself into action over the Canaries, creating a war room with
herself as Commander-in-Chief, which, as she reminded
herself, she was.

When Margaret Lee told her they were receiving copious
amounts of e-mail about the parliamentary crisis, Lise drafted
a message to comfort citizens, essentially saying: she had this.

Margaret Lee wasn't happy with the reference to "reserve powers" and she had some queries re the tone, and threatened to vet it with the PMO. Before the PMO even received it, Lise granted an interview to the CBC reporter on board, shared the draft, and the draft went viral. She watched Monsieur Triste's coalition address to the nation, which looked as if it had been taped in a jungle bunker in 1970s Nicaragua and beamed into the future, and listened to excerpts from Greg's constitutionally unsound responses to the opposition in the Commons.

Margaret Lee, on the satphone to the PMO, kept glancing at Lise as if she were committing treason.

After exiting at a private gate, Lise was met by protesters with white war paint and human proboscises exploding into fat red maple leaves. Her security made certain nobody came into contact with her, but did she sense a dose of laissez-faire about their mob handling? The press too cleared customs in record seconds, allowing them to join their peers covering Lise's highly anticipated return. They also seemed to know many of the placard carriers; she witnessed *hey-bro* and high-fives and *saluts* below the bobbing signage: *Non au coup!* WE VOTED ALREADY! *Gouvernement par élection SEULEMENT !* Do the RIGHT Thing!

Lise scuffed over the standard-issue red carpet in her stylish sealskin mukluks. Although she smiled graciously, that thick lick of fear kicked in, and she was relieved to see her limo move into position and idle outside the glass doors. As she stepped into the frigid air, which body-slammed her with an impact like a bomb, she heard a shot, at close range, and was suddenly seized by Corporal Robard and pitched into the rear seat of her vehicle, headfirst into a Tory blue goose down coat and the violent grip of leather gloves.

"Go, go, go, go, go," shouted Becky. "I've got her."

"Get off me," said Lise. *"C'était des feux d'artifice! C'est tout!"*

"Shut up," said Becky, "stay down," and she executed a back-stabbing fold-down on Lise that was so excruciating that Lise's rib chopsticked her own lung—or that was the sensation.

"The security code is cancelled," the driver said.

"I told you," said Lise, though she hadn't quite articulated that, sitting up and pushing Becky off.

"Take the Airport Parkway," Becky ordered. "To Riverside."

The driver grimaced. The limo was already at sci-fi warp speed, with RCMP squad cars front and rear.

"I'd still prefer you switch to Riverside," Becky said to the driver. "And then the Vanier."

"Becky," said Lise. "You can't commandeer my car."

"I'm sorry," said Becky.

"What's going on?"

"We need to talk."

"About—"

"Your boy. I didn't want to wait."

Lise's BlackBerry buzzed; she ignored it. "What about him?"

The driver butted in. "Your Excellency? Security is copying that Mademoiselle Yeung requests you answer your BlackBerry."

Lise answered her phone. "What?"

"Your Excellency, I'm in the limo directly behind you," Margaret Lee said. Lise did not turn. "The coalition leaders demand a sit-down with you."

"Yes, absolutely," Lise said, aware that Becky was listening. "This afternoon."

"I've already refused them," Margaret Lee said.

"What?"

"As your secretary, I must advise that a parley such as that would tarnish the office of the Governor General of Canada."

"That's my decision, not yours."

"It's not seen that way, Your Excellency."

"By whom?"

Becky crossed her legs and pulled out her own phone. She was tapping.

"I have read the history." Lise couldn't stop herself. "In French and in English. I have studied every single one of those dusty books. Governor Generals everywhere talk to whomever they want, whether they're serving in Australia or New Zealand or Jamaica or Belize or wherever tiny island. Even Tuvalu. I want to consult with the opposition leaders today. In camera. Do it."

"The Privy Clerk says that he will meet with you. He's on his way from Langevin."

Lise's voice rose. "Lord bloody Byng met with Arthur Meighen."

"Look what happened when he did," said Margaret Lee.

Lise sensed Becky looking out the window. If she was

tapping a message on her phone, she couldn't possibly be taping too, could she?

"What happened with Lord Byng had everything to do with the actions of the Prime Minister."

"That is debatable," said Margaret Lee.

"Look at Australia's 'Dismissal.' Governor General John Kerr. He obviously met with the Leader of the Opposition, and arranged a double dissolution behind the PM's back. Before lunch at Yarralumla!"

"Yes. I know. Very 1975. But that GG went behind the back of a corrupt and incompetent Labour government."

Lise bit her tongue.

Becky nudged her.

Lise said to Margaret Lee, *"Attends une minute, s'il te plaît."*

"Just FYI"—Becky leaned in closer to Lise; she couldn't be any closer—"my take-away from Australia was that the PM came second."

"How so?"

"If the PM had phoned the Queen first, Kerr would have been the one packing." Becky winked. "Just saying."

Lise filed this factlet as she clicked Margaret Lee back on. "I'll talk to you later." She clicked off and turned to Becky. "Niko."

"I am so sorry to spring this on you," Becky said. "And I apologize for overreacting like that at the airport. Please first let me say—welcome back from beautiful A-Freaka." She air-pecked Lise on both cheeks. "Did you have fun?"

"No."

"We heard that it was quite emotional."

"Yes."

"Look," Becky said. "Our country's in crisis. There has been nothing as dire as this since the Liberals almost internally nuked us with the 1995 referendum. And I appreciate your job is to make sure there's a functioning government. Period." She paused. "But we're both moms. *Premièrement.*" She said *prem-yay-meant.*

"So tell me," said Lise. "Please."

"He was okay at first," Becky said. "But lately he's been behaving quite oddly."

"How so?"

"Reclusive. Remote. And not just with me and Greg. Even Martha's noticed and been upset by it. She thinks he's depressed."

"Has he mentioned Corporal Shymanski?" Lise watched Becky closely.

"No. Not to me." She looked surprised. "Nobody's mentioned him since you and I talked."

"Niko's been upset since Corporal Shymanski, uh, disappeared . . ." Lise left this deliberately vague.

Becky didn't blink.

Lise didn't either.

Becky tucked her phone back in her purse in a case-closed gesture. "The other thing about Niko?"

"What?" coached Lise.

"He keeps making these faces. I'm not sure he's even aware of it. But Greg will be talking, or Peter, and Niko's lower lip is stretched right down to Brazil, you know. Like he's not quite on the planet. And whatever's in his mouth—spaghetti, sushi . . ."

"Did you say anything?"

"I tried to make eye contact, like, 'Hello, anybody home?' but no answer." Becky gave Lise's shoulders a quick squeeze, then: "Drop me off here," Becky commanded Lise's driver.

Lise muttered, *"Vingt-quatre promenade Sussex."*

Her driver pulled up to the gate, which wasn't quite as impressive as the U.S. embassy's fort-like stanchions. Becky dug back into her purse as if looking for a tip. The exterior Christmas decorations were already up: a manger with Wise Men, and shepherds, and—hark!—caribou, and buxom angels with longish, bouncy curls who resembled country and western singers, an Indo Santa wearing a bright red turban and bearing a sack of what looked like dolls and plastic deep-sea oil rigs, and a massive unlit menorah centre stage.

"Here's the note from Niko's school," Becky finally said, producing an envelope. "As acting guardian, I took the liberty of reading it. Not good. And," she added, "he totally stopped taking his meds."

"What?" Lise croaked.

"He refused to take them."

"For how long?"

Becky shrugged.

The gate opened and she disappeared.

—

She had Niko's school schedule on her phone; this block was PE. She ploughed through the doors and inhaled boy BO, which smelled wonderful to her, so healthy, hormonal and full of life, and also the weirdly comforting aroma of cafeteria cheeseburgers. The boys were in blazers, trousers and ties, and pranced through the halls like *jeunes* multicultural captains of industry; they were the sons of ambassadors and deputy ministers and IT lone rangers. Lise had emptied her afternoon, ditching Clark.

In the gymnasium, a basketball drill was under way, and she spotted Niko—she always did. He didn't seem to be in the regulation uniform; he was wearing voluminous swim trunks under his T-shirt and purple pinny. She couldn't follow what special play they were practising, darting in and out of the key, making shots, but Niko was involved, participating, and how good was that?

She climbed up into the bleachers and sat down in the same row as a hunched, engrossed parent, a father who looked as if he'd just come in from shovelling the driveway. Flushed cheeks, bright eyes. And she realized it was Monsieur Triste! She remembered that his son had transferred to this school from Sherbrooke in order to be able to spend more time with his dad. Monsieur Triste was probably picking up his son too. Indeed he was, he was waving to the boy, who was not paying a whit of attention—chattering away to his teammates in broken English. And then Niko was benched, it looked like. Sullen, glowering at his phone, perhaps reading her earlier message about a rendezvous and pickup.

Monsieur Triste eventually recognized her. "Ah," he said, "here you are." As if he'd been expecting them to hook up at their sons' gym all along.

"*Oui,*" said Lise. "*Enfin.*"

"The Prime Minister has lost the confidence of the House of Commons," he leapt right in with excellent English. "He cancelled the Opposition Day so that we wouldn't be allowed to hold this non-confidence vote. Now he wants to deny the right of 169 elected Members of Parliament, whose job it is to vote on behalf of Canadians. He wants to lock up the House of Parliament." Monsieur Triste was definitely more pissed than *triste*. "Tomorrow he will ask you to prorogue."

"I am here to pick up my son," Lise said.

"I too am here to pick up mine."

An announcement blared over the loudspeaker. "Niko Neeposh, please report to the office." And again, *en français*.

Niko barrelled toward the double doors, giving them a kick as he orbited out of the gym.

Lise stood, trying to distract from his exit. She was caught between flying after him and finding closure with Monsieur Triste.

"Excellency, I've just learned that you refuse to meet with the coalition."

"That is correct."

"Would it be fair to ask why?"

"No."

Triste's body wore this heavily. "We so wanted to give you the opportunity to understand our agreement."

"The Governor General has her own advisers." She paused, feeling the rise of nausea. "It will be a long night."

He nodded grimly. "As it should be." Then added, "I hope, though, that you will read the letter which contains the agreement. The coalition's strong and united, and it is the viable alternative. The Prime Minister's position is a perversion of our democratic principle."

Lise raised her hands. "Enough." But then she had to say it. "I respected your words last evening."

"Oh," he said, and she was disarmed by his surprise. "Seen but not heard."

Triste's son, now loaded with a heavy backpack, thin spectacles, not cool, very non-Niko, leapt up the steps and plunged into his father's wide arms with huge tenderness. Monsieur Triste scooped him up while Lise stole away to find her boy.

Lise found Niko in the principal's office, which was bright and overwhelmed with student art, much of it verging on porn. The school was much vaunted for its fostering of creative expression. The jet lag was starting to swamp her; the despair—it wasn't far behind. The principal, Mademoiselle Lebrun, who, like all Niko's teachers, resembled a character from *The Simpsons* whether Lise could identify them or not, provided the synopsis, in case Lise hadn't been aware of how her own life, and that of her son's, was going. Niko's behaviour in class had been borderline, she told Lise. The school was aware that Lise and Niko's stepfather had been abroad and that Niko had been staying with close family friends.

"Not friends," said Niko. "Definitely not."

In Niko's social studies class, there had been a discussion of current events, and apparently many students believed that the Governor General would have to cave and do whatever the Prime Minister asked because that's what GGs generally did. Niko had raised the King–Byng constitutional crisis, wherein Viscount Byng of Vimy, the then Governor General, overruled Prime Minister Mackenzie King and refused to call the election, and then asked the Leader of the Opposition to form a government. Niko's classmates thought that Byng's move, essentially, sucked. Niko became quite voluble and insolent in his remarks, and even rather derogatory of both prime ministers. As a result, for Niko's own protection, as well as that of his peers, the school was asking Lise to consider a break for Niko.

"A suspension," Lise said.

"You could call it that," said Mademoiselle Lebrun.

"Is that what's contained in the letter?" Lise held it up. She hadn't had a chance to read it yet.

"Pretty much."

Niko slumped beside her in his bathing suit, his face aching with acne and acrimony and his own defencelessness in this monstrous pickle of academic proportion.

"Niko and I will reflect with René," Lise said. "On this suspension. And also on whether this school is serving his needs." She folded her hands in elegantly loud viceregal deliberation. "We will reflect tonight and talk to you tomorrow." She turned to her son. "Niko, do you have anything to say to Mademoiselle Lebrun?"

"Yes," he said, "I do." He crossed his legs and tilted himself toward her. "This is a pussy school."

Lise and Niko had a quiet dinner together. She asked the cook to prepare a simple thin-crust pizza marguerite with butter lettuce salad, Diet Cokes, and they ate in their private family dining room with *Pirates of the Caribbean* on Blu-ray. Johnny Depp and his swordplay made everything better, really. Niko was voracious and she ended up ceding her slices to him.

"I appreciate you defending me in your class," she said when he was done.

"De rien."

"Niko, I have to know. Why did you stop taking your medication?"

"I never took it."

"What?"

"I faked it."

"Why?"

"I didn't want to be drugged."

"Does Dr. Pelletier know?"

"Ask him."

"No. You tell me."

"Yes."

"Why didn't he tell me?"

"You'd have to ask him."

Lise drained a whole glass of Diet Coke. Yes, she'd be asking him. Given that she was supposed to be on a statutory update. She fumed.

"It's better if I'm not on SSRIs, *Maman.*"

"Not if you're acting like a terrorist in the Senate. Not if you're holding your mouth open wide with sushi in it *comme un fou* and calling your school pussy."

He took the remote and paused the PVR. "It's a defence, *Maman.*"

"Tell me why you need it. Please, Niko. Why do you need a defence?"

"Taylor," he said.

Corporal Shymanski, *encore.* Niko started to describe what he'd witnessed at the Gory Horror.

"I know this, Niko, you've told me before."

"I didn't tell you that Taylor was being held by Becky."

"Held," Lise repeated. "How held?"

"She was kissing him."

Lise's breath stayed in her lungs.

"In *that* way."

Lise knew right away what way he meant.

Niko couldn't talk about it without becoming breathless, agitated. "And then he was seized by Special Forces. He was probably taken abroad to a black site. Waterboarded for fooling around with the Prime Minister's wife."

"*Mon Dieu,*" Lise said.

"*Et c'est pas tout,*" he said.

She waited while he chewed the last slice, noticing his mouth was completely closed.

"When I was staying at the PM's, Martha noticed I was down and she asked me about it," he began, watching his mother's face.

"Okay."

"I told her about what I saw happen to Taylor, without mentioning he'd been *avec sa mère*."

"Okay," Lise said.

"She became very upset. She told me she had her own relationship thing with Taylor."

Lise nodded.

"She'd fallen in love with him, even though he only had one leg. She's a strong Christian. And one thing led to another—"

Lise kept nodding.

"—to a baby, then to a therapeutic abortion that her mother kept secret from her father, and then Martha—she confessed this to her dad."

Lise reeled. More than she'd wanted to know, more than anyone would want to know. And definitely more than she wanted her vulnerable son to have to deal with. Her mind didn't know where to go next. She focused on pretending to be serene. "Did Martha tell her father before or after the Gory Horror?"

"*Avant*. That was when I started thinking Taylor had probably been killed for making the Prime Minister's daughter pregnant and also fooling around with his wife.

But I didn't know how to tell you. Or how to tell anyone."

Lise crossed over to him and put her arms around him. "I'm so sorry, Niko. I'm sorry you had to carry this."

She felt him relax in her grip. *"Maman,"* he said, "it was so hard to live there."

She soothed him. She told him she wished she'd never left him, which was true. She really wished she hadn't over-guessed herself and let him stay there under Becky's wing, and it was because Becky had seemed so secure, grounded, and had been the superior manipulator.

"And I'm afraid Taylor's dead," Niko sputtered.

Lise felt so helpless. This had everything to do with Niko's deceased father, and how people he looked up to, adored and admired tended to disappear off the face of the earth.

"Niko," she said, "I'm sure Taylor's just fine."

He wouldn't look at her.

"Look at me."

He did.

"I want you to have faith that Taylor's okay. Will you do that for me?"

"Why should I?"

"Because you don't really know what's going on."

"Neither do you."

"No, I don't." She couldn't tell him about Lieutenant-Colonel Aisha K. It was an official secret, part of her oath; it was a Big Deal. She said, "But I can say that I find it incredibly unlikely that anything like that is going on with Corporal Shymanski."

"He has one leg. You didn't see them beat him up, *Maman*."
He pointed dramatically toward the window. *"Là-bas."*

"Niko, I'm telling you, giving you my word, about
Corporal Shymanski, and you didn't hear it from me."

"Mrs. Leggatt doesn't sleep with him."

"Pardon?"

"Madame Leggatt doesn't share a bedroom with the Prime
Minister. Martha told me. She sleeps on a different floor of
Gross-Piss-Off. Twenty-four Sussex. They barely talk to each
other—well, they talk to each other now, but Martha told me
they didn't even look at each other for days and days."

"Niko, listen to me. Do this for me. You just selectively
forget anything that did or didn't happen while you stayed
there. Do you hear me?"

Niko looked away.

"Do you hear me? And never ever speak of this again. To
anyone. Not even to Dr. Pelletier. Have you told Dr. Pelletier?"

"Non."

"Jamais, tu m'entends?"

"What are you going to do, *Maman*?" Niko pinned her
with his stare. "Are you going to prorogue? For him?"

To Lise, he might as well have been asking, *Are you going to
be his bitch?* Then he made the face. The one that Becky had
described. As if he had a very bad, dead-rat taste in the middle
of his life.

15

——

RENÉ STORMED IN THE Rideau Hall side entrance after ten p.m. He'd been detoured due to the candlelight vigil being held by Conservative staffers, blocking Sussex Drive in the freezing December night. Lise was so relieved to see him that she skipped down the stairs and slid herself into his embrace.

He wasn't a muscle man, but he leaned in to her, and his spine was Ben Kingsley steel, and he edged his hip between her legs and then dipped, almost raising her off her feet with the force and girth of his quadriceps, and it felt ooh-la-la. His neck, his sweet scent, his lips holding her earlobe.

"I dismiss you," he said to Corporal Robard. "Begone all ye aides, ye lackeys, ye serfs, ye butlers, ye yeomen, ye maids—on second thought, the maids may stay. No, they must go. I dismiss you, for it is now I must have sweet concord with my dame, my ruler, my liege, my representative of the King, my wife."

The PMO had summoned René, so that each and every Canadian voter could rest assured that the Governor General would be supported by a calm and rational husband.

"Your Excellency, I'll just take your bags—" Robard said.

"Begone!" roared René.

Robard bowed away in mock subservience and René and Lise headed upstairs. Bedward.

But it was quick, businesslike bliss, as Lise experienced it. Afterwards, they lay cozily enough in their matching bathrobes on top of the king sheets, brocade curtains drawn against the now-sinister vista of the Hill, the lamps as low as possible.

When she felt ready, she told him the story of her day with Niko: the King–Byng incident in class, the suspension, her incredible conversation with Niko about Shymanski et al., with the twists and turns of Sussex Drive domestic life, including the fact that Niko had never taken the antidepressants in the first place. She ended with the face Niko had made.

René reacted immediately. "The boy knows too much."

"I know."

"And it's also dangerous for him to know what he does."

"I told him he couldn't talk to Dr. Pelletier about it."

"D'accord."

"Oh my God, René. What can we do?"

"The only thing I can think of is if we take him out of the city. Even out of the country."

"I can't—not right now, with—the prorogation, the Prime Minister."

"I have looping in LA."

"When?"

"Next week, but I could go earlier and take him."

"*Demain?*"

"*Oui. Demain.*"

"*Bien.*" After her son was safe, she'd worry about how she could hold the country together by herself. And handle *la Noël.*

He rose abruptly from the bed, hit the floor for push-ups, stood, put his glasses back on and adjusted them, although she loved when they slid down his nose. "After I check in with Niko about California, we need to talk about Romania. *Toi et moi.* Foreign Affairs."

"*Vraiment?*" But she thought, *Enfin.*

"*Absolument.*" He headed off to dress. "*Sans aucun doute.*"

And she thought, *Pourquoi?*

Downstairs hummed.

Margaret Lee asked if she'd like to view the petition that had just arrived. Lise did, and was handed seven original pages signed by 169 Members of Parliament from all the coalition ridings: Bonavista, Cardigan, Kings-Hants and Beauséjour, represented by the dear son of deceased Governor General Roméo LeBlanc; Miramichi, Rimouski, Chicoutimi and Toronto-Danforth; Ottawa Centre, Ottawa South and Sault Ste. Marie; Nickel Belt, Guelph, Wascana, and Vancouver East, South, Centre, Quadra, and all the way north to Nunavut, *un pays avec les sons d'un poème. Des mots—très simples.*

They asked the Governor General to not prorogue the Parliament and permit them to exercise their vote as they had been elected to do by the Canadian people. All original signatures—scrawled, emphatic, illegible, anally neat—cleanly dated. She knew how hard it was to corral these kittens even to sign a birthday card to their kid. She stared at the pages.

Back in Margaret Lee's office, the windows were shuttered and one sole halogen light illuminated her desk, occupied only by a Mac laptop and a nineties phone. A whiteboard exposing Lise's present and future dominated the wall. "I may have located a constitutional adviser," Margaret Lee said. "You don't know him."

"That dog won't hunt," Lise said. "I want one I know."

"They're all in the Caribbean."

"Right," said Lise. "And last September they were in Muskoka."

"They get around," said Margaret Lee.

Lise walked out. She wanted to review her Eugene Forsey, perhaps even to call one of these experts directly herself. She ducked across the first-floor corridor, the fragrance of a lovely new bouquet, overstuffed with lilies, choking her.

René was in her study. "Oh, here you are," he said.

"How did your talk go with Niko?"

"It was okay. Given everything. He's in crisis."

"He's inconsolable."

"Yes, and scared. He's on for California except he wants you to come, too. I explained to him why you can't. Not right now. He gets it."

"*Je t'aime.*"

"Hold that thought." He led her to the couch. "Lise, we need to discuss Romania." They sat down in unison. "On the Ceremonies Route, on the way to the Speech from the Throne, I told you I'd done some extracurricular work for DFAIT when filming was on hiatus."

"Yes," Lise said. "You told me you did it for me. To improve my relationship with the PMO."

"*Exactement.* I was still mad at them for that low trick of playing the Lévesque cleep on the Apoonatuk show. Trying to frame me as a separatist."

"And twisting my elbow so that I'd allow the writ to be dropped for an election that wasn't scheduled."

"Yes, and I guess I thought, let bygones be bygones. That our time in office would flow more smoothly if I played the game. So they approached me, DFAIT. They already knew I had some free days, I don't know how, and that it wasn't enough of a break for me to come back to Ottawa or go to Paris or London. They wanted me to do 'detailing.' Detailing, they called it. I told them I wouldn't do anything I disagreed with."

"Black ops," Lise said, nodding. Romania was known for that.

"So this was wine and dine. I met these Romanians, businessmen, being courted for a private–public partnership, something with natural gas. Their reserves are diminishing, and we have the technological companies that can maximize their capability. And we're at this fantastic restaurant, French, and before I know it, the restaurant's closed, it's turned into a private gathering, and out come the drugs, very good drugs—from the look of them, you know—and the girls, also very nice—from the look, for sure—and I'm out of there."

"Where were your bodyguards?"

"Nada. Because I wasn't on official business in Europe. And I tell DFAIT what happened, why I left, and they apologize for putting me in that position. And I wanted to tell you about it, but everything was so crazy. A few weeks later, I'm back on the shoot, and it was my big scene, *ma chère*, big, the DFAIT deputy shows up on set, can you believe? And he's got this photo, can you believe—"

Lise could.

"—and there I'm standing under the Romanian flag with this drug lord, convicted drug trafficker, in a big embrace."

Lise held her face in her hands. "So they've set you up again."

"Oui, ma chère."

"What did you say to DFAIT?"

"Fuck off."

A silence.

René continued, "We are here tonight on the cusp of history. I don't want to burden you with this when you must have all your wits for this monumental deliberation. I can't tell you not to prorogue."

"Shut up, René," Lise said.

"But if I were you, I wouldn't let the PM prorogue."

"Shut up."

"I'm finished with this regime, Lise. I'm done with this particular minority government, and if they're still running the country tomorrow, I'm done with Rideau Hall, and with serving as your consort."

Lise fastened her hand on his heart.

"*C'est tout. C'est fini.*"

"What about our marriage? Our boy?"

"You are free to follow your conscience. I love you now, and I'll love you tomorrow, whatever happens, and I'll wait for you to leave the office. I'll never leave Niko. He is my son now too. But if this government continues another day, I cannot stay. And if I *stay* with you, your days in government will be numbered."

"What do you mean?"

"Your life may be in danger."

From: "Rebecca Leggatt" < mschatelaine@gc.parl.ca >
To: "Lise Lavoie" < lagrosselegume@gg.rh.ca >
Sent: 4 December 2008 2:33 a.m.
Subject: Toi

Dear Lise,
Thinking of you. Try to get some sleep.

Your BFF,
Becky ;)

From: "Lise Lavoie" < lagrosselegume@gg.rh.ca >
To : "Rebecca Leggatt" < mschatelaine@gc.parl.ca >
Sent: 4 December 2008 2:35 a.m.
Subject: Re : Toi

Whatever.
LL

16
—

It was four a.m. in Ottawa. She should have slept; she couldn't sleep. Her thoughts pinged: what *had* happened to Corporal Shymanski, and where *was* Lieutenant-Colonel Aisha K., and poor Martha, poor young girl, and Becky having to deal with such a crisis while living at Sussex Drive. And ponged: how stupidly Roman Catholic could Shymanski be; and wasn't Martha exposed to sex education, and why didn't Becky pick up on their romance; and, *mon Dieu*, her own husband was threatening to resign from Rideau Hall and abandon her. Which would be disastrous for her son. And if René didn't resign, he'd bring down a scandal upon them. Also not good for Niko. She was devastated; she didn't know where to put her emotions. She had to stash them, along with what the anglos call *le baggage*, and so she did.

They were brisk at Buckingham Palace, but they connected her with Sandringham, which was where the King happened to be. "In a spot of trouble over there, are you?" The Governor General coordinator was wry.

"Yes," Lise said. "I, of course, understand that the Governor General of Canada is independent, as all Governor Generals are. However, I'd like to be able to consult with His Majesty, if necessary, later in the day, specifically five or six hours from now. Would He be available?"

"Excuse me, Your Excellency, I'll put you on hold."

When he returned, he was quite chipper. "His Majesty says it would be lovely to converse as long as you're aware that he'll be chatting unofficially. All to be kept on the q.t. Ta-ta."

He really did say that.

6:00 a.m.: she checked on Niko in his room. She loved his cranky snore and the little bit of fuzz on his upper lip, which made the acne stand out. She snooped around his desk and took his defaced juice-sticky student directory; the number she needed was in it.

6:06 a.m.

She called Stornoway.

"*Allo,*" said Monsieur Triste. It was clear he hadn't slept either.

"*Préparez-vous.*"

"*Pourquoi, madame?*"

"*Vous allez former le gouvernement.*" She hung up.

She opened the shutters in her study. The old-fashioned Christmas lanterns decorating the driveway offered an inkling of deceptively sweeter Victorian times. She thought she could hear the Canadian anthem being sung by live human beings. It was faint and it was close by. The demonstrators must have spent the freezing night parked at her gate.

She lay down on the couch, the one serially graced by Charles de Gaulle, Winston Churchill, JFK, Nelson Mandela, the Dalai Lama, Václav Havel, Salvador Allende, Lech Walesa, and pulled up the gift quilt from the President of Kazahkstan, which smelled of fields and rutting goats and winter and meat cooked till it fell off the bones over a fire, and drifted to the refrain, which seemed to be on repeat, "We stand on guard, we stand on guard." She'd never known until now that it was a lullaby.

She didn't dare think about Solange or her Samuel, or even if they were still alive. She was too spooked even to check the Internet.

"The PM's coming," René said, waking her up.

Lise rushed across the hall to Margaret Lee, also still wearing the same outfit as yesterday. "Constitutional advisers," Lise said, like ordering doughnuts at Tim's. "Who've you got?"

"I told you," Margaret Lee said. "Nobody's available."

"Akinfemi?"

"He's in Nigeria, international court."

"Thomson?"

"The Hague."

"I don't think you really tried," Lise said.

"I am truly sorry you feel that way," Margaret Lee said. "We've had short notice and are making best efforts. In serving you, I serve the government of Canada, and it's crucial, Your Excellency, that you are well supported and believe you are, today."

Lise retreated.

She showered, and then sorted through what the valet had chosen: skirt by Paprika, blouse by Neige, jacket by Diplomatic, hose from Hue. She stood there in her lingerie, chilled. *Brain from Fried. Nerves from Scrambled.*

"I'm sorry about last night." René was at her dressing room door.

"I am, too." She waited for him to say that he'd slept on it, thought about it, had changed his mind.

He came over to her and pulled her into his arms. His scent made her weak. "I haven't changed my mind, Lise," he whispered.

"Okay," she said. That was all she had left in her.

"Do you want to know the polls?"

"I can guess."

"You've guessed right. Karp-Deem and Rippo—average 85 percent in favour of prorogation."

"What about the other poll? The Standard?"

"It doesn't matter. The other poll didn't make the headline."

She hugged him back. "Niko?" she asked.

"*Il dort,*" he said. "When he wakes up, we'll hang out. Maybe play some shinny on the rink." He paused. "And I want you to consider the North."

"The North?"

"His extended family. Mistassini. Niko would be safe there."

"His father wasn't." She waited and he didn't bite. "And what about LA?"

"LA now. The North—later. Just think about it." He let her go and switched on the TV coverage. "I'm not going anywhere until you conclude this."

She saw another reporter doing a stand-up at the locked doors of the House of Commons, and then a shot outside Rideau Hall where a circus of TV trucks and crews were setting up. Live footage rolled of the Prime Minister's limousine arriving at the Prime Minister's private entrance downstairs.

"Good morning, Excellency," said Greg. His valet had gone the extra mile this morning: the PM sported a cashmere topcoat over his Harry Rosen suit, a crimson tie with an arrowhead motif, and his rim of hair was fluffed. He stamped his feet on the carpet, a Ferdinand the bull gesture. "Clark's right behind me. He's been held up by the very enthusiastic pro-government supporters."

"Of course," said Lise.

"Becky sends her regards."

"Yes."

"She may drop over later. Nick left some things at our place."

"Yes, thank you so much for your hospitality."

"No skin off my nose. I never saw the kid, to be perfectly frank."

"Good morning!" said Clark the Privy Clerk, filing in. He seemed a little crisp, his game face tightly on.

Margaret Lee joined them, gathering her weight in outerwear, then ushered them into the Governor General's study, which Lise could detect had been thoughtfully refreshed, with Kazakhstan folded and replaced on a decorative Mennonite table.

The Prime Minister checked his BlackBerry. "I've allotted a couple of hours. More for appearance than substance."

"Prime Minister, I have set aside the entire day."

"I understand, Lise, but I have another important media event—"

"The Ski-Doo dealership?"

"—to attend directly following and it can't be—"

"The Ski-Doo—"

"I heard you the first time, Excellency. Clark, outline the procedure."

"With all due respect, Prime Minister," Lise said, "I know it. I am up to speed on everything, *everything* that has transpired."

Greg took her measure. "Fab. Then let's cut to the chase, shall we?"

Lise made a temple of her fingertips. "I have studied the situation and I must let you know that in my opinion, and in using my reserve powers—"

"The reserve powers are really at the Prime Minister's discretion—" the PM said.

"—in using my reserve powers, I am not inclined to grant a prorogation at this time. *Pourquoi? Parce que* we just had an election, and you know, Prime Minister, as well as I, that Canadians do not vote in a president, it is the party with the most seats who forms the government. You were the leader of that party and formed a minority government. You can only govern as long as the other parties in the House align with yours to give you a majority vote and confidence. Confidence, *c'est le clef.* Right now it seems to me that you do not enjoy the confidence of the House, and if a vote is taken, your government will fall."

The Prime Minister stood. "Privy Clerk, Secretary, please entertain yourselves while I speak with the Governor General alone."

Clark murmured, "I must remain in the room."

"Everyone has to heed the call of nature," Greg said.

Clark didn't budge.

"Get out."

Clark and Margaret Lee headed out of the study and the PM closed Lise's door behind them.

Lise's heart was beating so vigorously she thought her Neige blouse might be visibly pulsating.

"Look, Lise, I may not be the sharpest knife in the drawer, and you're definitely not, but we both know that this country can't be taken over in a coup. It's not right, it's not on, and I won't stand for it."

"If I may be frank, Greg—"

"Well, as it turns out, Lise, you may not—"

"The hubris—"

"Excuse me."

"—behind *ce cirque*. And this is not a coup. This is what occurs day to day in Parliament, and is based on the evolution of our system from the Royal Proclamation of 1763, through the Quebec Act of 1774, to the Statute of Westminster, 1932, to the Letters Patent of 1947."

"Have you seen the polls?"

"I do not trust them."

"The press?"

"Ditto. *Même chose*."

"The general mood of the nation won't sustain—"

"You make it sound as if Canada, she's having her period—"

That seemed to repulse him and he shut up.

There was a knock at the door and it swung wide open, as in a Molière farce. It was René. He wouldn't look at Greg. "Your Excellency, I would like for to speak a minute with you." His *anglais* disintegrated when he was nervous.

"*Excusez-moi.*" Lise bowed to the PM, and led her consort into his own adjoining study and closed the door with gravitas.

"They're going over your head, Lise," René said. "A Privy Council member on Can TALKS says the Tories will go to the Canadian people and ask the Chief Justice to give the permission to prorogue. The PC member, she says you're an unelected official—"

"So is she!"

"—appointed by a defeated Liberal PM. She said—"

"Who is this?"

"Madame Alice Nanton. She said they'll explore every legal—"

"So if I don't do it, they attack this office."

"*Oui.*"

"*Mon Dieu, mon Dieu, mon Dieu.*"

"That is what you're dealing with."

"I am damned if I do, and if I don't."

René looked at her. "You must break the traditional silence of the Governor General. *Parle à la presse.*"

Lise walked purposefully back to the door of her study, even knocking so that she didn't barge in on the Prime Minister in case he was combing his hair, blowing his nose, et cetera.

But he was gone.

The door to the hallway was ajar and sitting on the polished oak floor, by the coffee table, was the little orphan Pablo, spreading out what looked like Kumon homework sheets.

"Pablo!" Lise said. "*Buenos días.*"

"*Salut,*" said Pablo.

"What are you doing here, bud?"

"Math."

"Where is your father?"

"He had to go do something."

Lise was about to cross the hall and hunt Pablo's dad down when Becky arrived, hauling a backpack stuffed fat with Niko's gear. She'd appeared seemingly from nowhere.

"Is this a bad time?" Becky asked, and before deigning to read the very plain answer on Lise's face, she said to Pablo, "Not in Aunty L.'s office, honey! Use the library next door, go on, go on, NOW! And don't tag any of the furniture, okay?"

Pablo collected his Kumon file and worksheets and trudged down the hall along with his wiggly worm eraser and fistful of automatic pencils. Lise noticed Pablo looked under the weather; decimals had done that to Niko too.

Before Lise could say a word, Becky said, "I think we're looking at home schooling here." She nodded in the direction Pablo had travelled.

"Becky, where's the PM? We're in the middle of the meeting," Lise said. "Thank you for Niko's stuff, but we'll have to catch up *plus tard.*"

Becky floated into an armchair *à la capucine* near Lise's desk. "Well, everyone's taking a break. Greg's huddling with Clark and Peggy in her office. I don't mean to butt in, but how's it going? And how are *you* holding up?" She gestured to Lise herself to have a seat. "I also brought fresh-baked blueberry muffins." She pulled out a blue gingham tea towel–covered basket from her huge tote, skimmed off the towel and offered them.

"Not right now," said Lise. But the smell got to her. "Oh, *tabarnac,*" and she took one.

Clark the Privy Clerk appeared in the open doorway. "Your Excellency, are you agreeable to meet again in ten minutes? The Prime Minister's finishing an international call." Messenger Boy.

"Bien sûr."

"Hello, Becky," said Clark, sighting her.

"Hi, Clark."

He waved and exited.

"Bye, Clark."

Lise sat kitty-corner to Becky.

"Word is you're not keen to do the deed," Becky said.

"Word is right."

"Well, you're the GG. You've got to do what you feel is best."

"D'accord."

"Far be it from me to offer any advice," she began. "I know I have no business talking with you about it, but we do go back, us ex-newbies, *vous* and me. So, I'll just say, take a moment to think about your legacy. And how it impacts your family long-term, particularly if you side with the coalition over a legitimately elected government and that splits the country in two. The press are mean. That CBC."

"*Many* are mean," Lise corrected.

"If you do it, Lise, nothing is lost. The coalition can come back in a few weeks, vote down a confidence bill and take over the reins of government. In a way, that's the best test. If they can hold together for a few weeks, maybe they can hang together for six months, nine, until the next election. But if the coalition sinks in the interim, nothing's lost. Greg's a world-class leader, almost a beloved icon. He's already served as Prime Minister and was resoundingly re-elected."

"I think you've mixed the crack in the Kool-Aid," said Lise.

"Okay, so not *resoundingly*."

That won an unwilling smile from Lise. "So you're saying that if I don't do it, I'm throwing the country to the wolves and will wear it forever."

"I'm not saying *that*," Becky said. "You know I'm not."

Lise's land line shrilled on her Napoleonic desk at the same time as Margaret dashed in. "It's King Charles!"

"Impressive," said Becky.

Lise picked up the phone and gave Becky and Margaret Lee the look. They both took their leave, Becky with a curtsy.

"Your Majesty," Lise said warmly.

"Our most flattering representative," King Charles said.

"Thank you for returning my call."

"Our pleasure. We received a message that you wanted to consult about the goings-on."

"Yes, Your Majesty, I did want to check in with you, at the same time as I'm fully aware that there are no restrictions on my completely independent reserve powers."

"Yes, completely true. How's your husband? Has he been in any film productions recently?"

"As a matter of fact, he has."

"Really? How splendid! I'm always telling our British producers that they should IMDb René and take a look."

"How kind." The director of *In Bruges* was Irish.

"And how was your African vacation? I'll be there next year. How's the suntan?"

Lise winced. "I know you're on a schedule, so I just wanted to ask about your experience or your mother's with this sort of Commonwealth crisis."

"You just missed our Mother, actually—"

"So—"

"Well, I watched all of the goings-on from afar when I was growing up. In the instance of your own prime minister, Vampire Leggatt, I'd like to stab a silver crucifix into his anti-environmental heart. And I have a few of those handy in the Abbey, my dear. But, that aside, what I've learned is that Governors General may be right, they may be wrong— but in the short term, the country always resents interfer-ence. Governors General do themselves no favour by standing up to their PM. How would the King Mum put it? 'It comes back and bites one on the arse.'"

"King–Byng," said Lise.

"Well, I don't recall that one," the King said, "but the Dismissal down under, that was a corker! Back in the seventies, of course. I admit our Mother did have a hand in that one."

Lise heard a commotion in the King's background.

"Your Excellency, it's been lovely catching up. Must dash with memories of the exquisite gown you wore at our first meeting."

The one plunging south of her coccyx. *Merci.*

"Our absolute pleasure."

"The other thing you could think about," said Becky, "is your own reputation." They were now upstairs in Lise's informal family room (with the famous photo of René's father being sworn in as the MP for Beauce by Governor General Vanier; a shot of teen-aged Lise and Solange in the

Bois de Boulogne; Brett teaching Niko to paddle) because Clark had locked himself in Lise's office due to the Prime Minister's demand that three venerable constitutional advisers be airlifted post-haste to Rideau Hall.

"Unblemished," Lise said. "I am an open book."

Becky leaned in. "Are you sure?"

"Absolument," said Lise.

"What about everybody else?"

"Whom do you mean?" said Lise. She felt sick. "Do you mean René?"

"If the shoe fits," said Becky.

Lise felt as if she could raise the couch with Becky on it and hurl all out of the gabled window onto the broadcast trucks below.

"I'm trying to help." Becky lifted her magic tote, dug until she found an envelope, opened it and slid a photo across the Doukhobor coffee table.

It was René, in a grizzly hug, apparently, with Che Guevera, but she knew it was the famous Romanian drug lord, bare-chested, drugged, drunk. Behind them, but not far enough, bare-breasted, bare-assed dancers were leashed to a spectacular dildo, a ten-footer, and she thought she could identify the famous drug spilled across the table.

"I just have to think," Becky said, "as your friend and neighbour, what would this do to your family?" She closed her eyes. "Imagine. To Niko." A pause. "I'm getting a headline: 'Who Put the Vice in Viceregal?' 'Left to His Own De-Vices.' 'Who let the Vice out?'"

Lise wanted to ask where Becky got this, but she already knew, the way she knew they had photos of her on the ground at the Former Slave Depot, or in conference with the ex-president of St. Bertrand, and every other move she'd made or hadn't. There was no point in asking, filing a complaint; she was done.

Lise stood. "I must ask you to leave my apartment. *Immédiatement*."

Becky did not. "Because you, Open Book, were also seen in a tête-à-tête with the ousted president of St. Bertrand."

"Our paths crossed in an airport in Africa."

"I heard. Like Stanley and Livingstone."

"Neither was seeking the other, which you already know. You have that photo *aussi*?"

Becky folded her arms. "Jean-Louis Raymond isn't on our A-for-Allies list. He didn't help us out." She paused. "And it also wouldn't help if folks knew the Green King was interfering."

Lise sat back down beside Becky. She restrained herself from spitting on the photo of stupid René with the stupid stupid drug lord, and those poor enslaved girls. "All right," Lise said, "let's talk *dinde*."

"Ding-Dong," said Becky.

"Turkey."

"*Dindon*," said Becky.

"Whichever you wish," said Lise. "I will prorogue on the Prime Minister's advice."

"You'll come to see the wisdom, Lise."

"On a few conditions."

"This isn't a negotiation."

"Yes. It is."

Becky didn't answer.

"*Numéro un.* The secretary resigns right now."

"Peggy?" Becky was mock shocked, and Lise supposed that this was because the first condition was so very, very easy. "But the PMO—"

"Fire her," said Lise. "And further—"

"There's more?"

Lise took a breath, then exhaled. She'd assumed this role, carried this enormous Dominion on her slim shoulders, to help her country, to help the world. She was already on the edge of losing her husband, and her son might be having a breakdown. It was clear now that she could do nothing at all to help Canada. Its democracy had early-onset Alzheimer's. Its democracy was in a media-induced ethical coma; it had permanent parliamentary amnesia—her mind was raving.

"*Numéro deux,*" Lise said. "St. Bertrand. My native land. Canada is to forgive the debt."

"You've got to be kidding," Becky said.

"*Numéro trois.* St. Bertrand *encore.* Stop the privatization of telecommunications."

"If we don't do it, the States will. Or France," Becky said. "Lise, this is naive. You've made a far left turn here. Take two Tylenol and burn your Naomi Klein, seriously."

Lise reached across and clutched Becky's arm and held it very, very tightly. She was pinching it. "*Écoute-moi,*" Lise said.

"They think they know about us, me and René, the photo, the chance meeting. You have the nerve to sit here and tell me about my own family, how my decision will affect them."

"Let go, Lise, please," said Becky, softly.

Lise dug her fingernails into Becky's flesh.

"I'll deck you," Becky said. "I'm stronger."

"I know, though, that your family is also going through things—"

Lise had never seen a human flush blood out of her head faster than this woman. She witnessed a living illustration of physiological brain drain. Becky turned so white. It was beyond fight-or-flight.

"And I know that it would not be good for your own family if certain information about them—got out." Lise timed her next words. "To the base. *N'est-ce pas?*"

Becky sank into herself. She looked like the Wicked Witch of the West when Dorothy threw the pail of water on her and she melted. Except Becky wasn't wailing. And she was a redhead. Silent, savvy, and far more cunning than an MGM witch. Plus her husband, with CSIS, CSE, RCMP, NATO and CENTCOM, could summon more than flying monkeys.

When Becky finally spoke, she stared down at her lap. "The children pay the price."

"Yes." Lise swallowed. "Children everywhere." She picked up a blueberry muffin from Becky's basket and threw it at the TV. "Long-term."

Becky shook her head. Lise saw that she had to ask. "What do you know?"

Lise didn't hesitate. *"Tout."* She threw another muffin.

"Truly?"

"Oh, yes."

"What do you know?"

"Your daughter." Lise caressed the familial noun.

Becky sat up tall, squared her shoulders, took a breath and left the room. Lise waited. Outside, the sun shone brilliantly, and Lise could see, on the slightly crumby TV screen, that the crews outside Rideau Hall, where she was collared and leashed, had started shooting the winter rainbow that had just now rooted itself in the middle of the Ottawa River behind the Hill. She heard, "Meanwhile, the PM's looking for his own pot of gold."

It was less than ten minutes later when Becky returned. She passed Lise the handwritten letter of resignation from Margaret Lee. "Effective immediately. Embargoed until the New Year."

"The debt."

"Forgiven."

For Canada, a drop in the bucket. For St. Bertrand, perhaps a future.

"Telecommunications?"

"Best efforts." Becky produced the prorogation document. "Clark says sign here and here."

Lise did. She had a wild urge to add one of Becky's emoticons to her signature but was able to restrain herself.

"One final thing," Becky said.

Lise regarded her with detachment.

"Who told?" Becky asked. "Niko?"

"I will never say," said Lise.

"Shymanski," Becky breathed.

From the empty rooms above the Rideau Hall front porch—
an area of suites known as the Mappin—Lise moved aside
the curtain. Below her, the Prime Minister was in makeup.
Becky was magically redelivered from a limo that slipped in
up the drive. She wore sunglasses and a long dark coat by
Arabesque, with a knotted red and white scarf—she was
Pablo-less now, and Greg completely ignored her presence,
even when she tugged the sleeve of his protective duster.

A helicopter landed on the pad by the skating rink. Three
men rushed from the pod. Constitutional advisers, she presumed. Too late.

"My fellow Canadians." Greg launched into his speech. Lise
stared down at his bald spot. He was audible because every
channel in the nation was broadcasting this, and every television in Rideau Hall was tuned in. "The Governor General and
I have concluded a productive two-hour session, the longest
in camera discussion between a Prime Minister and the representative of the monarchy in Canadian history. She has, in her
infinite wisdom, granted this government a prorogation
until—" and he named a date she couldn't register because
René had appeared in the door, his carry-on luggage in hand.

He looked at her and put his hand on his heart. She
walked to him and bowed her head; he rested his lips on her
neck. Niko was just behind him, also with a carry-on.

René said, "My resignation is on Margaret Lee's desk."

Lise nodded. It was all too much. "The North," she said. "Mistassini might be a good idea."

René squeezed her hand.

"Niko," Lise said, "I want you to relax in California, go surfing, just get away from here and have a good time."

Niko said, "You sold out."

And they left.

Later that night, alone, Lise turned on the news.

The prorogation was already ancient history.

Monsieur Triste had resigned as Leader of the Opposition.

Instead of opening a Ski-Doo manufacturing plant, the PM had called yet another media conference at the Press Building. Flanked by Afghan ambassador Jabar Khan and a few pertinent ministers, he announced that the Canadian government had negotiated the release, without paying any ransom, of the beloved Lieutenant-Colonel Aisha K.

"Lieutenant-Colonel!" he said. The camera moved to a wide shot. The PM gestured to a dark-haired babe poised in the wings.

"*Tabarnac!*" Lise knocked over her wine.

It was the first time Canadians had seen the Lieutenant-Colonel without her full-coverage burka; they didn't know what she looked like at all. That went through Lise's mind as she studied the woman on her screen. Her walk was a glissando—no rhythm, no slight weave and bob. She wore a camel jacket, matching short skirt, calf-clenching black leather boots, tasteful gloves, and more closely resembled the sultry TV anchor from the Kabul breakfast show than any memory Lise had of her own mature and maternal Lieutenant-Colonel Aisha K. This Aisha's hair was beauty-pageant ready; she wore winged eye makeup and lashes thick enough to flip a hummingbird. And where was Shymanski?

Greg showed all his polished teeth. "Welcome to democracy."

She'd never seen that woman before in her life.

March 18, 2009 10:00 a.m.
Room 151, Centre Block
CANADA

Special Committee on the Canadian Mission of the Military Police Committee in Afghanistan

Comité special sur la mission canadienne du comité de polices militaires en Afghanistan

***

The Chair (Mme Margaret Lee Yeung, Kelowna–Lake Country, IND): I'll call the meeting to order.

Lt.-Colonel Aisha K., welcome. We have all been looking forward to your appearance. Are you ready to proceed?

Lt.-Colonel Aisha K. (Afghan National Police, Kandahar, Kandahar, Afghanistan): Thank you, Madame Chair. Congratulations to you on winning the by-election in Kelowna.

The Chair: Thank you. It is an honour to continue in the service of this great country. Lt.-Colonel, please begin.

Lt.-Colonel Aisha K.: A little bit of background. I joined the Afghan National Police in 2002, in Kandahar, Kandahar Province, Afghanistan. My primary duties were to investigate crimes involving female perpetrators and victims, and to assist my superior ████████, who was assassinated in ██████. After my superior's murder, I was the primary female officer in Kandahar and it was my role to liaise with military and police personnel from NATO, which in Kandahar was primarily Canadian.

In 2005, I was partnered with Corporal Shymanski. His role was to liaise with my unit, provide bodyguard services when there was any possible threat to me or my cases. In 2006, I visited Canada and toured with him in order to publicize the situation for girls and women in Kandahar and to commend Canada for its commitment to my people. At that time, Corporal Shymanski was a great guy.

In the fall of 2006, this changed completely. Corporal Shymanski became involved with a prostitution ring run out of the governor's mansion's basement. He coerced ANP recruits to become involved. He recruited young Afghan women to become involved. And there was heavy involvement with drug trafficking. In January 2008, when two neophyte ANP reported his actions to my superior, they were murdered by taser. The Taliban claimed responsibility, but tasers are not weapons they routinely use.

At that time, ███████████████ ordered me to work undercover in the prostitution ring. I will not go into detail here, but my investigation revealed Corporal Shymanski's extensive involvement in criminal activity at every level.

In February 2008, when I was delivering critical evidence to the ANP chief and RCMP superiors, my convoy was attacked. There was an explosion and in the chaotic aftermath, I was abducted by ████████████████, rescued by ████████████████, and lived in ████████████████ until the brave Canadian forces liberated me in December 2008.

With the clear understanding that Corporal Shymanski lost a leg in that same explosion, I offer that this was an unfortunate consequence but does not exonerate him of accountability in this action.

The Chair: Please take all the time you need. A glass of water.

Lt.-Colonel Aisha K.: To the best of my knowledge, Corporal Shymanski acted alone. No superior RCMP officers were involved in this operation.

The Chair: Lt.-Colonel K., thank you for your brave testimony.

I turn this over to the Honourable Committee member from Buntzen Lake.

Hon. Bibbo Hedge (Buntzen Lake, B.C., NDP): Lt.-Colonel K., these are serious revelations and unsubstantiated, perhaps defamatory, accusations. Did you see first-hand Corporal Shymanski commit any crime?

Lt.-Colonel Aisha K.: Yes. He had a taser. In Kandahar.

Hon. Bibbo Hedge: Did you not have a successful visit to Canada with Corp. Shymanski in 2006? Did you not say, and I quote, "he's a great guy"?

Lt.-Colonel Aisha K.: Yes, at that time, he was a great guy. Then, he wasn't.

Hon. Bibbo Hedge: With all due respect, that doesn't make sense.

Lt.-Colonel Aisha K.: War does not make sense.

The Chair: Thirty seconds, Mr. Hedge.

Hon. Bibbo Hedge: The last time I heard testimony like this in Special Committee was—

The Chair: I'm going to make an executive decision here. Let's break for lunch.

April 2009

SODOM AND GOMORRAH
(with thanks to "Somewhere Over the Rainbow")

From *Temptations: The Rock Opera*

Sodom and Gomorrah
Where'd you go?
Birds drop over your ashes
Oh how I wish 'twern't so

Sodom and Gomorrah
I'm still here
Yes, I'm one lonely pillar
Gone is my spouse so dear

I knew it was my lot in life
To Honour being my Lot's wife
I got i-i-i-i-i-it!
But then all our people they were bad
And Our Nice Father he got mad
And here we find me
(Licking our salt wo-wo-wo-ounds)

Sodom and Gomorrah
My heart cries
Urban centres I sinned in
Make me so sad I sigh

WORDS AND MUSIC BY GREGORY LEGGATT, B.Sc., M.Sc.

17

—

April was the cruellest month and therefore optimal for a G20 in London—hosted by British PM Gordon Brown and his wife, Sarah. They were Labour. Becky and Greg had been chauffeured in the early morning English gloom, past baton-waving Met police and frazzled cherry blossoms, to the conference site at Docklands, where Becky would make sweet and Greg would rub brains and elbows with Angela Merkel, Cristina Fernández de Kirchner, Nicolas Sarkozy and others, including that rabid Kevin Rudd and American newbie and infidel Barack Hussein Obama, still on his global honeymoon. As fate would have it, as soon as Greg had tactically bolted to the reception area washroom, Becky bumped into the FLOTUS.

"Becky!" said Michelle Obama, as if they were sorority sisters.

"Michelle!" Becky had to look up to her—everybody did, because the First Lady was Tall. And clearly extremely intelligent—a lawyer, after all. Harvard. And a proactively parenting Chicago mom, which made her cunning. Yet dressed in a poodle skirt, peasant blouse and Crayola pink cardigan, she resembled the teacher, super-sized, on *Magic School Bus*.

Plain Sarah Brown, her name an onomatopoeia, sashayed between them, resting a cold hand on Becky's shoulder. "Meesh," she said to Michelle. "I see you've met Becky."

Michelle smiled graciously. "Heya, Sarah. Yeah."

"If our countries, Meesh, the U.S. and Britain, have this so-called 'special relationship,' how would you characterize relations between you and Canada?"

"That's easy," said the POTUS, playfully inserting himself into the troika. "Friends with benefits!" With a huge grin at Becky, Barack slid his arm around Michelle's waist.

"Barack, you're bad." Michelle mock-tapped his wrist.

"Becky, am I right?" said POTUS.

On the spot, Becky thumped her purse against her thigh. "Hell, yeah! And this friend would like to bend your ears about the pluses of Canadian oil sands!"

Chuckles ensued. Becky laughed along, making sure she lasted the longest, while Sarah Brown fussed and gathered the other First Ladies (and the bemusedly lost "First Laddies," spouses of the female leaders) to talk about security and the escalating G20 riot.

In the distance, she saw that Greg had returned to their VIP area, but he seemed to be avoiding her gaze.

—

The truth was, Greg had been avoiding *her* for months. He hadn't spoken to her, privately, since the prorogation. They hadn't spoken to each other publicly either, unless there was a teacher summit, kid's birthday or Valentine's Day photo op when she baked a smiley heart cake she wanted to crush and schmear in his face. He'd been outraged at the December negotiation with the Governor General, that Lise and her rogue son had threatening intelligence on their daughter. There hadn't been a whit of gratitude for her extraordinary efforts around the constitutional crisis or the deliverance she dealt up to him with her own family values on a platter with her soul. His mood was generally irascible, and had seeped into the civil service, the ministries, the culture, the very warped woof of Ottawa, the texture of the snowflakes, the sharpness of the knifelike icicles, the march of pedestrians with their malevolent shoulders, and more. She'd felt the chill enshroud her from the PMO to the PCO, from the Parliamentary Library to the Rideau Mall parking garage to the Beaver Tails stall at the ByWard Market.

As a result, all that Becky thought about was her upcoming meeting with Nina Madrigal, Greg's first love. For it was on the following week. In Ottawa, mind you. Becky had thought about the enigma of Nina so often, replaying her conversation with Alice Nanton on that fateful day late last November, that she felt as if she were embarking upon an affair.

But first, the G20. On the London Eye, Becky was trapped with Svetlana Medvedeva. (Becky kept all appendages folded, crossed, tucked and intensely Kegeled; any Russian in London made her nervous after the radiant death of their ex-KGB guy.) She survived.

Then there was the visit to the Royal Albert Hall for a concert predictably performed by choirs from alternative schools ("Jerusalem," "It's a Small World," "That Sheep May Safely Graze" and "Stronger" by Kanye West, more of a poke than a nod to the African-American First Lady, and completely inappropriate). Trust Labour!

That evening, Becky attended the First Lady event at Number 11 Downing Street while Greg dined next door (working dinner) at Number 10. The theme was "Your Art is Your Life, Your Life is Your Art," and Sarah Brown was slightly apologetic when she confessed that the epigram originated from Henri Matisse, a non-Brit. "However, we're all artists," she declared. "Brilliant!"

Before dinner, the First Ladies toured Number 10. It was massive, with more than a hundred rooms, including apartments, parlours, nanny cave, Jacuzzi, private garden, nuclear bunker, and an empire that expanded into Numbers 11 and 12. Well-meaning Sarah Brown had done her decorating best, pointing out where she'd moved a Gainsborough hither, a Turner sunset thither.

Becky was seated next to the Children's Book Author. She'd noticed that people who wrote children's books were never called writers, they were called *authors*, while adult authors were simply *writers*. Their table also included two tiny spouses from countries whose first language was anything but English, and Mrs. MI6, wife of Britain's spy chief—which made social sense to Becky, because she knew that many of the spouses were married to former intelligence czars.

Becky was hyper-aware of the CBA's works, a critically lauded, unusually lucrative series about a juvenile (delinquent) warlock fighting the Followers of Light, who finally saw the light himself but only after six volumes and the equivalent in billions of pounds. She'd found it heretical, anti-Christian rubbish, and had herself signed one of the petitions to have the books banned (burned!) in Canada.

Over the cherry port charlotte dessert, the CBA zeroed in. "So, Ms. Canada"—she pointed her fork—"why's your man so keen on killing the Kyoto Protocol?"

"Oh, crumb," Becky said.

"Why do you say that?"

"I have only one mission at the G20."

"Which is?"

"To never talk politics."

The CBA, an earnest activist, obviously didn't hear. "I've been watching Canada very closely since he came to power, and the country's gone totally wacko. You've abandoned AIDS initiatives in sub-Saharan Africa, slashed budgets, and told your provincial leaders to privatize medicine, water and education, and you're inflating your military budget, and your surplus—that amazing buffer built by the previous administration—has been splurged on, quite frankly, cheap vote-bribing wanks."

Becky stared across the daisy-and-rosebud-festooned table at the CBA. She was lithely starved, her hair swept up in a ponytail of preposterous ringlets, and she'd obviously been brainwashed by fellow lefty billionaire eccentrics. George Soros. Bill and Melinda Gates?

In the hush: "Canada's really none of your *beeswax*," Becky said.

"Pardon me?"

"I wonder you have the time to write," Becky mused. "So many fac-*turds*, so little time."

The CBA pushed away her Royal Wedgwood.

"Oh, look," Becky misdirected, and pointed into the corridor, cluttered with yet another portrait of Winston, "there go the First Laddies." The female leaders' husbands were stealing away.

But the CBA launched into the plight of First Nations reserves. And the PM had loosened restrictions on food sanitation, with corporations policing themselves. How many have died from listeriosis? Did Becky know? Or care?

"Hey," said Becky, "I think you've mistaken me for Svetlana. You know, Mrs. Medvedev? Over to our extreme right?"

Becky saw Sarah Brown glance their way. Even Meesh. Becky would have loved to take off her figurative gloves and attack the CBA for poisoning the precious minds of children with toxic literary magic, but she knew better. She'd been trained by American PR experts. So she blinked back a tear.

"You have children," said the CBA, reading Becky's mind, "do you not?"

And with that, Becky was impaled.

For Greg had been wooing her natural-born children away from her. Day by day, he'd slowly isolated her with tactical disses and invited their allegiance to Club Greg. She was home-schooling Pablo, so still had a maternal and elementary oar in there, but Peter was long gone from her reach, now on Ritalin for ADHD and unspecified issues, and his eyes were glassy, his answers to her clipped.

And her girl. Martha had become protectively close to her father, vetting his gospel rock opus and truly singing from his song sheet. She'd finally applied to colleges, but they were in Ottawa—U of O, Carleton—as her father had advised, so they could continue to create beautiful Christian art and together disseminate. Peter had become more attached to his older sister, a convert to the choir, perhaps because he was the only child not actively claimed by a parent.

"Adopted, are they not?" said the CBA.

"One," Becky said, "is."

"How do you sleep with a man who refuses to protect their future?"

Where was Becky's hostess? Where was New Labour when a guest victim really needed them? Were they Labour or not?

The CBA had her in a chokehold. "A dissembler?"

Becky's chin went wildly out of control. She set her jaw and covered her lower face with her hand. Mrs. MI6 passed a glass of port.

"A bully?"

Becky pushed down the noise climbing from her core into the elevator of her throat.

"How do you *sleep?*" the CBA demanded.

"You *bee*—" Becky began.

The CBA looked over Becky's head with pure loathing.

"—*ach*," Becky finished.

Greg's hands landed heavily on her shoulders. She was mini-Raptured out of her chair and suddenly found herself at Carla Bruni's table soiree. The talk was of electrolysis and Rouen. Greg stood guard.

Just behind them, Michelle Obama ostriched over the CBA and extended her black hand. "Jane!" she boomed, shaking the author's lily-white paw. "Pardon me, but I've just got to tell you how much my kids LOVE *Warlock*. Barack and I take turns reading, and the girls made me promise to have you sign their copies."

The CBA was diverted, at last.

Sarah Brown appeared by Becky's side and announced that they would all receive personally signed editions of the CBA's celebrated books, which would then be retrieved from the First Ladies and donated, in their country names, to an auction for British charity. "Isn't that brilliant?"

Mrs. MI6 approached Greg and leaned in. "Your art is your *wife*, sir."

Greg didn't get this but Becky thought that she did.

After the Barack Hussein Obamas had piled into their armoured Beast, the press exhaled. The rest of the ruling classes toddled, all hail-fellow-well-met, into their limos and crept back into the dankish London dark, avoiding the "kettled" rioters in the City.

In their car, Becky and Greg were, as usual, absolutely silent. She could discern that he was in a horrible mood. Rudd the Radical always got under his skin, Sarkozy was a mosquito, Berlusconi a putz, and the orgasmic cacophony about the U.S. president was hard for any Conservative prime minister to take.

Becky's near slip hadn't helped.

In the few months since Becky's family room prorogation deal, much had changed: Chief was gone (and she'd had nothing to do with that, *nothing*), Doc was Chief, while Clark the Privy Clerk, like that kitchen slated for renovation but in desperate daily use, remained.

However, sitting three feet away from the PM tonight in this low-tech armoured car, in a domestic Iceland, the CBA's assessment of her husband and his policies rang true-*ish* to her. For the first time.

He was on the BlackBerry, previewing a new ad campaign to brutally erode the reputation of the new Leader of the Opposition; suppressing late-breaking fallout from the RCMP drug ring scandal in Kandahar (which had gained traction); deflecting blistering orders from Obama's own Chief of Staff, Rahm Emanuel (a.k.a. "Orahma"). Yet she didn't feel a shred of empathy for his mini-concerns.

Her isolation had pushed Becky to reach out to old friends back in her Whitehorse home, and this new Internet necklace of past acquaintances, the "How's so-and-so?" or "Whatever happened to?" had led to fastening the clasp on the location of Nina Madrigal, Greg's ex. She was living in Gatineau, Quebec—could you believe it? right across the river from them in Ottawa—and had lived there since splitting up with Greg and shedding the Yukon. She could probably have peeked in their bedroom window if she was so kinkily inclined and owned binoculars.

She'd agreed to meet Becky back in Canada. Was it right? Was it wrong? Becky didn't know. She could no longer live with the silence, the mystery or the potentially outright lies he'd fed her. She'd put the Privy Council member's revelations out of her head during the prorogation—for the party, for the majority, for Greg—but afterwards, with the unrelenting chill emanating from him and then her children, she'd thought of nothing but Nanton's details and Greg's tearful description of his breakup with Nina right before Becky made love with him in the front seat of his car.

Nina had nixed the secret service. It had to be private. Becky had to be alone. And no recording devices.

Greg and Becky arrived at Clarence House, passing the topiary pigs, big as army tanks, spotlit on the Mall. "Art" cultivated and curated by the Green King.

"Hogwash." Greg picked imaginary and real lint off his lapel. The King Mother had insisted they stay with her at Clarence during the G20, if they could ignore the solar panels her progressive idiot son had installed on her roof.

The limo stopped.

"Get your act together," Greg said, then hoofed it into the House.

When she caught up, Lawrence Apoonatuk, the new Canadian ambassador to France, even though his French was pretty *pauvre*, was attached to Greg's ear in the foyer. Apoonatuk gave Becky a contemptuous pro forma bow, then followed Greg into a suite of offices with the Canadian delegation for the midnight briefing.

Chest-shaven Doc, now the new Chief—she called him Choc—closed the door in her face.

Choc off.

Greg hadn't said a word about Becky's loveliness. She'd been draped tit to toe in skin-tight, cumulus-white Absolution couture with a peekaboo chiffon midriff. Her auburn tresses had been teased and glossed. He hadn't even fucking once slipped a casual arm around her silk waist.

It was enough to make her fantasize south of the forty-ninth.

Before Becky could remove herself to their suite, the Clarence House steward, the night version, appeared. "Madame, I hope you had a good evening."

"Yes," Becky said. "Brilliant."

"Your daughter has retired."

Martha was with Becky and Greg in London. Becky believed Greg had invited her on a multi-tactical whim—as a human interest buffer, teen mascot, a curiosity for the Canadian media tagging along. Citizens would love to see

Canadian "royalty" hook up with one of the princes. Fortunately, from Becky's POV, Prince Harry was in Helmand, calling in bombs on the Taliban insurgents and Pashtun-speaking newlyweds.

"Thank you," Becky said to the steward. She stepped back outside for a breath of air. She was in the private garden, a stone's throw from Buckingham Palace, spectacular until the King shut down the lights at eleven to conserve energy. Behind the high walls, there was the rumble of London traffic and the peculiar *eeyore, eeyore* sirens of the police cars. Big Ben struck.

Becky phoned her mom. She was staying with the boys at 24 Sussex.

On the first ring, "What's he like?"

Of course, Obama.

"I'm just watching CTV and it looks as though you and Greg arrived at Docklands right behind him and Michelle."

"We met," Becky said. "How are the boys? Is Peter taking his pills?"

"And she just looked so elegant. She's tall, isn't she? I just caught a glimpse of you in that silly hat beside her."

"Mom, is Peter taking his—"

"Yes, Becky, yes, everything's fine. Peter's missing his big sister and Pablo's missing you. The boys—they're saying the author of the *Warlock* series was at the dinner too—"

"Yes."

"Well, the boys want books autographed."

"Right."

"Being married to the PM of Canada is one thing, Becky, but when you're breaking bread with President Obama! Be still my heart, and he and that Michelle have such chemistry! The way he folds his arms around her waist, and how they look at each other, and how he took her hand when they were waiting to meet King Charles and he whispered in her ear and made her laugh. So natural. So in synch."

"Put Dad on," Becky said.

She'd studied the White House website herself and the official photographer's thousands of shots. The one she came back to was taken in a service elevator between inaugural balls, with Barack and Michelle's hands on each other's shoulders, foreheads locked, eyes open and steady, and his jacket draped over her Canadian designer gown to ward off any chill. PR had nothing to do with *that*.

"Hello, sweetheart," Glenn said.

"Dad."

"How's my Second Lady?" he said. Her mother's giggle echoed in one of the vast chambers of drafty, gloomy Gorff.

"Super," she said, exhausted. Becky did find it odd that she spent more time talking to Glenn lately. In fact, *she* mostly called *him*. At Christmas, when she'd taken the children back to Whitehorse without Greg, she'd played long chess matches with Glenn; she'd snowshoed by his side for kilometres on the golf course.

"Hang in, princess," he said. Her dad had unloaded his Hummer, joined a men's group, was stoked about balance and sobriety. He laughed more, with big bursts from his belly. That explained her mother's giddiness, her chirps about the Obama intimacy, as if she'd been relocated at Viagra Falls.

Oh my God, Martha, in her nightgown, was walking out the main entrance of Clarence House.

"Mom?" Martha peered into the darkness. Her hair was nun short and she was Communion wafer thin, as if erasing her body or acting as surrogate dieter for the father who couldn't stop stuffing his face.

"I'm here," Becky called to her. "Coming." She yelped, "Later," into the phone. She was at Martha's side before security could mobilize. "What is it, honeybee?"

"Taylor."

"What about him?" Becky was so ready for Martha's vulnerability.

"He called."

Becky put a firm hand on her daughter's back and steered her into Clarence House, past the curious servants and up the elevator to their third-floor quarters. The virgin Diana Spencer had stayed here before her marriage to the then ring-a-ding-ding prince, but best not to dwell on that. Once Becky had the door secured, she guided Martha to a settee.

"What did he want?"

"To talk. To you."

"Me?"

"Yes."

"About?"

"He wouldn't say."

"Where is he?" But Becky already knew that he was in Resolute, Nunavut, about as far north and as far away as he could be within the realm, held in the grip of the North until his appearance before the Military Police Commission next week. Martha wasn't supposed to know about the reprehensible Kandahar business.

"Nunavut."

"He's blocked on your phone."

Martha averted her gaze.

"Is he blocked on your phone?"

"Yes."

"Then how could he get through?"

"He called from a different number." She reached up for a half inch of hair and pulled it. "To call from."

"Have you been talking to him? Honeybee?"

"Yes."

Becky realized she wasn't surprised. Where would a young woman put the trauma? Becky had pretended to herself that Martha was unscarred, that the medical abortion was less mentally and physically arduous than the old-fashioned primitive route. She even remembered saying to her daughter that the procedure would be like an unusually heavy menstrual period. At night in bed, she'd told herself that Martha's youth had protected her from the crushing guilt still affecting Becky's oldest girlfriends, now mothers, who ticked off phantom birthdays every year with unbearable melancholy.

And where would a sweet girl like Martha bury her love for a decent crippled war hero, with mutton chops and puppy dog cheeks, who'd been put on a pedestal by her father the Prime Minister?

"You miss him," Becky said. "Don't you?"

Martha closed her eyes. "Yes."

"Does he talk about your decision?"

"He just says he understands. That it was my choice." Martha folded over into Becky's lap. "I'd be in the third trimester, Mom."

Becky held her. The pattern of the candelabra imprinted on her daughter's cotton nightgown.

"Do you know why I liked him so much?" Martha raised herself on an arm.

"Why, honey?"

"He was so gentle. He wasn't angry, you know? So different from Dad."

Becky took that in. "That's important," she said.

"It is," Martha said. "Isn't it?" She was quiet. "Night, Mom."

18
—

"TAYLOR."

"Mrs. Leggatt, thank you for calling me back."

"You're in a lot of trouble, Taylor," Becky said.

There was an oil portrait of the older, well-seasoned Princess Di in the sunroom. Her blue eyes egged Becky on as she paced with her cell.

"Mrs. Legg— Becky."

"*Numero uno*, you are not to contact my daughter using any form of communication on earth, be it phone, mail, carrier pigeon, text, telepathy, prayer, nothing. It constitutes harassment and there are charges for that. *Numero dos*, if I were you, I'd be focusing upon that appearance next week in Ottawa, where you've become the star of an international disgrace for Canada and NATO, jeopardizing security and the sacrifices made by your fallen brothers and sisters in uniform. Impugning your superiors. Exploiting the young women—"

"That is what I want to talk to you about, Becky."

"There is nothing under the sun or moon or stars you could possibly want to talk to me about. Unless you want to discuss your betrayal of our trust, the national trust, regarding your intimate relationship with my daughter. How did you think it would look—running a drug and prostitution ring with the Afghans and then ruining the Prime Minister's daughter? My own girl! Do you have a clue?"

"That is what I want to talk to you about."

"Talk!" Becky surged. "Now."

"I have had a lot of time to think, Mrs. Leggatt. Since the IED fourteen months ago—"

"I don't want to get into—"

"Pardon me, but you don't know the whole story."

"I do."

"With respect, you do not. They have only my testimonies with redactions—"

"Fair enough," Becky said.

"The hit was targeted," Taylor said.

"Of course it was targeted. That's what the Taliban do, sweetie."

Taylor was flustered. "I need to talk to you in person. I need to give you something."

"That's just so not on."

He persisted. "You need to know that my relationship with Martha was, how to say it, engineered."

"Excuse me."

"It was set up."

"You're dreaming."

"I was being shut up."

"You have lost it."

"Kept close and kept focused."

Becky did remember that after Corporal Shymanski's rehabilitation, he was posted directly to the Prime Minister's entourage and treated by Greg in particular as a welcomed member of one big happy family. Martha was suddenly invited by her father to tag along for pancake breakfasts, fishing trips and strolls at summer fairs, where security pushed her right up against the limping Corporal. It was around that time that Greg had started composing the *Temptations* tunes.

Oh my God, she thought.

"I was silenced," he said.

Becky said, "Okay, let's meet."

A few days after she and Greg had jetted back to Ottawa, Becky waited for Nina Pearce (née Madrigal) to unlock the door of her cream 2004 BMW M5. They were in the outdoor parking lot of the Casino du Lac-Leamy, in plain sight in a congested area by Lac de la Carrière. Gatineau. Becky had stashed her Harrington Lake Jeep a few rows away. The lock snapped and she slid into the vehicle and positioned herself beside her legendary predecessor.

"You weren't followed?" Nina said.

"No." As far as the PMO knew, Becky had checked into a day spa for treatments.

"Security?"

"No." The Beamer interior smelled of smoke and

cinnamon, and in the back seat there was a Maltese with a plastic cone around its head and workout gear, a towel.

"May I check your purse?"

Becky was insulted. "Be my guest." She passed over her Roots hobo bag.

Becky stole a few looks while Nina rummaged around. She was a more vivid iteration of Becky, for sure, the non-maternal version, now a salon redhead, with the eyebrows receiving as much attention as her pet. But she had laugh lines too, which Becky had never factored into her Nina projections.

Nina handed it back. "I'm an executive secretary at a publicly traded firm," she said, explaining the anti-spy shakedown.

"I know."

"So I know what I'm doing."

"Are you going to check me for a wire?"

"No. You don't have one of those."

"Is your dog sick?" Becky asked.

"No. She just feels more secure wearing the cone." Nina didn't reveal the dog's name. "I won full custody of her in the divorce."

Becky removed her sunglasses. "Do you know why I needed to meet with you?"

"Do you know why I agreed?"

"I'll level with you," Becky said.

"Don't. Please—"

"But—"

Nina gazed out at the lake but didn't seem to be taking it in. "Since Gregory became the PM, I can't tell you the number of journalists who have stalked me. My family's been bothered, my marriage was plagued, my phone bugged, and I've been fortunate that my corporate security at work has given me the tools to keep my private life private."

Becky knew she was the gatekeeper for a Kanata bigwig. A solid Tory supporter.

"Why did we break up? Whose idea was it? It was decades ago, but everyone wants the true story."

"Including me," Becky said.

"Clearly," Nina said. "Do you mind if I smoke?" Her hand reached for the Dunhills in her coffee holder.

"I do mind," Becky said. "Sorry."

Nina laughed. "I respect that."

"You see," said Becky, "there are competing versions."

"Yes," Nina said. She was enjoying her power just a little.

"Serious depression versus restraining orders," Becky prompted.

"I know," she said. She looked out the window and absently reached back to pat the snout of the no-name pooch. "Look, I have to have a smoke." She grabbed a cigarette from the pack, a lighter, and got out. She headed to the sidewalk by the lake and lit up.

Becky waited a minute and then got out of the car and came up beside her.

Nina punched her key fob and the Beamer beeped.

"This is what I want to tell you," Nina said. "Here's your

take-away. I've watched you and Gregory over the years. You have a beautiful family—"

"Thank you for affirming that."

"—two of your own and that sweet little boy from South America. You've stuck by Gregory through thick and thin." She took another drag. "He's a politician. As are you. It's always about spinning a story. Even if the story is saying, hey, by the way, blue is red."

Becky nodded and moved out of the exhalation of smoke.

Far behind them, the motorcoaches roared up to the casino to deliver loads of day gamblers, dreamers and seniors.

"So," Nina said. "He was a man who made up a story. It happened to be about me. It was a story he needed to tell because he was so hurt."

To Becky she sounded protective. Revisionist.

"Hurt that you ended it," Becky said.

Nina ignored her. "The story allowed him to survive to carry on. To meet you, keep you and have a beautiful family." She flicked the ash. "To live happily ever after."

Becky stared out at Gatineau. So he'd lied. Not only had there been a restraining order, he'd disparaged his lover.

"They took care of me," Nina said.

"Excuse me?" Becky said.

"Covered my airfare, six months' rent and change. Pastor Grant still sends me a Christmas card."

She felt ill. "I really have to go," Becky said.

Nina crushed her cigarette under her Cole Haan pump. Becky had the very same pair. "Well, that was fast."

Becky had already turned around and was walking back toward her Jeep. As she passed Nina's car, the Maltese started to yap; it was just a cute face in a cone. She kept walking. "Your dog needs to pee."

Taylor was late. She waited in yet another parking lot, the deserted one at the Mackenzie King estate near Kingsmere Lake. Nobody was here except for Mackenzie King's ghosts and herself.

Out in the bush, she could see the green creeping out onto the trees.

Which would be worse—the history that Nina Pearce had been carrying for two decades or the information Shymanski wanted to unload?

The tongues of Ottawa were wagging. The Parliamentary Committee was scheduled for tomorrow and there was internal wrangling about parameters and redactions. She'd also heard on the news that the Afghan ambassador, Jabar Khan, had been recalled to Kabul and President Karzai wasn't disclosing any details. Colvin's detainee case was also on the boil.

Where was Taylor? She phoned him.

"Becky."

"Where are you?"

"I'm on the Champlain—"

"You're late."

"I'm sorry—"

"Just get here."

"I'm sorry, the Governor General, I had to—"

Trust Lise to have her fingers in this. "Hurry," Becky cried.

He wasn't far. There wasn't even time for her to walk up the hill to the house, closed now, and wander through the ruins. What had that prime minister been thinking with his seances? And how well Ottawa had kept its secrets over the years. Imagine if any relatively current PM was dabbling in the dark arts!

She heard the car. And then it was visible on the stretch of Chemin Mackenzie King. A green compact, an eco-rental, an Honour-Car: she could see the familiar logo on the driver's door. It was Shymanski, and she wondered what she could possibly have been thinking. Meeting this wild card, this publicly accused ANP murderer, trafficker and daughter deflowerer, in the middle of the wilderness.

She stayed in the Jeep while Shymanski pulled into the parking lot. She watched him fiddle with something in the car and then her phone rang.

"Becky—Mrs. Leggatt, do you want to walk?"

"Yes," she said. "In the ruins. Up the hill and to the left. Join me in five minutes."

"D'accord."

She threw on Greg's Tilley hat and her black scarf. She wondered if by appearing here she gave credence to Taylor's notion that he'd been set up with Martha. There was too much to think about.

It was a gentle climb. She was up by the cottage. Not far away, she saw the colonnaded ruins, suitable for a performance of the Scottish play. A soft mist choked the lawn.

She heard the blast. It shot right through her, a battle, and then she found herself and she was running back to him as fast as she could.

The Honour-Car had been tossed. It rested upside down in flames. Acrid black smoke was already towering high. She screamed his name and ran past a leg, real or prosthetic. He'd been expelled in the driver's seat, with the door attached, and it seemed absurd to be trying to open a door to reach him when he wasn't actually inside. She hunted by feel. She didn't dare breathe. There was no logic to it. She had to unfasten his seatbelt, but it seemed to have melted into his hoodie, which became his torso, and then her hand seemed to be inside his cooking lung. He had to be dead. Then her hands reached up to the seatbelt clasp and fused.

By the time the operatives stepped out from behind the trees, the hands were ice. What were they doing there? Who were they? In seconds she was dragged from the explosion and rolled, under their heavy guy weight, to extinguish her jean jacket, her flaming hair under the smoking Tilley.

Then she heard the ambulance.

At the Gatineau Emergency, where she was attended by the very same Pakistani physician who'd treated Greg the previous fall, Becky thought she'd been granted a do-over.

She saw his familiar face, and that's where she went in her brain.

They prepared her for an airlift, working to minimize the impact of smoke inhalation and to reduce her heart rate and vascular resistance, assessing her TBSA, her fluids. Her hands, with second-degree partial-thickness burns and some third-degree coverage, were raw under the cling film. She tried to find the right words.

"You turned back time." She was deliriously grateful. "He's alive."

"She's in shock," he said.

EX-MOUNTIE AMPUTEE BURIED IN QUEBEC

The funeral for ex-RCMP corporal Taylor Shymanski, 26, of Sherbrooke, Quebec, was held in his hometown today.

Shymanski died just hours before his scheduled appearance at the Military Police Comission in Ottawa after his rental vehicle spontaneously exploded in Kingsmere. No one else was injured in the blast. Shymanski served with CAF in Afghanistan, 2005–2008, where he lost a limb in an IED incident and was awarded the Medal of Meritorious Valour. He also served within the PMSS (Prime Minister's Security Service) and had recently resigned from the RCMP. Shymanski is survived by his parents and a younger sister.

(STAFF, *CANADIAN ATLANTIC PRESS*)

May 2009

19

At William Randolph Hearst Burn Center, New York Presbyterian Hospital, Becky was registered under her maiden name, Holt. The administration knew how to protect Canadian privacy. For morale and more, though, she'd adopted a brunette wig, shoulder length, the Julia Roberts.

Greg visited once, briefly, not wanting to run up costs for suffering taxpayers. She discussed her treatment: the skin graft, the infection she'd incurred, the cosmetic prognosis for her hands as a whole, and certain digits and her right thumb specifically. Greg nodded appropriately.

Her parents had been taking care of the children, staying at Sussex Drive and flying down to spend time with her on weekends, but had recently left for a long-awaited trip to China. Glenn had told her he was sending Greg daily texts: "Wish you were here."

"And how are the kids?" Becky asked.

"Don't ask," Greg said. Pablo wasn't causing any trouble,

but Greg had had to punish Peter for insolence and various transgressions. And then Greg was infuriated at Martha's hysterical reaction to his disciplining of Peter.

Becky's hands almost took on a life of their own; they wanted to wring her husband's neck until he was unconscious and softly compliant on the floor.

"Greg," she said. She had to ask. "Did Taylor's death have anything to do with our daughter?" She wasn't referring to suicide; she knew Greg knew that. She was so far past the posthumous spin touting the young Mountie's PTSD and his expertise with incendiary devices.

And while she waited for him to speak, Becky admitted, if only to herself, that the alternative theories would be too hard for her to live with and also make it impossible for her to continue living with him.

"Do you think I care about two kids in the bush?" he said. "About an illegitimate bun in the oven?" He stood up and towered. "I am working for a—"

She heard *Ma* emerge from pressed lips like *mother, maman, ma belle.*

novembre 2009

20

———

AT THE PREMIERE OF *Nun from Bucharest*, by the writer-director of *In Bruges*, Lise sagged in her rhinestone- and ruby-barnacled bolero, heavy enough to serve as an in situ workout. Her palms sweated. She sat thigh by thigh with her distant ex-consort in the darkened Paris, a retro art house cinema near Central Park in Manhattan (which they'd entered on a red carpet not her own, to the scent of buttery topping and fresh *merde* from the horse-and-carriage rides). It was the birth of the cerebral movie season, the week before American Thanksgiving.

René's role was award jailbait: priest, death, *derrière*. There was already an Oscar hiss; he was reputedly a lock for a Best Supporting Actor nod. Advances in the trades were rapturous: "Claude is Cinematic Catnip from Canada," "René-nian Rhapsody!" And they were in the same row as Benicio del Toro and Penélope Cruz, along with their significant plus-ones, such as Javier Bardem.

Niko sat on René's other side.

It had been months since Lise had hung, so to speak, with René. Hollywood was all over him and he was stewing about a stack of features, an AMC series. Not only that, but he'd spent months with Niko in the North, Mistassini, last spring, embedded in the Neeposh family, bonding in a complex form of Cree Outward Bound, and running, reading, talking and ruminating. They were both stronger, infuriatingly spiritual, and lean.

The Romanian threat to René hadn't played out, at least not yet; the Canadian public had adapted to his resignation, almost a year ago, with either a mature detachment or vicarious interest. Lise had just missed him.

Niko had returned to his mother in midsummer, and they'd drifted away from Dr. Pelletier—*pas vraiment un pique-nique*, particularly after Niko learned about the tragic, terrible, gruesome death of Corporal Shymanski last April. But he'd become even closer, to Lise's surprise, in mutual bereavement, to Martha. Lise was partnering again, reluctantly, with Becky, recovering from a bad barbecue burn, on the next ArtsCAN! Martha tagged along with her mother to Rideau Hall and Niko lurked, listening to her rehearse Greg's misogynist songs on Glenn Gould's piano. Afterwards, he'd lead her out, in her black leggings and Juliet blouse, her cumbersome silver cross hanging like a middle breast, to his all-season tent, behind the tennis court.

Martha was around *beaucoup*.

As the final credits started to roll, *Nun from Bucharest*

received an ovation like a cannon shot. René and Niko clung; Penélope Cruz's bodyguard fist-humped with Lise.

The Sony Classics after-party was held twenty blocks north in a Byzantine ghetto at the Met Museum. The guest list ran the gamut, a *méli-mélo* of the Broadway A-list, the LA elite and boring politicos from the Beltway. She met René's new agent from WME, and his newer manager from wherever, both short, loquacious juice guzzlers. Javier pumped Niko about sleeping naked under the northern lights on stacked spruce boughs.

"You must be so pleased, René," Lise said. "With how things have turned out."

"Oui, vraiment. Mais il y a quelque chose qui manque."

She waited, hopeful.

"I realize that by pushing you into accepting the GG position, I sublimated my own need. Denied my heritage."

Before she could pursue this further, he left with Niko for a loft in Nolita. *Bye bye.*

Lise sat up when her BlackBerry buzzed. She had to squint to decipher the caller ID. It was the middle of the night back at the Waldorf Tower.

"Prime Minister," she said.

"Sorry to call so early," Greg said. "Can we talk?"

"Certainement. What's the matter?" She realized she hadn't checked in with her secretary, Noel, since the screening of *Nun from Bucharest.*

"I want to prorogue."

"Prorogue what?" It was late.

"Parliament."

"Again?"

"Been a year."

"You've got to be kidding."

"I'm not."

"It's crazy."

"Nope."

"What about protocol? You don't just phone me. That's not the way it's done."

"It is when the Governor General isn't in the country. As usual." Prime Curtness.

"I'm back in Ottawa tomorrow."

"Will you or won't you?"

"Why do you want to prorogue?"

"This Parliament has run its course."

"That's it?"

"Yup."

She gathered her wits. Documents requested from the government by the media about high-level RCMP involvement in the Kandahar drug and prostitution ring, all supposedly under Freedom of Information, were being withheld by the PMO for national security reasons. Even the embattled Leader of the Opposition wasn't allowed to take a peek. Then it dawned on her.

"Does this have anything to do with *my* scheduled appearance at the Parliamentary Committee on the Military Police Commission matter in Afghanistan?"

She heard Greg breathing.

"*My* upcoming testimony regarding Corporal Shymanski and the Lieutenant-Colonel?"

"That's an insult."

"Does it? Because if I give permission to prorogue, I'd be postponing my own testimony."

She hung up on him.

Last April, before his car spontaneously combusted, or he committed suicide, Shymanski had phoned her private number. "Your Excellency." Taylor's voice was low and shaky.

"Where are you?" She locked her study door.

"I just quit the force."

"Where are you?"

"Here. I testify in two days." He paused. "Your Excellency—"

"We have to meet," she said. "Privately."

"Where?"

"Niko's school." He knew it, of course. He'd sometimes driven Niko there or picked him up, or met him at his locker. "This time tomorrow."

"*D'accord.*" And he was gone.

The next morning, she went unaccompanied; the principal and secretary were used to her dropping in to collect Niko's homework. So she headed down the hall right into the gymnasium, which was pitch-dark, and hit the switches, but felt his presence. He was right by the door.

Corporal Shymanski was gaunt in his civvies—jeans, a hoodie. If he'd seemed disturbed, haunted, in Afghanistan four months ago, he was a different person now. He had a frenzied beard and looked older, defensive, and in some way as desperate as he would have had to have been to carry out all the criminal activities he was being accused of. He said to her, "I have been framed."

"I know."

"That woman isn't Aisha."

"She's an imposter," Lise said. Then, "Where's the real one?"

"I don't know."

"We were with her in Panjwai. What happened? Did she even get to Canada?"

"I don't know. Can you help me?"

"I want to." She paused. "But what about the Prime Minister's daughter? Martha?"

"That was a mistake." His face softened. "But she was so kind. So sweet. I can't imagine what she must think of me now, with all this—talk."

"Who abducted you from Rideau Hall?"

He didn't answer.

"CSIS?"

He shook his head.

"The force?"

He didn't respond.

"Because of Kandahar?"

"Yes. I'd finally submitted a statement to the Commission about my superiors. I blew the whistle. And later I found out that because Aisha had been found—the real Aisha, in Afghanistan—the RCMP couldn't keep it covered up. The

Afghans told her she could talk to anybody about what she knew—even Al Jazeera."

"*Mon Dieu.*"

"*Oui*, or Iran—Afghanistan needed leverage. They needed to keep NATO troops. And she knew a lot. She'd been undercover. And I knew what she knew but had been too scared to talk. For a while."

Lise shivered.

He handed her an envelope, disc-size. "Find her," he said. "You're the only one who can."

She was suddenly worried for him. "Where are you going, Taylor?"

"I'm meeting Mme. Leggatt now. I'm late."

"Do you think that's wise?"

"Yes," Shymanski said.

"She's treacherous."

"She's also Martha's mother."

Lise presumed, then, that this had to do with Martha, perhaps giving her a message.

She hugged him tightly. "*Bonne chance.* I hope it all goes well at the Committee."

"*Moi aussi,*" he said.

"You leave first," she said.

And he did. She could hear his footsteps going down the hall, and then the bell rang and his distinctive pattern disappeared in the rampage of the boys.

An hour later, he was dead. That was seven months ago.

—

Of course, Lise tried to hunt her down. The real Lieutenant-Colonel Aisha K. Niko and René were on walkabout and she couldn't think about anything but her.

But it was tricky. At the reboot of the new session of Parliament back in January, Greg had shuffled the Cabinet. Defence was now Environment, DFAIT was now Health, and the Brigadier General had retired to Bogotá, but many deputies were still in place. Lise welcomed them warmly to receptions and ribbon cuttings, then selectively put them on the hot seat.

A long-ago aide-de-camp had been posted to Mannheim, Germany, to handle CIMIC communications, so Lise made the annual call on her birthday.

"Were you actually present when Lieutenant-Colonel Aisha K. was reunited with her children?" Lise asked.

"The Lieutenant-Colonel's children were never at Mannheim," the aide said. "I heard they were staying with relatives in Quetta."

Then in early summer, when Lise met privately in a plane hangar with the U.S. president, Barack Obama, on his three-hour Ottawa for Dummies tour, she failed to convey half of what the PCO had instructed her to divulge. Instead, she answered Barack's barrage about her prorogation decision. He'd heard Rumours, had Concerns. Canada was supposed to be the *democratic* neighbour.

Lise told him everything, everything, he was so disarming, he was her African brother, my God, he was black too.

And then he said he owed her one. A big one.

She'd said, "I need to find an Afghan mom."

"Liz, I'm on it," Barack said.

"It's Lise," said Lise.

He pointed at her and grinned. "Jeez, Louise," he said, "Lise!" and then had dashed off to break beaver tails with Greg at the Peace Tower.

And when Lise chaired a conference at Carleton University about development issues in Asia, and met a leading centrist-left feminist from Pakistan who'd heard of Lieutenant-Colonel Aisha K., she pounced.

"I'm searching for her children in Quetta," Lise said after the PowerPoint presentation.

"I'll do some digging," the feminist said.

She called Lise to let her know that the children had indeed been in Quetta, but had mysteriously disappeared from their uncle's house.

Meanwhile, the PMO-endorsed Lieutenant-Colonel Aisha K. thanked Canada on July first for its cordial welcome and low-key press. In a parlour at the Afghan embassy, she said, "I am retiring from public life to live in peace and raise my family."

Her imaginary family.

On Labour Day weekend, Lise received a call from Meena Karzai. She and Hamid had just spent the day on Martha's Vineyard with the Obamas, all very hush-hush, very low-low-key, and she was so sorry they weren't going to visit Canada, their wonderful NATO ally.

"Listen," said Meena. "I've just been talking to Meesh, and I understand you're looking for Aisha."

Suddenly there was a jumble of conversation in the background.

"Lise, is your line secure?"

"Who knows," Lise said.

"I hope so, *inshallah*. You're looking for Aisha *Karzai*."

Lise said, "I don't know if that's her last name."

"That's her last name. She's Hamid's cousin."

Lise could have fainted. "His cousin."

"Yes." A pause. "My husband has hundreds of cousins, and she's one of them."

Another pause.

"Babur! Babur!" she called to her son. "There are sharks in the Atlantic Ocean, my sweet, my *habibi*! Sharkies! So beeeg! And electric eels! And men-of-war!"

Lise said, "Meena, you were right. I don't think we can have this conversation on the phone."

"Lise, listen to me. Aisha kept an eye on Kandahar for Hamid. A close eye, and he looked out for her, too. Trust me. He tried to reason with her. But you have to look at the beeg picture, and I know you do that all the time as the King's representative. You have to, I know. And in Afghanistan we look at the beeg picture and we see that we only have NATO troops helping us fight the Taliban when the countries—Britain, France, Germany, Netherlands, Canada—support the war enough to send their children to fight it."

"I'm hanging up, Meena."

"She couldn't be embarrassing your mountain police, Lise."

Lise was silent. Until she had to know. "And her children?"

"No worries. No worries. We are taking good care of them."

"Where are they?"

"In Islamabad. With Indira."

"*Qui?*"

"Jopal."

The Pakistani president's older sister.

It was the usual mini-disc.

Aisha, 11/25/2008, Panjwai. Jerkily printed.

Lise hit play.

On her laptop screen, it was the real Aisha, in goatherd clothes, and Lise believed what Aisha said, that she was shooting the video herself on Corporal Shymanski's phone and she was secluded in a jerry-rigged bathroom in a military tent by herself. With an army close by. Back in 2008, late November.

It was her beautiful face, and she was scared.

She talked about the promise of the Witness Protection Program in Canada.

She named her children: Khaled, Abdurachman, Malalai, Omar.

Lise watched the video over and over, over and over again.

It finally made sense.

She composed a letter to the Special Parliamentary Committee of the Military Police Commission, stating that she was submitting evidence regarding the Lieutenant-Colonel Aisha Karzai and Corporal Taylor Shymanski case, the deaths of two ANP recruits, and RCMP corruption, at the highest level, in Kandahar, Afghanistan. She stated that she was fully aware she was contravening her viceregal oath regarding Official Secrets but that the violations of the Charter of Rights and Freedoms and Canada Criminal Code must take precedence.

She addressed it to her former secretary, Chair Margaret Lee Yeung.

Signed with her special stamp, special seal, the Right Honourable Lise Lavoie, Governor General of Canada, Commander-in-Chief.

In New York, the day after René's premiere, Lise overslept at the Waldorf Tower. Room service rushed breakfast to her suite, Niko phoned to say he was on his way uptown in a taxi, and Lise watched *Good Morning America* while showering, dressing, grabbing a bite. René was on, promoting *Nun from Bucharest*.

"Sultry," the host said after the clip. "What's next?"

"I'm quitting the business," he said.

Lise dropped her croissant.

"I'm running for federal office in Quebec when my wife steps down as Governor General."

"Who for? Which party?" asked the host. "The Democrats?"

"Yes," René said. "We call them the New Democrats."

"Ooh," she said. "Like New Labour in England."

"*Non,*" said René.

When Lise and Niko arrived back at Rideau Hall, Greg was pacing the driveway by her front door. In wait. It was a warmish day for November, freakish shirt sleeves weather, and he looked hot and tubby in a pink cashmere sweater. He shoved a couple of bunches of zingy yellow tulips her way.

Niko evaporated indoors.

"Ready to prorogue?" Greg gritted his teeth.

"No."

"Then I guess you haven't heard."

"What?"

"About St. Bertrand?"

"What about it?"

"There's been a coup. The Communist dictator Jean-Louis Raymond has seized power," Greg said.

"He was the democratically elected president in 2004, Greg. Canadian observers ratified that election."

"The death toll is rising."

Lise swallowed.

He said, "I—DFAIT wants you to fly to St. Bertrand immediately as a non-official envoy."

"In the midst of civil war?"

"No better time."

"This is about the prorogation, isn't it?"

"I appreciate how you're staying on topic, Lise. It would be smart to prorogue before you depart."

"I'm going to go Republican on you, Greg. Read my lips. I refuse."

"That's not Republican, Lise. That's rogue. Hey, I've brought your constitutional advisers along. Again." He pointed. In the back of his limo, three white-haired heads, of varying shades and textures, were engaged in gesticula-tions. "A couple of your favourites."

"They're not ice cream, Greg."

"Fresh from the mausoleum."

"This is unbelievable," Lise said. "We shouldn't even be having this conversation without our seconds. Where's Clark? Where's my secretary, Noel?"

"Lise, Rome is burning and by extension your capital of Jolie Ville. My understanding is that you've already estab-lished a relationship with this usurper—"

"Oh, puh-leeze."

"And your Communist sister is behind him—"

"Be careful what you say, Greg."

"The Western allies would appreciate your first-hand take on the situation. Remember, Canada has granted debt relief to St. Bertrand. We don't do that every day. Not when we have a military to feed. And we've left their telecommu-nications alone—"

"Are you ordering me to go?"

"It's an ask."

"So it's an order."

"Let's put it this way. I'm not *not* ordering you."

"Will I have military bodyguards?"

"Yup."

"Do you know if Solange is all right?" For she knew Greg knew everything.

"All right?" he guffawed. "Ask Vice-President Soleil your-self when you see her."

"She's veep?"

"Apparently."

"I'll be back for my appearance before the Parliamentary Committee." Lise was forced to take a deep breath. "Count on it."

Greg ripped off his sweater and hurried back to his limo. He climbed in and the driver hit the pedal. The three-headed cluster jerked backwards then forwards.

Lise headed toward the entrance, but a movement in the Mappin window caught her eye. Becky was adjusting a curtain. *The nerve.*

"My mom's here," Martha said.

"*Bien—*" Lise said passing through the Long Gallery, "*sûr.*"

Martha and Niko unknitted themselves on the piano bench. Niko's hair was already mussed and Lise surmised that the practising in progress had nothing to do with *Temptations.* But she didn't have time to lament that Niko's person of interest happened to be Greg Leggatt's damaged Christian progeny.

"She went upstairs," Martha offered.

Lise stamped her feet on the landing.

Before locating Becky and lynching her, Lise turned in at her bedroom to drop her purse and immediately noticed the note on top of her mahogany dresser—heavyweight bond redux, this time handwritten, in a feminine cursive.

You are the patriot.
Becky

"Becky," Lise growled.

She was standing by the altar in the Right Honourable
Georges and Pauline Vanier Chapel, her gloved hand
maintaining contact with the crucifix. The wee bedroom had been converted into a non-denominational
sanctuary back when Georges had served as the most
penitent of Governors General. "Lise," Becky said. "It's
urgent that we talk. I hope you don't mind my letting
myself in."

"Get out." Lise simmered.

That took her aback. "Lise."

"Get out of my house."

"It's not actually yours—" Becky swallowed.

"It's a private apartment and you can't trespass, as you
do whenever it serves your husband's interests."

"I take your point, but it *is* Canada's house, the peoples'
house."

"They're welcome any time. You're not."

"Lise."

"Please leave before I summon security."

"Lise! Listen. I know you're breaking your oath to testify before the commission."

"Why are you privy to that? It's classified."

"I know Greg wants you to prorogue. That's why I've

come to talk to you. And that's why I had to hide here."
Becky held Lise's gaze. "From him."

Lise assessed. This was a huge prosecutable admission
and Becky appeared sincere. But she always had, in a self-
assured way.

"It's another tactic, isn't it, Rebecca? I have been manipu-
lated by you in every conceivable way since you moved
into Sussex Drive. And even before. Not only that, but
threatened, humilitated, and slandered, and in my own
defence and that of my family, have been reduced to com-
batting you in ways that are completely counterintuitive to
the way my life operates. Why are you here?"

"To warn you—"

"About what? That you're back to destroy my husband?
Further destabilize our son? Bewitch him with your daughter? Debtor-fuck my country? Assassinate my sister?"

"Close," Becky said.

Silence.

"Which one?"

They were on their knees, side by side, on an uncomfortable
Vanier prie-dieu. That way no staff would dare interrupt.

"When I learned you were appearing before the
Parliamentary Committee, I knew Taylor had shared information with you."

Lise didn't indicate anything one way or the other. She
wasn't going to talk to Becky about the mini-disc. She said,
"I had no choice. A woman who risked her life for our

country and turned to Canada for sanctuary may be dead.
Four children orphaned."

"Is Greg sending you to St. Bertrand?"

"Yes."

"Right away?"

"Tout de suite."

"What about the prorogation?"

"Becky, please—I can't disclose."

"You have to testify, Lise. Don't let him stop you."

Lise read the alarm on Becky's face and, yes, anguish.
"Becky?"

"I was supposed to meet him that day. Taylor." Becky
gripped the book rest of the prie-dieu with her gloved hands.
"Last April. After you. He wanted to give me something. And
I think they knew this and that's why they blew him up."

Lise was sick with horror, even though she suspected that
she'd always known this.

Becky slowly pulled off one long silk black glove and then
the other. Her hands were mottled by grafts and scars, like
some marbled ghost cheese. This was no barbecue mishap.

"Oh, Becky."

"I couldn't help him. His hoodie was on fire. His silly
beard. He was melting into the seat. I tried—" Becky started
to weep.

The noise of her grief was sickening. Abhorrent. Lise
had to turn her head.

"The operatives were in the woods."

"Pardon?"

"Don't go to Africa," Becky said.

"You're afraid I won't be back in time to testify?"

"You won't be back at all."

Lise absorbed that.

Becky sat back on on her knees. "I am sorry, Lise. I've trespassed against you. I regret many things I have done."

"I appreciate your apology," Lise said. "I'd suspected many people of leaving that note last November. But never you. Why?"

"Because I could," Becky said. "The most important thing I've learned is that I can do horrible things to people. Then—dump them. Deny. Deflect. Ignore. Or even accuse the person I've hurt."

Lise didn't say anything.

Becky collected herself. "In case you're wondering why I'm still at Sussex Drive, I've been informed that if I pull a Maggie Trudeau, he'll take sole custody."

What a world, Lise thought. What a man.

Becky said, "Will you pray with me?"

Lise's hand shook in Becky's scarred white claw.

They were silent until Becky said, "Amen."

"Amen," said Lise.

"Amen," Martha said.

Lise's eyes flew open. How long had the girl been standing there? And Niko right behind her.

"What did you hear?" Lise asked.

Niko was composed. "Everything."

21

By the time Lise and Corporal Robard landed in Bujumbura, Greg had anecdotally mentioned her mission at the conclusion of a press conference about the upcoming 2010 Winter Olympics.

René had returned to Rideau Hall to burn sacred sweet-grass with Niko.

After a fitful sleep at the U.S. embassy, Lise was joined by four other quasi-official envoys: Lawrence Apoonatuk, renaissance pundit and current Canadian ambassador to France; Greg's former Chief of Staff, now an International Monetary Fund mandarin; and an American, Alexander Manson, introduced as a "Bush-squared" fixer, who'd been active in both Republican regimes. Manson seemed cozy with Greg's former Chief of Staff.

The fourth *homme* worked in the Australian Privy Council: Paul Leggatt. A relation.

Lise didn't trust any of them even to open her Pellegrino.

They flew by Chinook with a Black Hawk escort from Burundi to Jolie Ville. Their plan for a briefing with Jean-Louis Raymond kept changing, primarily because they couldn't make contact. Lise was able to get through to Samuel, her sister's husband, and then finally reached Solange, who'd indeed been sworn in as the interim veep. Lise spoke to her as the Chinook sped over the spiced jungles and terraced hillsides of St. Bertrand.

"The last time you were here, Excellent sister," Solange said, "President Raymond was seized and deported."

"I had nothing to do with that."

"You were obviously tracked."

"I don't know. Maybe. I *am* a head of state, Solange—"

"So am I—"

"Well, you weren't then."

"You're flying in with assassins."

Lise stared at the Ray-Ban men, her fellow envoys in milky chinos and Boss polos, except for Apoonatuk's Armani ensemble. She held the phone up like a mic. "Tell me now if Navy SEALs are en route to remove Raymond."

Manson's jaw twisted, a puppet dino's.

"If that's the case, we need to turn this bird around to Bujumbura," Lise said daringly.

None of the men answered. Paul Leggatt hadn't even said hello to her yet.

"See," Lise said, back on the phone.

"It's not the weather, little sis. There's no forecast. They're just going to do it."

"The allies would appreciate a sit-down to see what's on Raymond's mind. It will be a ten-minute talk. *C'est tout.*"

"*Un instant, s'il te plaît.*" Silence.

Two minutes later, Solange was back. "Jean-Louis agrees. Our terms. Our turf."

Lise signed off. "*À bientôt.*"

"May I have your attention, please?" Robard jumped in immediately, waving an arm. "May I have your attention, please? Your Excellency, gentlemen, your attention—I need your attention. We have a CENTCOM update."

Lise and the Ray-Bans paid attention.

Robard summarized quickly as they were only a few minutes from Jolie Ville airspace. Jolie Ville was experiencing scattered gunfire and grenade blasts; the death toll was in the hundreds. The capital had been without electricity or water for a day and the food supply was disrupted. The airport was closed. Looting was anticipated. The previous Western-backed president was MIA. International aid agencies were ramping up but days away from on-the-ground assistance. The nearest U.S. forces were back across the border in Burundi. The Black Hawks would circle the outskirts of the city.

To complicate matters, Mount Agogo, the volcano overshadowing the city in the south, had started to seismically act up. Hundreds of earthquakes, minuscule on the Richter but nerve-racking in number, had set a record for swarm activity. It was expected to blow within minutes, knocking off the spatter cone and releasing the lake of lava within the crater at speeds of sixty miles per hour. All this with the attendant silica content of pyroclastic flows, ash, cinder, smoke and dust—none of it good for airborne craft.

Nobody mentioned pathetic fallacy.

Or reversing direction.

Alexander Manson continued undressing her in his head. It was obvious.

Lise was surprised when the Chinook made landing by the Former Slave Depot on the shore of Lake Victoria. "I thought Raymond HQ was at a Catholic church," she said to Robard.

Robard pointed at the sooty white steeple set in amongst the eucalyptus.

"Let's say howdy," Manson said. "See what this *hombre* has to say."

Before they could exit the Chinook, it was surrounded by soldiers—a mix of indigenous St. Bertrand militia and Chinese military.

"Only the lady," the leader said. "Her only."

"We all go," Robard said. "She can't go unaccompanied."

The militia and soldiers replied in a chorus of fluent pointed Kalashnikov.

"Then she can't go," Manson said.

"Let her go," Apoonatuk advised.

"My sister's in there," Lise replied.

"They're expecting her," Apoonatuk said.

Manson slipped a capsule into her fist. "It's quick," he said. "You'll be dead. Before you feel. Anything. I like. You."

"What?" Lise held it in her palm, then worried that it could eat into her skin and kill her in seconds. She stuffed it deep in her pocket.

"Or use it. On somebody else. In a pinch." Manson nodded meaningfully.

"You need to get back here fast, Your Excellency," Robard said, gazing at the volcanic smoke. "Pronto."

Paul Leggatt just watched her.

Lise stepped out of the helicopter and drunk-walked up the trembling stone-lined path toward the wooden church. The Chinese soldiers escorted her. The Africans, with the Kalashnikovs slung over their shoulders, remained with the Chinook. The scene felt movie-like, as if these extras weren't taking their roles seriously enough. Over the white picket fence, she could see the slave sculptures in the pit: the family chained together and stuck in place. Ashes settling on their heads and shoulders.

When the ground shook again, a flock of papyrus canaries spilled upward into the darkening sky and took off for the north. These were the birds that had awoken her when she was a child, curled in the same bed as her sister; they'd imitated them and irritated their father, and he'd been so angry he'd chopped down the tree they nested in.

Lise was swept along through the nave, to the chancel where Raymond and his workers were buried in a serpentine set-up of CPUs and rudimentary monitors; it also served as a primitive broadcasting centre. His suit still hung from his frame and the arm of his spectacles was taped with a Band-Aid.

"Thank you for agreeing to meet," she said.

"Solange," Raymond said.

Her sister emerged from behind the apse. She was wearing a boxy business jacket and very casual shorts, dressed like a news anchor for whom above-the-waist viewing was what counted. Solange nodded toward them and kept going.

"She's talking to Clinton," Raymond said. "Hillary."

"It takes a village," Lise said.

Solange finished her conversation and approached them. "*Allo*, Lise."

Lise embraced her sister, and the smell of deep fear, perspiration and the essence of their mother. "I have been told that I can't stay long. Mount Agogo—"

"We understand," Raymond said.

"Let's backtrack," Lise said. "As you know, I asked the government of Canada to take steps to ameliorate problems here. St. Bertrand was granted debt relief, was it not?"

"Yes," Raymond said. "And right after Canada wiped out our debt, the IMF devalued our currency and we owed other loaner nations quadruple the amounts—staggering sums."

"Buggering numbers," Solange said.

"Beggaring. So it made no difference," Raymond said.

"It made it worse," Solange said.

The ground shook violently under them. The church swayed and rattled.

"How about telecommunications?" Lise said. "We didn't privatize that, right?"

"No. You didn't. But France did, and then Canadian tele-communications firms got a cut."

"A hefty cut," Solange said.

"The people of St. Bertrand have not seen a dollar."

"Or heard a ring tone."

Lise felt sick. It was hopeless, wasn't it? "Okay, so what about China? I see by your soldiers you've managed to get them onside. And they're no slouch."

"China's stepped into the Canadian role," Raymond said.

"Seizing our resources and squeezing us later, Lise."

"Although they've been critical these last months," Raymond acknowledged.

"So we're done here." Lise nodded sagely. "I'll take the message back to the Prime Minister."

"Have a safe trip," he said. "I'm going to deliver the evacuation message to Jolie Ville now," and he turned and did exactly that. "My fellow citizens," he began, "people of Jolie Ville and neighbouring villages . . ."

"I don't know if I'll ever see you again." Lise pulled Solange aside.

"Odds are zero."

"Do you remember the day we left for Canada? I remember you packed all your Babar books in a little suitcase."

"You," Solange said, "hung on to your doll for dear life."

Lise pulled her close and kissed her older sister's hot forehead.

Solange said, *"C'est bien que tu aies eu un fils, Lise."*

Robard rushed in through the narthex. "Your Excellency,

come now. We have to go. It's going to erupt. The city's evacuating. The Black Hawks are leaving."

Solange squeezed her arm. "Don't get in that helicopter."

"I don't have a choice," Lise said. "I'm not afraid of 'detailing.' I've been deeply 'detailed' before."

"I'm telling you—" Solange said. "Is Leggatt's step-brother on it?"

"Yes."

Solange slipped something heavy and gun-like into Lise's blazer. "Take it."

Lise slipped her hand around it. It was a gun. *"Es-tu folle?"* Then she felt the nub of Manson's pill, and she pinched it between her fingers and pressed it into the fist of her sister. "And here's cyanide."

"Ah," Solange said, dropping it into the interior pocket of her jacket. "Take one and don't call me in the morning."

"Not for just any headache," Lise said forcefully.

"Eh hehn. Eh hehn." And then Solange shoved her out the door. Lise heard it barred.

Lise stayed imperfectly still for a second outside the church in the darkening morning. Banana trees heaved on the sway-ing earth; the waves of the lake were whipped into fierce oceanic whitecaps. Like volleyballs on fire in a deranged video game, bombs of magma randomly struck, one hitting a stack of used tires only a short distance away.

Robard wildly beckoned her into the Chinook. Apoonatuk, Manson and the IMF rep were already strapped in and Manson was clearly ordering the pilot to take off.

"Come! Come now! Come now! It's going to explode."
Robard.

Manson looked at her and pointed to the lake. "Lise," he
said. "Go by water."

"What?"

"Get! A boat."

The earth undulated. Lise fought to keep her balance.

Paul Leggatt fished for her hand. "Get the fuck on!"
he said.

"I'm staying," Lise yelled, waving him off. "Go!"

Lise was stunned as the Chinook miraculously started to
ascend. It was immediately caught in an updraft and lifted
heavenward, as if scooped by a celestial express elevator
only to be given a good shake by God. Then it settled and
flew northward over the lake, following the invisible path of
the papyrus canaries.

Lise waited for an explosion. And waited. Still. And then
she didn't hear the Chinook anymore.

Three Toyota SUVs sped away up the dusty road and
made the left onto the Jolie Ville highway, really a one-lane
bus road to Burundi. Solange and Raymond were gone.

Lise didn't hesitate. In her job with *oui*Care, she'd seen a
lot. The Q-tip arms and wobbling craniums of malnourished infants, teenaged mothers with obstetric fistula, geni-
tal mutilation, and the impact of a banquet of diseases: Rift
Valley fever, malaria, cholera and the rest. Perhaps more
importantly, she'd handled herself when she'd been robbed
at gunpoint at her neighbourhood Caisse Desjardins

withdrawing cash on Christmas Eve fifteen years ago. Instinct had kicked in.

Her strongest drive was to get onto the water and far away. At the dock of the Former Slave Depot, now a tourist stop, she saw the red-sailed dhow used to illustrate the mode of transportation for slave trafficking. A man threw a goat, a kid, to a woman and children on the dhow. He was in a big hurry and obviously stealing the boat and live provisions. She bolted toward them, running pell-mell down the dock.

"Take me with you," she said.

The man turned. "No." He shoved her. "Go 'way." The woman on the dhow started yelling at her too in an indigenous dialect but it was clear she wasn't extending any hospitality.

Lise said, "Money. I'll buy more goats." She pointed at the kid.

He ignored her, working quickly to cast off.

"I have Visa."

The woman pelted her with carcasses gutted from coveted Nile perch. The perch had decimated the fish that had sustained St. Bertrand natives for centuries and was flown out to European dining tables.

Lise pulled out the gun and shot it in the air. She'd once practised with the King's Own Guards, the first time she'd worn the uniform. She had their complete attention.

"I'm on the boat," she said.

He offered a hand. Still keeping the gun trained on him, Lise swung herself across the dhow and then stayed a safe distance from them.

The dhow reeked of rank bodies, pee, and excrement. *Les poissons*. The children, with their bloated tummies, looked away from her, their hands busy stroking the kid. Lise detected shifty ideas in the eyes of the father.

She kept her gun pointed at them. "I am the head of state of Canada. I shoot to kill. Bujumbura, now. *Vite.*"

A second later, the volcano erupted.

MOTHER MARY'S SONG TO THE "OTHER" MARY
(with thanks to A.L. Webber and T. Rice)
From *Temptations: The Rock Opera*

You do know how to love him
How to give, how to serve him
He's the boss, the biggest boss
In these past few years, he's grown so much
He seems like someone else.

You do know what to do next.
You understand why he's the leader.
He's so right. He's very right.
And he's so so right, it could keep you up
At night
He's right as rain and more · · ·
Go Praise the Lord!

Should you build him up? (Yes)
Should you bake and sew? (Yes)
Should you bathe his feet? (Yes)
Text him on the phone?
You have to accept your female fate
And cede your life to him.

Girl, I hope you heed my advice
I'm his mom so I should know
He's the boy who's always been
So smart, so sure, no thought impure
Leading every charge (no leftist dupe)
A man writ large.

He's writ so large
(Did someone say writ?)
He's your boss.
Love your boss.
You're just a rib.

WORDS AND MUSIC BY GREGORY AND MARTHA LEGGATT

LINDA SVENDSEN

Excerpt from edited redacted copy Page ■ of ■
November 26, 2009
CANADA

**Special Committee on the Canadian Mission of the Military Police
Committee in Afghanistan**

**Comité spécial sur la mission canadienne du comité de polices militaires
en Afghanistan**

***

The Chair (Mme Margaret Lee Yeung, Kelowna–Lake Country, IND): ▮▮

The Right Honourable Lise Lavoie: ▮▮

[340]

The Chair: Au revoir.

Arts CAN!
ANNUAL GALA

— CO-HOSTED BY —

THE RIGHT HONOURABLE LISE LAVOIE
Governor General of Canada

— AND —

MRS. REBECCA LEGGATT

Mistress of Ceremonies
MS. SHELAGH ROGERS

— WITH —

ARCADE FIRE, MICHAEL BUBLÉ,
DIANA KRALL, YO-YO MA, MITSOU,
OLIVER JONES TRIO, LLOYD ROBERTSON,
TEGAN AND SARA, NIKKI YANOFSKY

— AND VERY SPECIAL GUESTS —

Thursday, November 26, 2009
Reception 7 p.m., Curtain 8 p.m.

NATIONAL ARTS CENTRE, OTTAWA

22

STAGE RIGHT.

Becky was tremendously worried. Lise still had not arrived.

Greg and Martha, and their well-oiled band, were performing *Sodom and Gomorrah*. They were the second-to-the-last surprise act; midset. Beside Becky, Peter and Pablo, tuxed and bow-tied to the max, were anxious for the curtain so they could hit up the 2010 Team Canada hockey players for autographs; the athletes were now benched until the grand finale. Peter was also obviously embarrassed by his father wearing a cool, black, tight T-shirt and control-top jeans. Children had limits.

Martha's voice soaked the National Arts Centre barn. She wasn't Céline, Shania, or that new girl but she sang with moist emotion, as if she were to be guillotined at dawn with a dull blade. Mr. Yo-Yo Ma, gracing the cello, laced Lot's wife's ballad with a hint of despair. Watching from the opposite wing, Niko, now gone Native with a ponytail, his acne Accutaned away, swayed with requited lust. He didn't take his eyes off Becky's own girl, thin as a stretchy stick of chewing gum, in her short white sleeveless sheath. He gripped a conspicuous white feather.

"Thank you," Martha said with a bow. The applause slowly blossomed.

A stage left skirmish. And then Lise, her commoner co-host, appeared, offering a big thumbs-up to Becky.

Becky nodded, relieved, and sent her a very meant kiss.

Lise had testified before the Parliamentary Committee that morning, resigned as Governor General after lunch, and moved from number 1 Sussex Drive to an undisclosed hotel. For Becky, it was a miracle that Lise was even alive, ambulatory, and on the cognitive ball. Becky wasn't clear on the African recovery details. She'd heard not only that U.S. Secretary of State, Hillary ("It takes a Black Hawk") Clinton, had personally controlled ops—from an aircraft carrier loitering in the Gulf of Oman—and rescued Lise in a mini-raid near Mwanza, but that King Charles vacationing in Mombasa, Kenya, had become involved and sent a Prince in a heli. Or a personal jet. Or both. And then the reliable Trenton commander, their regular pilot, had flown the Challenger at Greg's command to deliver Lise safely home.

So rumours had been flying, literally.

However, the Canadian media had overlooked the rescue drama to shine significant light on Lise's bizarre behaviour in Africa, where she'd threatened indigenous boat people at gunpoint, committed a dhow-jacking, declared herself Canadian head of state, and eaten "pet goat" meat.

Op ed columnists queried the GG's relationship with her bipolar sister, the Communist terrorist, and the unauthorized clinical trial conducted on innocent African children by the doctor brother-in-law, and also spared column inches to note that Lise's deceased first husband had had radical Cree aspirations. And there had been a leak about Eastern Europe: Romania.

Any mention of Lise's testimony about the possible murders of a young Mountie hero and an Afghan mother was missing.

"Our final song on this memorable evening," Martha said, "is called 'Mother Mary's Song . . . to the "Other" Mary.'"

Was it Becky, or did that shallow titter indicate restlessness? Martha began. "I——————"

Greg strummed, all diligent service and rock posture.

Before the gala, when Peter had hounded Becky about Lise's resignation, she hadn't known what to say. The media made it sound as if Canada was well rid of her, but Becky knew, of course, that Lise's action had everything to do with her approbation about the deeds and direction of the current government. Daddio. She hadn't dared say that to her son.

But Peter had addressed the pause. "Bet she quit because she couldn't stand Dad."

"What?" said Becky. "Who said that?"

"Nobody," Peter had said. "It just figures," and then he'd gone back to fantasizing about the Team USA roster.

Now Martha was yowling, *"Should I bake and sew?"*

So Canada was without a Governor General and Clark the Privy Clerk was going squirrely nuts across the way in the Langevin. Forsey was being parsed and re-parsed, Becky knew. And the country, despite the censorship surrounding Lise's resignation, and the blatant character assassination, was still smitten with her. Lise's approval ratings were soaring on the CBC poll: stratospheric numbers for integrity and patriotism.

Becky surmised that this was perhaps the natural disaster bump. Becky, Lise and the powerless ArtsCAN! board had agreed to donate half the gala proceeds to relief efforts in St. Bertrand. Not to be outdone in chequebook empathy, Greg had agreed that the government would pony up an undisclosed amount to a specified cap for "PMOpproved" charities. But when she checked the customarily Tory-fawning Karp-Deem and Rippo polls, during the chorus, the results were the same. Lise was off the charts!

Suddenly, Martha couldn't be heard. She'd had a tremulous catch in her voice and stopped singing mid-verse. Greg strummed on while the drummer gunned the beat, but Martha was zombie-stalking off the stage into Becky's silk-gloved hands.

"What is it, honeybee?" Becky said. "Honey—"

Her daughter's eyes streamed. "I can't do this. I hate him."

Becky knew what she meant: she hated him perfectly too. Hated his feet in his socks, his socks in his shoes, his tread on the stairs, his earwax, his snore and torso and digestive system, and what he stood for and what he'd done.

Greg was right there. He snagged his daughter by the arm. "Martha, come back out and finish—"

"I can't."

"Martha Leggatt." That tone.

It was Peter, in his stupid tux and cummerbund, who rushed over and kicked his father's shin and then again, repeatedly. Then he aimed higher with direct effect. Greg suddenly released Martha and pinned Peter under his arm.

Then Martha's hand flew with a steely will of its own.

Greg flinched and the hot-fingered imprint burned his cheek. "What in hell—?" he said, instinctively dropping Peter to raise his hands and ward off another blow.

Which the newly-arrived Niko mistook as a threat to Martha and before the PMSS was even aware, or Becky could insert herself between them, Niko's fist met Greg's nose. Or maybe, lip. It bled copiously—on Becky, reaching into the bodice of her Olympic gold ballgown to fetch a tissue and press it to the PM's mouth. Martha's dress was streaked, too, as if she'd been grazed evading snipers in Kosovo.

"*Mierda,*" Pablo pulled his big sister away. "*Que te jodan! Me cago en todo lo que se menea!*"

Becky hurriedly covered his mouth. "*Palabrotas.*"

Greg's security approached en masse to restrain his children. Niko, already familiar with the drill, lifted his arms in surrender and Greg seized the opportunity to grab the white feather and further staunch the flow of blood.

He turned away from his family and his guards to lumber back toward the stage, then suddenly stopped. Becky actually wondered if he might be concussed. Then she heard it, too.

Cheers exploded. A resounding wave of applause bounced off the ceiling. It was a wave that could lift a country to the top of the podium or selective UN councils. Becky thought the hockey team had jumped the queue and she was ready to reprimand Shelagh Rogers or whoever was running the show. In shock herself, perhaps, she peered out.

It was Lise at centre stage. She'd stepped forward to segue from Greg's catastrophic closer to the Olympic finale. The audience was on their feet and stamping them. Cellphones celestially glowed. The applause deafened. All for Lise in the spotlight in a sane and soberly grey dress. A new normal.

René entered from the stage door and Becky saw him pause to honour his wife.

They chanted, "Chief, Chief, Chief, Chief, Chief, Chief, Chief . . ." Becky realized that they were either echoing Lise's remarks at the Press Building after stepping down or petitioning her to run. "This morning I testified as your Commander-in-Chief. And now I will return to be just *Maman*."

Lise took a very steep and a very long bow.

Then the trumpets blared and the hockey players glided onstage. While Becky and Lise saluted the gala stars, the players performed a chorus line cancan which brought down the house. Then, in a burst of uncharacteristic nationalistic spontaneity, the players raised Lise in her plain dress and Becky in her bloody gown to their shoulders.

The women bounced on Luongo and Iginla, Weber and

Brodeur, Crosby, Toews, and Bergeron, on forwards, defence, and goalies. When they met, in the middle of the mosh, they hung on to each other and embraced. So tightly.

"Thank you," Lise said to Becky.

"*Merci beaucoup*," Becky said to Lise.

Peter and Pablo, unable to restrain themselves any longer, invaded the stage for autographs. The recently approved Can Mox broadcaster captured all their frolicking for future presentation pre–prime time.

When gentle Mr. Doughty lowered Becky back into the sudden respectful silence, a place that was new to her, she turned and made eye contact with her husband for one last time. He stood in the wings. His nose was clean, his hair recombed, and any blood that was shed did not show because he wore black.

They looked at each other. Then he looked away first. And she thought, *He's just a man.*

As his security safely removed him, the house lights went up.

OTTAWA CLARION
PM PROROGUES AGAIN

TORONTO GAZETTE

LEGGATT GOVERNMENT IN CONTEMPT OF PARLIAMENT SHYMANSKI-KARZAI FILE WITHHELD

ACKNOWLEDGEMENTS

I am grateful for the assistance and support of the following people, publications, websites and institutions:

The Creative Writing Program, our students and alumni, and Office of the Dean of Arts, University of British Columbia; The John Simon Guggenheim Foundation; The Social Sciences and Humanities Research Council of Canada; Robin Straus; Anne Collins, Deirdre Molina, Scott Richardson, Adria Iwasutiak, and Random House Canada; Lesley Harrison and Elina Levina; Brian Rogers; Michael O'Shea; J. Yaniv; the Farrs; *Parliamentary Democracy in Crisis*, edited by Peter H. Russell and Lorne Sossin; *How We Almost Gave the Tories the Boot: The Inside Story behind the Coalition*, Brian Topp; *Canada's House: Rideau Hall and the Invention of a Canadian Home*, Margaret MacMillan, Marjorie Harris and Anne L. Desjardins; *Rideau Hall: Canada's Living Heritage*, Gerda Hnatyshyn; *Heart Matters*, Adrienne Clarkson; *The Prime Ministers of Canada*, Christopher Ondaatje; CP; JM; Carol Cunningham; A. Scott; T. Ades; TL; Shelley Gibson; G and K, and their father; Government of Canada (www.canada.gc.ca/home.html); Governor General of Canada (www.gc.ca); National Capital Commission website; *Ottawa Book of Everything*, Arthur Montague; *Frommer's Ottawa*, 4th Edition, James Hale; and Canadian political coverage in *Maclean's*, particularly Aaron Wherry's blog, the Vancouver *Sun*, the *National Post*, the Toronto *Globe and Mail*, and on the national broadcasters; Wikipedia (http://en.wikipedia.lorg/wiki/Timeline_of_the_ Canadian-Afghan_detainee_issue); Aristide.org (www.aristide.org/ articles/Aristideinexile.htm); and Clara Sörnäs, for her sculpture *Memory for the Slaves*, adapted and transplanted from Stone Town, Zanzibar, Tanzania, to imaginary St. Bertrand.

LINDA SVENDSEN's linked collection, *Marine Life*, was published in Canada, the U.S., and Germany and her work has appeared in *The Atlantic, Saturday Night, O. Henry Prize Stories, Best Canadian Stories* and *The Norton Anthology of Short Fiction*. *Marine Life* was nominated for the *LA Times* First Book Award and released as a feature film. Svendsen's T.V. writing credits include adaptations of *The Diviners* and *At the End of the Day: The Sue Rodriguez Story*, and she co-produced and co-wrote the miniseries *Human Cargo*, which garned seven Gemini Awards and a George Foster Peabody Award. She received the John Simon Guggenheim Fellowship in 2006. She is a professor in the Creative Writing Program at the University of British Columbia.

A NOTE ABOUT THE TYPE

Sussex Drive is set in Monotype Dante, a modern font family designed by Giovanni Mardersteig in the late 1940s. Based on the classic book faces of Bembo and Centaur, Dante features an italic, which harmonizes extremely well with its roman partner. The digital version of Dante was issued in 1993, in three weights and including a set of titling capitals.